Advanced Praise

Tender and charming, *Everything You Love Ends Up in a Yard Sale* is, at its core, a book about friendship. With a deft hand, Braunfels avoids the saccharine with wry humor and a sprinkling of apt sarcasm. Readers will finish this book reluctant to leave the new friends they've found in Annie and Grace.

— Jennifer Dupree, author of *The Miraculous Flight of Owen Leach* and *What Do You Want From Me?*

At the heart of *Everything You Love Ends Up in a Yard Sale*--Jennifer Braunfels' hilarious, heartfelt, and deeply hopeful debut--is the unlikely friendship between Grace and Annie, two women navigating a place familiar to any reader who has also been battered by life but still stubbornly held on to joy. Braunfels' wise and funny story is a beautiful reminder that the pain of loss is sometimes the clearest reflection of the love we've shared and the strongest sign of the strength we still have to carry on.

— Brandon Dudley, author of *Hazards of Nature*

Everything You Love Ends Up in a Yard Sale is quietly bold: equal parts humor and heartbreak. Jennifer Braunfels redefines the contemporary beach read, intertwining love and loss with both clarity and complexity. An introspective romantic comedy with a strong literary bent, this remarkable debut novel is for anyone who's ever sought a home away from home in order to situate themselves in the modern world. Jennifer Braunfels writes for the wanderer and homebody alike—guiding each eager reader on the journey they need most.

— Court Harler, Founding Editor of *Flash the Court Literary Magazine*

Everything You Love Ends Up in a Yard Sale

Everything You Love Ends Up in a Yard Sale

A Novel

Jennifer Braunfels

First Edition

Library of Congress Control Number: 2025948849

Casebound ISBN: 978-1-62720-621-1
Paperback ISBN: 978-1-62720-622-8
Ebook ISBN: 978-1-62720-623-5

Design by Cecelia Durborow
Editorial Development by Solange Lazzari & Chase Lawson
Promotional Development by Caroline Drennen

Published by Apprentice House Press

Loyola University Maryland
4501 N. Charles Street, Baltimore, MD 21210
410.617.5265
www.ApprenticeHouse.com
info@ApprenticeHouse.com

This book is dedicated to my mother,
who gave me her love of stories and the ocean.

1

"Liar."

I pull my sunglasses down to the tip of my nose and stare at the front of the rest area. It's still vacation season, so the service plaza is packed with cars and SUVs. Liam's coming out, pushing one of the doors open with his forearm and texting with his free hand, which makes my heart thump in my chest. Who the hell is he texting?

"Liar," I repeat to the stale empty air of my car.

When he's almost to his truck, Liam slides his phone into his pants pocket, glances up, and waves at me. Flashes me his patented smirk. Meet Liam. He's swipe-right handsome with his sleek black hair and those piercing blue eyes. There's a lot to like about him. He's a hard worker and very driven to be successful. Another great quality is that he cares about others. But lately, when I look at him, it's like something has shifted, and I feel like I don't know him at all.

Liam bends to adjust the tongue of his "Hey Dudes." He stands and then jogs to his truck, parked one row in front of me. He stops when he reaches the side of the vehicle. He gives me a wink, unlocks the door, steps onto the running board, and slides into the front seat.

When I see his reverse lights come on, I put my car in drive and pull out ahead of him, and once I've safely merged back into the traffic on 95, I do what I often do: I make a pros and cons list in my head. I'm trying to focus on the positives, but one thought keeps pinging around in my brain: the affair. Now, Liam claims he didn't have sex with his coworker back at home in Exeter. He says they had more of an emotional office fling, a work-wife thing, so that's not technically cheating, right? I've had this very question on my mind for a solid month now.

Yet, by the time I'm halfway across the big green bridge connecting Portsmouth to Maine, with Liam following me in his shiny new truck, I'm able to convince myself that if I live isolated and content in Maine for a full year with him, everything about our seemingly doomed, broken relationship will fix itself. Self-delusion isn't an unusual habit for me. I do it quite often and quite well.

About an hour later, as we near US-1 North, I push my sunglasses up higher on my nose. I search for Liam in the rearview and see him right behind me. He's got his damn phone in one hand, looking down at the screen, smiling. My stomach churns.

As we exit Route 1, I roll down my windows to breathe in the August air. Summer in Maine always makes me feel alive. The foliage will remain a vibrant green for a few more weeks, and the annoying, biting black flies will have peaked already. I lived in Maine most of my life, but when I went off to college, my parents sold their place here, making the big move to a condo in New Hampshire. Some of my favorite childhood memories are of my best friend, Say and I riding the waves at Popham Beach all day on our boogie boards, then stuffing ourselves sick with roasted marshmallows every night. I make a mental note to text Say when we arrive at the beach cottage.

We sail through familiar small towns, past country stores and corn fields. I see a handpainted wooden sign with a picture of a pie on it. You can't put a "Pies Ahead" sign on the side of the road and not expect me to stop, so I turn my blinker on. Liam sees my signal and rolls down his truck window; he sticks his left arm out and motions for me to keep driving. Now all I can think about is pie.

A half hour later, I adjust the rearview mirror to look for Liam again. I don't see the silver grill of his Ford F-150, although I'm sure he is still somewhere back there. What I do see is my wild hair. Liam would hate that I had the windows down because it's air conditioning all the way for that guy. My tangled hair would be too much for him. I roll the windows up partway and attempt to pat the jumble of curls back down into place. Maybe I'll be able to look somewhat presentable by the time we get to the rental house.

I stop looking at myself in the mirror and put both hands on the wheel when the road begins to snake through the marshes. The familiar sulfur odor of my childhood seeps in through the car's windows. I sit straighter in my seat to better take in the scenery. I'm transfixed by the dune grass blowing in the breeze and the barnacle-covered rocks. I round a sharp corner, and off to the left, a line of surf comes into view. I glance up one last time. No Liam. Just a mile or so more to the rental house.

As soon as I pull into the driveway, I jump out of the car and breathe in the salty smell of the ocean. I want to dive right into the waves, but Liam would want me to get right down to the business of unpacking. I open the trunk, only to try and then fail to lift out an overpacked suitcase. As I do my best to unload as much as I can before Liam arrives, I smell cigarette smoke, which stops me.

To my left, a woman stands in her front yard. She stares at me, then takes a slow drag off a slender cigarette. I, too, know the pleasure of a slim, cool and minty Misty. I used to wait tables on summer break to help pay tuition. We waitresses would fight over the packs of smokes the older ladies left behind. They never left good cigs like Marlboros or Parliament Lights. At the end of a long shift, though, nothing tasted better than a Misty under the flickering lights in the parking lot.

The woman's cigarette dangles between two fingers with long nails that resemble white picket fence posts. In her other hand, she holds a diamond-studded dog leash that trails down to a small white poodle with blue bows tied onto its ears. At no point does this woman try to look away from me. Instead, she purses her lips and, with God as my witness, blows the most perfect series of smoke rings I have ever seen. As the afternoon sun beats down on me, I have to squint to get a better view of this bold woman. I smile and wave.

She nods in my direction, blowing out the last of her cigarette smoke. She drops the butt and mashes it into the grass with the toe of her pink flip-flop.

This new neighbor of ours is wearing an orange tube top with a matching pair of velour shorts. She's short, wide, and at least sixty years old, but her curls still shine brown. Her skin shines brown too, so tan it could cover a couch and pass as actual leather.

The poodle yanks the leash toward me, but the woman jerks the dog back to her side. She wins the tug-of-war, and the two walk up the short path back to their house. I'm still watching her when Liam pulls up behind me on the street. He parks, hops down, winks at me again, jogs to the back of his truck, and opens the tailgate.

I try again to lift the clunky suitcases out of my trunk, and when Liam sees me struggling, he comes right over. "Grace, let me help you with the heavy stuff. Please?"

Liam sets my first suitcase on the ground with a grunt. I extend the handle and roll the suitcase up the walkway. He has both eyes on me—I can feel them boring into my back. He has a certain way of doing everything. As I drag the suitcase up the porch stairs, the plastic wheels bang against each step. I finally manage to finagle the load onto the splintered wooden porch.

"Grace, you got it?" Liam calls from the yard.

"I'm fine," I say with a wave, though I now have a painful cramp on my right side. I rub the sore spot, and the stitch goes away.

The rental property is a small cottage just a few streets over from the oceanfront. The faded wooden siding reminds me of glossy, beach-life magazine covers. I peek in through the wide front windows: simple planked flooring and white wainscoting on the walls. The rustic, comfy furniture in the living room probably came from some upscale shabby-chic store.

On the porch, Liam balances a box on his thigh. "Well, what do you think, babe?"

"I think everything about this year will be perfect."

I lean back to kiss Liam on the lips, and when I open my

eyes, I see the woman from next door on her own porch with her dog under one arm. We make eye contact; she nods again, then whirls away. I'm about to mention this nosy new neighbor to Liam, but I stop when I notice him lowering the box he was holding onto the porch. He fishes for his phone in his pocket. Sudden anger makes my cheeks flush. I cock my head to the side and place a hand on my hip. Liam glances down at his screen and grins, then pockets his phone again. "That was just Mom checking in. Ready?" he asks with a smile, bending to pick up the box again.

"Ready," I say in a flat tone.

As I watch him walk into the house, I shake my head to try to clear my negative thoughts, but still, I can't help but feel that there's something going on with Liam that he's not telling me.

2

It's only seven in the morning, and I already have my hair piled up off my sweaty neck. Muggy Maine air makes my hair look like a beehive made of brown cotton candy. My real focus right now, however, is on the damn toilet in the half bath near the kitchen. The toilet won't flush, and I'm frustrated. That frustration stems from the fact that I work at the kitchen table, and I'm much too lazy to use the bathroom upstairs.

We're finally unpacked, except for a few cardboard boxes here and there. I like to rearrange furniture for no good reason. Reorganizing marks a genetic trait passed down to me from my mother, but I've only moved the living room around three times so far. I've managed to do actual paid work in between my pointless maneuverings since we arrived three days ago, but I have not attended to my research as much as I should have.

I slide my yellow rubber-gloved fingers into the tank. The oily water smells like hardboiled eggs. This kind of chore usually does not make me gag, but right now, it's all I can do not to vomit. I've watched three YouTube videos on how to fix a toilet, so now I'm an instant expert, of course. I jerk the rusty chain because that technique worked in all the online videos.

Only a few minutes have passed since I began this nasty job, and I'm already ready to throw the top of the toilet tank out the back door. It doesn't help that this half bath is so tiny. The toilet and sink are practically on top of each other. Sweat drips into my eyes, so I take my hands out of the murky water and swipe at my forehead with my forearm. Brown water drips off the yellow glove and hits my bottom lip. I dry heave, then retch in earnest, though nothing's in my stomach but a few cups of coffee.

I attempt to yank the yellow gloves off my hands one finger at a time, but even my slender fingers are swollen from the heat. Cursing, I strip off both gloves by the wrists and throw them inside out onto the tile. Liam would hate that I threw those sopping, stinking gloves onto the just-mopped floor. The mere fact that the gloves remain inside out would send him right over the edge.

I turn on the bathroom faucet and bend to put my lips under the steady stream of water. The water turns so cold it feels almost antiseptic. After a few solid seconds, I lift my head and wipe my mouth with the hand towel on the rack. When I stand up straight, I get a good look at myself in the mirror above the sink. My hair juts out in frazzled strands.

"Christ on a crutch," I mutter at my reflection.

A knock at the back door makes me jump. Way too early for Liam to be home.

"Yoo-hoo!" calls a person whose voice I don't recognize.

I step out of the bathroom to find the woman from day one now standing at the screen door. She holds Tupperware in her hands. "Goo-ood morn-ing," she singsongs.

"Goo-ood morn-ing to you too," I echo.

The woman doesn't even wait for me to open the door but

somehow manages to pry open the metal frame with her foot. When she steps into the kitchen, the screen door slaps closed behind her. Her long, picket-fence nails press into my skin as she shakes my hand.

"I'm Annie Whitney from next door, and this is little Chance. I thought we'd pop over to introduce ourselves."

Annie immediately scans the floor around her ankles. "Chance!" she hollers, and I startle backward.

A moment later, the little white obedient poodle, now with a blue-checked bow tie around its neck, comes sniffing to the back door. The dog's toenails make small clicking noises on the wooden deck. "Jesus, Chance! Why do you always run off on me like that? I could've had a heart attack, for chrissakes!"

Annie forces the screen door open with her foot again; the dog yelps and jumps to the side just in time to not get clipped by the door. I can see this sequence is a dance they've done about a million times before. Chance scoots inside, making it in just before the screen door slams shut on his tail end. "This dog will be the death of me," Annie gushes, "I swear to God. I'm sorry, what was your name, hon?" she asks, with one of the thickest New York accents I've ever heard.

"I'm Grace. Come on in and have a seat."

Annie hands me the Tupperware, plunks herself down in a spindled kitchen table chair, and then grabs her lower back. "Ooohhh, my sciatica."

"Are you okay?"

"Grace, when you get to be old like me, everything goes to shit." Annie lifts both her breasts and lets them flop onto the table.

I slap my hand over my mouth just before I burst out laughing. I can't stop cackling, and Annie joins me. Chance tilts his snout and looks at us like we've lost our damn minds.

Finally, I gasp out, "Can I get you some coffee?"

"Oh honey," Annie wipes her eyes, "I shouldn't past nine in the morning. My doctor says caffeine isn't good for me, with my health and all."

Annie pauses for a moment to gather Chance to her knee. "But...well...maybe just a little bit. If you already have some made. I wouldn't want to impose—"

"You've got it."

I pour the morning's leftover lukewarm brew down the sink and move to make a fresh pot. I could use another hot cup myself.

"Tell me," Annie begins, "why did you come here to our little town?"

I take down two chunky mugs from the cupboard. "Do you take sugar?"

Annie scoffs. "Not a chance. Do you have any Sweet'N Low?"

"I have Sugar in the Raw, but not Sweet'N Low."

"Well, that explains a lot," she mumbles.

I can't help but smile. This woman reminds me of my very kind but very overbearing aunt Sally, who was like a second mother to me. I find these over-the-top dramatics strangely calming and comforting. Must be another genetic anomaly.

I pour fresh coffee and sit at the table with Annie. I smile but don't speak.

Annie huffs. "You *still* haven't given me an answer. Tell me everything about you, Grace."

She quick-taps her white nails against her ceramic mug.

"Well..." I begin, "Liam, my boyfriend, works for an architecture firm. We moved here so that he could oversee a remodel of the house of a wealthy man in town. The owner insisted that one of the architects be on-site as construction was going on. I grew up in Maine but left after college. So, when Liam said he got this gig, I was really excited to come back."

Annie slurps her coffee. "Perfect. Nice and strong, just like I like it. What do *you* do?"

"I work for a media research company based out of Portsmouth. Big companies hire us to research whether their products look positive or negative in the media. I read through collections of news articles and product reviews and annotate as I go. The end result is a final, boring report for the company. My last project was about tires."

"Tires?" Annie suppresses a snort.

"Yes. Tires. Thank you for not laughing, but I also find it funny that I get paid to read hundreds of online articles about stuff like tires. My current project focuses on a pest control product used by the government in Iraq. I'm what they call a 'reader,' and most readers get to work from home. I only go into the office for a day or two when I complete a project, which is why I'm here with Liam for the next year."

"Fascinating," Annie drawls. "What qualifications does it take to land a job where you read about tires and bug spray?"

"A BS in English, I guess. My mother always jokes that 'B' and 'S' are the key initials in that degree. Mom says that if you graduate with an English degree, you wind up with nothing except a whole lot of debt—"

Annie interrupts me. "Your mother's not wrong."

I laugh, then grimace as I think of my student loans.

"Sorry," Annie says. "Continue." Annie mimics zipping her lips.

I go on but purposefully leave out any of the strange feelings I'm having about Liam. No need to share my entire life story with this stranger.

"My life in a nutshell," I finish. "Nothing too crazy to tell. What about you?"

Annie doesn't hesitate. She tells me that she and her husband, Bill, moved to Maine almost thirty-five years ago. They have a grown daughter named Kelly and a couple of grandkids, but she's not on speaking terms with Kelly's husband, Asshole Tommy. "That Tommy is a no-good, lazy bastard. What else can I say?"

Annie makes the sign of the cross, then pretends to spit on my kitchen floor. Many, many more minutes pass while Annie prattles on about Tommy the Slacker; then Bill, a very handy man to have around the house; and, of course, Chance. Chance has been around for seven years, and from the way Annie talks about him, I can tell that she loves her dog more than anyone or anything else.

Annie only pauses half an hour later when she sees the toilet tank lid on the floor in front of the bathroom door. She points with one long fingernail. "What's all that about?"

"The toilet's not been right since we got here."

Annie shakes her head and tsks. "What about your boyfriend? Can't he fix the toilet? What kind of man leaves his girlfriend home all day with a shit-show toilet?"

My stomach churns at the mention of Liam's name. I clear my throat. "He's just been so busy with the house remodel for Peter Thorndike."

Annie sputters coffee out onto the table and snatches at her paper napkin. She first wipes her mouth and chin, then the spattered table. She says nothing, just grunts once, then again while I sit back and watch her antics.

"I take it you're not a fan of Mr. Thorndike?"

"I have nothing to say about that man." Annie pauses for a second, then can't keep quiet. "That man *loves* his money, and he *thinks* he's better than everyone else around here because of his *big* bank accounts. But that's all I have to say. For now. To be continued."

I tilt my head at her.

Annie raises her eyebrows and pretends to zip her lips shut again but then unzips them.

"I'll send my Bill over to have a look at that toilet."

I refill Annie's coffee cup, and she shares all the neighborhood "news" with me about people I've never met. Finally, Annie takes a dramatic deep breath after one last big gulp of coffee. "I have one more question. Will you cut that coffee cake I brought over? I'm wasting away over here."

I decide right then and there that Annie Whitney is the most obnoxious person I've ever met. I love her immediately.

I push myself to my feet and make my way over to the counter, but as I reach for a knife in the dish rack, something catches my eye. Jutting out from the side of the lease paperwork and stack of forwarded mail is a small yellow-lined piece of paper. I tug the corner of it and lean in close. There's a name and a New

Hampshire address I don't recognize scribbled on the paper in Liam's handwriting. "Something something Anderson," I mumble to myself. I squint to try to make out the rest of the name and the address, but Liam's known for his terrible handwriting.

Who the heck is that?

A tingling sensation races through my belly, followed by a sharp tug on my right side. I wince as I rub away the pain, and when the twinge subsides, I shrug my shoulders, telling myself this scrap of paper is probably something to do with Liam's work. And maybe he's right. At some point, I will have to let go of everything that happened at home in New Hampshire. I shove the paper back under the heap and begin cutting the coffee cake.

3

"This is it. I have to work today," I say aloud to the empty kitchen. When I raise my arms to stretch, that pain in the lower half of my belly returns. When I lower my arms and take a deep breath, the strange cramp retreats.

On recent mornings, I've gotten up early (for me) and annotated a lot of online material before noon, but that's about all I've managed to accomplish so far, workwise. Walks on the beach and quick peeks into the quaint, main-street shops have appealed to me much more than desk work. I also write every day in a journal file I keep open on my laptop. I've chronicled the road trip here, as well as my bizarre encounters with Annie.

Liam usually leaves before I wake in the mornings. Most nights, he gets home after I'm asleep, either in our bed or on the back sleeping porch. The back porch happens to be my favorite spot in the whole cottage. I'm drawn to its worn wicker chairs, comfy loveseat, and the nostalgic coffee table in the middle of the room, cleverly made of an old lobster trap with a smoky glass top. Scattered throw cushions add color: crisp blue, pale green, and a dusky rose-cream. A white paper lantern hangs in the corner for nighttime reading. This porch is paradise, at least to me.

Liam *never* sits out there.

I startle when the yellow rotary phone on the kitchen wall rings just as I sit down to work. I realize, until this very moment, I had thought the vintage phone was just there for decoration. I had no idea it actually still worked. Who has a landline these days?

I lift the receiver. "Hello?" The hardened plastic feels clunky in my hand, not like a cell. But still, I can't wait to call someone else with this phone after this call. I haven't spun a rotary dial in two decades.

"How are things over there? You should see the sweat rings under my arms. The heat, my god, the heat."

It's Annie, of course, and *of course* she somehow knows this house number.

"Life's good, although I do need to get some real work done today."

I pace and twirl the phone cord around my index finger, just like I did as an obnoxious teen.

"Okay, I won't keep you."

"No, wait. We can chat for a few more minutes."

While Annie updates me, I pour myself another cup of coffee. Annie tells me more salacious details about Tommy, her "no-good-son-of-a-bitch-son-in-law."

After five full minutes of unrelenting rant, I have to interrupt. "But...can you tell me how you *really* feel about Tommy? Because I don't quite have a clear picture yet."

Annie clucks into the phone, then follows it up with a dramatic pshaw and an exaggerated pfft. I laugh at her weird noises. "I'm kidding, Annie. He does sound like a real jerk. Trust me, I believe every word you say about him."

I've now got the phone receiver tucked between my ear and shoulder like I'm sixteen again. Just as I bring my hot mug to my mouth, Annie bellows into the phone at Chance. I spill coffee all over the Formica countertop. It runs and drips onto the linoleum and splatters my bare feet.

"Annie," I yelp, "I've just made the biggest mess over here. I gotta let you go. Talk soon."

I have to detangle my forearm from the spiral cord before I can replace the receiver.

After I wipe my spill, I go back to the phone and lift the receiver to hear the steady hum of the dial tone. I stick my finger into one of the bottom circles and ratchet the dial around until my index finger hits the metal stop, then release and watch it spin-snap back. What a trip, but I know this phone is just one more way to distract myself from work. I hang up the old phone, plop down at the kitchen table, and open the project folder on my computer. Time to get productive. But then I look down and see a huge coffee splotch on the front of my white tee shirt.

Just like my mother would do when I was a kid, I pull that section of my shirt to my mouth and suck at the stain. Mid-suck, I hear a gentle knock at the back door. Looking up, I see a very plain man outside with a metal toolbox in one hand. A few long hairs rainbow the top of his head. He wears wire-rimmed glasses, a simple red polo shirt, and tan khakis.

I jump to my feet but then cross my arms over my chest because I don't have a bra on. And I'm wearing a white tee shirt. A wet one.

"Hello, there. I'm Bill. My Annie said you might need some help with your toilet?"

I honest-to-God cannot believe what I see before me. I'm not exactly sure to whom I pictured Annie happily married all these long, loud years of her raucous life, but this meek, gentle man isn't him. Can't be him. He doesn't even raise his voice above a mumble.

I finally gather myself together enough to say, "Yes, I do, in fact. Please, come in."

I uncross one arm, open the door, and Bill and I exchange a weak but warm handshake. As Bill steps inside, the screen door smacks shut, as it tends to do. "I'll have to get to that screen door next," he says.

"Would you like a cup of coffee while you work? Or better yet, a tall glass of ice water?"

I eye Bill's long pants and think he must be sweltering.

Bill waves me off. "I'd rather get right to work...if you don't mind. You should get to work too. I understand you have a lot of reading to do for your job."

I smile, sure Annie's told Bill every single personal detail about my life. I won't have to repeat my life story for Bill, at least. Now, I can really and truly get down to work.

But first, while Bill goes to the bathroom to work on the toilet, I run upstairs to put on a bra and a clean tee shirt. Now's also a good time to wash my face and brush my teeth. And ditch the sweatpants. *Maybe* I should drag a comb through my unruly hair too.

When I look in the bathroom mirror, I discover my bed-frazzled hair is even worse than I'd thought. I've never seen an actual rat's nest in person, but I'm sure I've got one prime example on the top of my head right now.

Once I've made myself as presentable as possible, I sit at the kitchen table and (finally) review the latest articles. Bill doesn't make a sound while in that tiny bathroom, but despite my best intentions, my mind wanders from my work. I wonder yet again what in the world the attraction could be between Bill and Annie. Married for decades, Annie had said. Opposites attract? What a silly old saying, but don't clichés persist for a reason? Still, how do they possibly cohabitate? And then I think about Liam and try to picture us in our retirement. I abandon the thought and tell myself I have to get back to work.

About twenty minutes later, I can see Bill packing up his tools out of the corner of my eye.

I clear my throat. "Please stay for a cool drink," I insist. "Or maybe some leftover blueberry coffee cake as payment?"

Bill shrugs. "Well...I really should go."

"Okay, but at least take a piece to go. Take one for Annie too." I feel fresh sweat rolling down my temples and hope Bill doesn't notice.

I wrap two large pieces of coffee cake in a shiny swath of tin foil. I hand the makeshift doggie bag to Bill. He tips an imaginary hat my way, and then his brow furrows. "Grace, are you okay? You're looking a little pale."

I force a smile. "I'm fine. Just a little tired still from the trip here, I guess."

"Well, okay. Take care of yourself, you hear?"

Bill leaves out the screen door, which closes behind him without a sound.

I shut my laptop and rub my eyes. Liam and I haven't seen each other much at all these past few days. When we do, it's often very late, so I just sit and watch him devour the leftovers from my earlier dinners. As he eats, Liam tells me about his days in great detail, and I listen. He eventually asks about my days, but I can tell that he's too tired to care about the responses I give. Besides, I have nothing much to report: I try to work when Liam isn't here, and I talk to Annie when I can't. Sometimes I capture events in my journal. That's all—work, gossip, journal.

I stare out the kitchen window, trying once again to picture me and Liam at Annie and Bill's age, but all that goes through my mind are images of Liam and his coworker, Sophie. He's told me repeatedly that nothing physical happened between them, but still, I have to wonder. Nausea clutches at my stomach.

I jump when I hear a bang on the porch. I whirl around and see Annie standing on the other side of the screen door. "Let's go. I haven't got all day to wait around for you," she announces as she barges her way in. Today's outfit: a hot-pink, short-sleeved jogging suit straight out of 1987.

"What's the holdup? Get dressed. We need to exercise." Annie acts as if we've walked together every day for years and years.

Suddenly, the room is spinning. Annie puts a hand on her hip. "Hey. Are you okay? You look like you've seen a ghost."

I swallow hard and steady myself against the wall. "I'm just.... I'm tired. I've been overwhelmed with work. I could use a break, I guess."

Annie leans forward and places her hand on my forehead. "Jesus. You're burning up. Are you sure you're just tired?"

"Yeah, I'm fine. I'll take a quick walk with you. Though I shouldn't go too far. I have a deadline for work in two weeks."

"You look about half dead, so let's just take a quick jaunt on the beach. Plus, I have to drive straight to an appointment after our walk."

"Give me a minute to change."

I grip the railing the entire way up the stairs, taking deep breaths in through my nose and out through my mouth. By the time I reach the top of the staircase, I'm feeling a little steadier. I tell myself I've got to find a way to let go of the anger and suspicion I still harbor toward Liam because I suspect all this stress is what's making me feel sick.

Since our houses are only one street over from the beach, Annie and I take little time to get to the shore. There aren't many people on the beach yet today. We're in the midst of an Indian summer; by noon, this beach will be full of lounge chairs, plastic pails, and frantic moms with babies in dirty, sand-filled diapers.

Chance struts ahead of us on his leash. Annie pumps her arms up and down, and while I'm impressed by her speed, her breathing is too labored just a few more minutes in. "We need to stop and stretch," she commands.

I'm glad for the break too, because the twinge in my lower belly won't seem to go away. I tell Annie, "I should've had more water this morning and less coffee. I have an awful cramp in my stomach."

"Listen. You just need to do some stretches. Watch me." Annie bends down and performs some moves that look like they came from a workout video. Chance sits at Annie's feet and stares up at her. I join in but then stop after just a couple of shallow squats. The cramp now shoots off sparks of pain into my hips and thighs. I stifle an involuntary moan but still pretend to keep limbering up my legs.

Minutes later, Annie straightens from one last side stretch. She takes out a pack of Mistys and a lighter from the back pocket of her jogging pants. She places a cigarette in the corner of her mouth and lights it. I'm amazed Annie can flick the wheel of the lighter with those nails. Never in my life has a stretch break included a smoke break.

I back away from Annie and fan the smoke out of my face. Annie notes my grimace, takes one more drag, tosses the cigarette to the ground, still lit, then yanks on Chance's leash and takes off power walking again. I snub the cigarette with my foot before I follow them.

"How do you like it here so far?" Annie asks between labored breaths.

"I like it, but...."

"But what?" Annie stops to stare at me.

"I don't know. All of my friends are back in New Hampshire. Say is in New York. Liam's been really busy since we got here."

Annie interrupts, "What's up with Liam, anyway? I've never met him. I haven't even seen him up close. The day you got here, he looked tall. How tall is he?"

She pauses, completely winded from her game-show-host style line of questioning. She inhales sharply and runs her forearm over her damp brow.

I'm a little alarmed at her winded condition. "You'll meet Liam soon. The remodel has just been so hectic."

I slow my own steps.

"Liam's too busy to make time for you?" Annie rolls her eyes.

Her lungs seem to be working better at this more leisurely pace, but her face looks extra puffy and beet red.

Now I really feel like I'm going to cry. My nose tingles. The sharp cramp in my side returns. "Well, why don't you and Bill come over for dinner next Friday night? You can meet Liam then," I propose.

Annie stops dead in her tracks, which halts Chance as well, and I almost trip over the bedazzled leash. "Well, okay then! What can I bring? A dessert? And will you be serving Mexican?" Annie fake-whispers out of the side of her mouth, "Because if the meal has a lot of dairy, you should know that Annie's southern region struggles with a variety of cheeses."

I laugh then have to take some more deep breaths to ease the pain that has extended from my side to my stomach. The accompanying twinges are starting to feel more like lightning bolts across *my* "southern region." Probably something I ate.

But then the cramp becomes unbearable. "Hey, Annie, I kinda feel terrible all of a sudden," I gasp.

It feels like sweat is running down my legs. Must just be the heat, but I feel gross and sticky everywhere. "Can we turn back?"

"Of course."

I try to smile and talk like a normal person. "We should do this again...soon. Maybe when I'm feeling a little better."

"Agreed." Annie gives my wrist a gentle squeeze.

We fall quiet as we walk back, but Chance darts around my feet and barks. At one point, he tries to climb my legs. Annie snugs the length of the leash and pulls Chance to her. "I don't know what's wrong with him today. Chance, will you just knock it off!"

I follow Annie back to her house, walking very slowly, trying to nurse the pain in my abdomen. Annie opens their back door, unhooks his leash, scoots Chance into the house with her foot, then snaps the door closed behind him. "There. Finally, some damn peace and quiet." Annie swings around to say goodbye.

"I think I'll go lie down for a bit," I say as I turn and take a few steps toward my own back door.

"Grace!" The sharp, shrill note in Annie's voice freezes me. "Sweetie, honey, I think something's wrong."

"What do you mean?"

"There's blood."

"What?"

"Look," Annie blurts out, pointing to my lower half.

I look down at my soggy leggings. Jagged red streaks line the insides of my thighs.

"Holy shit."

"Are your periods always this heavy?"

"Not at all. The opposite, in fact."

"When was your last period, Grace?"

I do some mental calculations. "I don't know. Three months ago, maybe four? They've never been regular." My pulse rises, and I start to breathe hard. Too hard. "My period has never been this way," I repeat, frozen on the walkway.

"Let's get you inside."

Annie takes my hand and wraps her arm around my waist to help me back to the cottage. I keep my legs spread wide to prevent the blood from smearing more. "Here we go, here we go, here we go," Annie repeats when we reach the porch. I pull my house keys from my pocket and hand them to her. She grunts as she tries to figure out the correct key but finally opens the door and pushes it wide for me to enter first.

Annie follows me through the living room into the kitchen. I totter to the bathroom and close the door. I push my leggings and underwear down and see a lot of bright, chunky blood.

My vision blurs. "Annie!" I cry out as I grip my own knees for balance, afraid I'll pass out.

From outside the door, Annie says, "Sweetie, tell me what I can do to help."

"Do you see a roll of paper towels on the counter?"

"I've got you, Grace. Don't worry."

Still sitting on the commode of the tiny half bath, I open the door just enough for her to pass me the jumbo roll. I yank a wad of the roll and press it between my legs. What the hell is going on?

"Grace," Annie pleads again from behind the cracked door. "What can I do?"

A ringing screeches in my ears, and my body flashes with heat. I want to lie down on the cold tile floor. "Annie, I think maybe you'd better take me to the hospital."

Fifteen hectic minutes later, we arrive at the local hospital's emergency room entrance.

Annie hits the brakes too hard, and I jerk forward against my seatbelt with a guttural moan.

"Sorry, sorry," she whispers as she shifts into park.

A security guard stands by the entrance of the ER. Annie jumps out and waves her arms at him. "My friend needs a wheelchair."

The stout uniformed man nods and steps in front of the

wide double doors, which glide open for him. He reappears almost immediately with a wheelchair. His black walkie-talkie garbles muffled, crackling voices as he pushes it toward Annie's car. Annie opens the passenger door for me.

Seeing her there, helping me, makes me feel helpless. "I'm fine," I manage to protest. "Annie, really, I don't need a wheelchair. I can just...walk," I yelp as the cramp hits me again.

"As if!" Annie huffs and tsks. She snatches the handles of the wheelchair from the security guard and pushes the contraption toward me.

A gush of thick, hot blood floods my underwear when I stand. Before we left, Annie had fetched me a pair of clean underwear and yoga pants from my bureau upstairs, and I had added a thick overnight pad.

Woozy again, I have to clutch the doorframe to steady myself. "Maybe I'll take you up on your offer for that ride after all," I try to joke. Annie frowns at me.

As the doors slide apart once more, Annie steers me directly to the admissions desk. The rubber wheels of the wheelchair thud against the uneven tile. Annie clears her throat and says, "My friend Grace needs your help. She's bleeding. A lot."

The woman in purple scrubs behind the desk stands to peer down at me.

I take a deep breath and say, "I think I might be having a... miscarriage." My voice croaks on the last word.

The receptionist nods and picks up the desk phone, pushes a few quick buttons, and then speaks into the receiver. Her words sound muffled in my ears and don't make any sense to me.

I look up toward Annie, and she squats to lower her face to

mine. "What else can I do?" she whispers. "Do you...want me to call Liam for you?"

I grimace and look away from her. "How about I get checked in and let them take a look? We'll go from there."

Annie brushes my bangs to the side, then leans in more to kiss the crown of my head.

"Sounds like a plan to me, sweetheart."

The receptionist hangs up the telephone. "I'll take you right in to see the triage nurse."

The receptionist's sneakers squeak against the clean tile as she comes around to me and Annie.

"Family only," she states. "Otherwise, you have to wait out here."

Annie swallows so loud I can hear her gulp, and then she pats both my hands with both of her own. Her hands feel too cold to me. She says, "I'll stay right here in the waiting room."

I am cold all over now, shivering even, but I still manage to say clearly, "Thanks, Annie. You're the best."

The nurse wheels me away. I glance again over my shoulder at Annie and try to wave.

My whole arm trembles, and I drop it back down into my lap.

"It will all be okay," Annie calls out, "I'm right here for you." Annie shifts her purse from one shoulder to the other, then sits down in a hard plastic chair at the end of a long row of other hard plastic chairs. She holds her chin up, meets my eyes one last time, and watches me go.

4

Liam opens the passenger door and leans across me to unbuckle my seatbelt. He helps me out of the truck with a gentle hand at my back. As he closes the door behind me, I make my way toward the house, triggering the motion sensor, which sprays a beam of light over the wet tar of the driveway. I guess there was a rain shower while I was in the hospital waiting for Liam to pick me up. I didn't notice. Still holding my stomach, I trudge up the front steps and let myself in through the front door.

I stand only for a moment, trying to decide if I should plop myself down on the couch or go straight to bed. I glance at the clock on the wall. It's almost midnight. I might as well go upstairs.

Halfway up, I hear Liam let himself into the cottage. I don't stop.

In the bedroom, I click on the lamp on my nightstand as I kick off my sneakers. I ease myself slowly under the covers, prop myself up on my pillow, and start scrolling through my phone, not really wanting to text anyone in particular. I could text Say, but I'm not ready to discuss what happened. Yet. I want to call my mom, but my cheeks flush with heat at the thought. I'm not embarrassed about the miscarriage. I'm mortified that it took nearly six hours to get Liam to respond to my repeated calls and texts, and then an additional hour for him to come to the hospital, from wherever he was.

I could have called Annie, but I'd already sent her home late in the afternoon, and I didn't want to bug her to come back to be with me.

Liam ducks his head into the bedroom. "Need anything from downstairs before I come up for the night?"

I still can't bring myself to look at him. I continue to scroll on my phone. "Nope."

Part of me wants to ask him where the hell he was all that time and why he didn't respond. But I'm exhausted. And I have a headache. And I feel nauseous. And I'm not sure if the gravity of it all has hit me yet. This morning, I was pregnant...and now I'm not. And since I had no idea that I was pregnant, I don't even know what I should be feeling, exactly.

Liam returns and goes directly to his side of the bed. He lowers his skinny chinos and then struggles to step out of them. Once free, he drapes them neatly over the back of a chair in the corner of the room and then does the same with his button-down shirt.

When I reach over and switch off my lamp, the room goes completely dark, except for the green glow from my cell phone. Liam lets out a playful "Heyyy," so I reach over and click the lamp back on.

"Sorry."

I continue to stare at my phone. The room is silent.

"Grace?"

I don't respond. I want to ignore Liam for the rest of my life.

"Grace. Are you okay? Is there anything I can do? Can I get

you anything?"

And then, without meaning to, I bark, "Where the hell were you?"

Liam's mouth drops open.

I know I shouldn't do this now. It's late. I'm beyond exhausted and in pain. But this is the one time I just can't let him off the hook. I sit up straighter, but my voice cracks. "I was there, all by myself for hours, Liam. So many hours. Why didn't you call me back or text me at least?"

"Grace, I...." Liam stops, then starts again. "Like I told you, I was so caught up with work with Peter that I didn't even glance down at my phone."

"Yeah right," I huff. "Whatever."

I lie down and roll over onto my side, my back to him. I can feel Liam tense behind me, getting defensive. "Not *whatever*. It's true. You don't know what it's like working for that man. He wants what he wants, and he wants it now. I thought he was on board with the master bath design, and then he up and changed everything at the last minute. I had to come up with a whole new set of plans with the building crew breathing down my neck."

I feel him shift onto his back, then slap his hands down on the duvet.

Before I can stop myself, I mutter, "Sounds like you've had a real rough day. I'm so sorry today was so hard for you."

"Grace. That's not what I meant, and you know it. I know you had an awful day today, but you asked where I was, and I wanted you to know. I'd never ignore you."

Tears form in my eyes and spill down my cheeks, and I'm angry at myself for reacting to him, to his excuses. "Liam. It was humiliating. They discharged me and I had to sit by the entryway in a friggin' wheelchair waiting, hoping, to hear from you." I swipe at my eyes and nose with the back of my hand. My lip trembles.

Liam leans over and attempts to rub my back. I stiffen under his fingers.

"Grace. I'm so sorry. Had I known, had I seen my phone, I would have come right over to be with you. I was out in the guesthouse drawing up new plans. I turned my phone off and didn't even look at it because I had to finish those new plans as fast as I could, and I didn't want the distraction."

"Mm-hmm," I mumble.

Liam squeezes my hip. "I'm so sorry, Grace. Truly."

I do the mental math in my head. Peter's place is maybe twenty-five minutes from the hospital, and that's only if you're doing the speed limit.

"It was so bad, Liam. The baby, well, I mean, the leftover tissue had to come out, and I had to push...."

I stop, overcome. I can't help but openly cry. The room is silent except for my sobs.

"Grace. I swear to you, I will never leave my ringer off for that long ever again."

I bring my knees up to my chest, and as I do, I feel a warm gush of warm blood between my legs. "Great," I say, swinging my legs over the side of the bed. I squeeze my legs together and shuffle to the bathroom.

I close the door, pull down my yoga pants, and sit on the toilet. I let myself continue to have a good cry, my face cradled in my hands. My shoulders shake, and the tears streak down my face, and I don't stifle my sobs.

I hear Liam shuffling on the other side of the door. "Grace, sweetie. Can I come in? Please?"

And as much as I don't want to let him in, he barges in anyway. Liam kneels on the floor before me, puts his arms around me, and buries his head in the crook between my head and shoulder. I feel his warm breath on my neck. He doesn't even seem to mind that I'm sitting here, bare-assed on the toilet, bleeding, with my yoga pants around my ankles. He rubs big circles on my back with his hands and whispers, "It's okay, it's okay..." again and again.

I lean into him and cry until I feel truly exhausted. Liam continues to hold me.

Finally, I glance at the full-length mirror hanging on the door behind Liam and catch my own reflection. My face is swollen, red and blotchy, almost like Annie's that morning on our beach walk. My curls are moist along my hairline and jut out all over the place in crazy strands.

I sit up straighter. I take a long, deep inhale and then exhale.

Liam places his hands on my bare thighs and looks up at me. "It's all going to be okay, baby."

I unravel a wad of toilet paper and blow my nose. Liam grabs hold of the edge of the vanity and pulls himself to his feet.

With Liam out of the way, I stare at my reflection again. Feeling sorry for myself, I say, "I mean, I wouldn't blame you for ignoring me today. Look at me. I look like total shit."

More tears roll down my cheeks—I can't stop them now. Usually, I would try to cover at least part of my weeping face because Say has told me my entire life that even though we're not related by blood, we both possess the same ugly cry gene—but tonight, I'm too exhausted to care what Liam sees me do or not do, despite what I just said to him.

Liam bends forward and places his hand under my chin. "Hey. Look at me."

I allow my eyes to meet his. He tucks some of my wild hair behind my ear. "You are so beautiful to me, and we will get through this together," he says with a sad, sweet smile. His eyes shine even more blue than usual.

"You promise me you were at work today?"

Liam's smile fades. He straightens, and it takes him a few seconds to answer. He sighs, then leans down to my level again. "I swear I was caught up at work today. Had I known what you were going through, I would have been there in a heartbeat."

He swallows hard, and it looks like he has genuine tears in his eyes. "You shouldn't have had to go through what you did today alone, and I'm so sorry. Truly."

I want to believe him—I really, really do— but part of me just can't. Maybe he was working, but I wonder if he has tears in his eyes because he realizes that while he was off doing God knows what, I was going through the worst thing I've ever been through in my entire life. That's enough to make anyone cry. And as the tears continue to roll down my face, and I stare up at Liam, I start to doubt if we'll ever be able to recover from what happened today.

5

"Look. Bill's already seen the insides of my toilet and Annie's already seen the insides of my uterus smeared down my legs. You can't get more intimate than that. Why not throw a dinner party into the mix as planned?" I stick my head in the fridge's freezer, grab an ice cube to rub on the back of my neck. The ice melts, drips down my spine, and I shiver.

Liam looks at me with raised eyebrows. "It's only been two weeks. I don't think it would hurt to push this dinner another week."

"Do you want to postpone the dinner because of me? Is that the real reason, or does this have something to do with a work deadline?"

Liam shakes his head. "No. I am *trying* to look out for you."

He walks to the kitchen sink and fills a glass of water from the tap. As he guzzles, I hear each swallow, and his Adam's apple bobs up and down.

Time to get back to breakfast. I whisk eggs with a fork in a ceramic bowl. When I turn to pour the mix into the hot pan on the stovetop, some sizzling butter splatters onto my stomach, and I jump back. "Shit."

I pull up the hem of my tank top to run a dishcloth across my stomach. I know I wasn't that far along, but my belly still seems slack. I drop the cloth to place my hand on my stomach, which happens a lot lately, I realize.

Liam sees my gesture and removes my hand. He cradles my tightened fist in both of his hands to keep me still. "Why don't you let me finish here? Go sit, get some work done."

Liam loosens his grip to lift my hand to his face and kiss my knuckles.

"Thank you, Liam." I readjust my shirt on my way to the living room.

I collapse onto the couch, lean forward to drag the coffee table closer. I put my feet up, then exhale. Wonder if Annie will stop by today.

I hear the metal spatula scrape the bottom of the nonstick frying pan. I hunch over to rub my hands along the two-week stubble of my leg hair. I really need a long shower today. And a thorough shave.

Liam comes in with a plate in one hand and silverware in the other. He sets the plate down next to me on the couch. I tuck my legs onto the couch to make room for him. I hear his knees creak when he squats in front of me. "Do you want to talk about anything? The baby?"

My cheeks flush. That's the one topic I have avoided talking about for two weeks.

I shake my head. Liam leans closer to me.

"I just want to make sure you're okay."

I nod. "I'm fine."

Liam rises, puts my plate on the coffee table, and sits on the edge of the couch beside me.

"Okay. If you say so. I need to get to work. I just want to make sure you're okay before I leave."

My mouth feels too dry to eat, or even speak, like I've eaten dirt. I close my eyes. I try to get my thoughts straight before I open my mouth. I know my hormones have been all over the place since the miscarriage. My mind feels too sluggish to keep track of all of my swirling emotions. "I'm fine," I choke out. "Let's talk about something else. Anything. Please."

Liam nods but says nothing.

I press both temples with my index fingers. "What I *do* want to talk about is what to make for dinner tonight. I want to impress Annie because she's such a good cook. I've looked at recipes online, and I think pork tenderloin with garlic mashed potatoes, a green salad, and a fresh fruit cobbler for dessert sounds impressive. What do you think?"

Liam squeezes my upper arm. "That sounds perfect. I'll try like hell to be back in time, but as I said, I'm behind at work because of...everything."

I unfold my legs. "Wait, you're behind at work because of... *me?*" My voice trembles. "Because of...our *dead baby?*" I force myself to stop speaking, afraid of what else I might say.

Liam tightens his jaw. "Grace, that didn't come out right. I didn't mean...."

"That everything's all my fault now? I bet you think I did something wrong."

Liam's mouth drops open. "Wait. Where'd you get that idea? We didn't even know you were pregnant. All I meant was that I lost time at work, and now I'm behind schedule. I've got these sketches for the guest suite that Peter wants done, like, yesterday."

I sigh dramatically and cross my arms over my chest. My breasts are still a tiny bit tender, so I uncross them immediately and wait for whatever bullshit he'll say next.

Liam continues: "I know this dinner tonight means a lot to you. I'll do my best to be home by five to help you prepare the meal. Or maybe six. I promise."

I lock eyes with him. "Thank you for all you have sacrificed for me lately. I'm sorry it's been so rough for you."

Liam takes a step back and nearly bumps into the coffee table. "Grace. I know I have a lot to make up for here. I'm trying."

I pull my eyes away from him to gaze down at my nails. I chip at the aqua nail polish. When I've pried off several loose spots, I brush the flaked remains from my lap onto the floor.

Liam bends and kisses me on the forehead. "We'll talk more later. I've got to get to work. I'll see you tonight."

Nausea grips my guts. I clench the jumbled blankets with my fists.

When Liam opens the front door to leave, a wave of heat enters. The temp's been on the rise all week. He swings back around and blows me another kiss before he closes the door.

From the couch, I flip him off with both middle fingers, which makes me feel better, even though he can't see me.

Images of Portsmouth and Liam's coworker, Sophie, spring into my mind. I crack my knuckles one at a time as I tamp the images back down. I pick up the plate Liam brought me and stab the fork into the eggs to take some bites. I shove more and more food into my mouth, but I know if I keep up this way, I'm going to choke, for real, so I set the plate on the coffee table and concentrate on chewing. Slowly. I breathe in again and again through my nose: deep inhales. I need to focus and make a plan.

I know I can't just sit on this couch all day and repeat the miscarriage in my mind. If I do, I'll lose my shit. Besides, I've had on the same frayed tank top and ratty pair of Liam's boxer briefs for two days. A shower and a change of clothes will clean me up and cheer me up. I toss the blankets to the side. Stretch. Moan. Yawn. Put one foot in front of the other. Move toward the staircase.

Like most older homes in this area, this house showcases a small stained-glass window at eye level on the landing of the stairs, and framed photos travel up the walls of the stairwell. I've seen these pictures many times, but one of them catches my eye as I slog up the stairs.

The photo was taken at sunset, and the sky's that pure pink color that glows at night on the Maine coast. The photo depicts the dark silhouette of two people from the back. In the photo, the couple holds hands as they walk toward the horizon. The shorter figure rests their head on the other person's shoulder. I take the photo off the wall to study it. I stare a few more seconds at the happy couple but then hang the picture back up and drag myself up the rest of the stairs.

The shower helps cool me down, but my head starts to feel hot again when I see blood run down the drain. I close my eyes for a few seconds, and when I look down again, I don't see any more blood.

I step out of the shower and wrap in my purple robe. Sweat beads cling to my forehead. I've got to get out of this steamy bathroom. I grab a towel off the rack and rough-dry my hair. Too hot for a blowout anyway. I toss the soaked towel onto the counter. I pull the length of my hair forward, braid, and toss the wet rope back over my shoulder. I should get some work done. I'll hit the grocery store this afternoon.

I dress and return to my nest on the couch. I lift the small oscillating fan from the floor and place it at my feet on the coffee table. I slip into work mode, but can't concentrate, so I close my laptop and set it on the couch beside me.

I snatch Liam's leather portfolio off the coffee table. I open the cover and flip through the yellow legal pad inside filled with sketches of rooms and measurements. Boring. I flip through a few more pages and am about to close it back up when something catches my eye. The corner of a photograph sticks out from one of the back pages.

I tug at it and pull it out. My heart thumps and my jaw goes tight. It's a photograph of Liam and Sophie at a Red Sox game. They're part of a group photo of the people he works with. Most everyone is raising plastic cups of beer toward the person taking the photo. But I can't help but notice that Liam has an arm around Sophie's shoulders, and she has one hand behind him, presumably on his lower back, while her other hand rests on his chest. He's facing the camera with his big toothy grin, but she's turned sideways gazing at him. She's laughing as if Liam's just said the most hilarious thing she's ever heard. My cheeks burn, and there's a tingling in my chest. I study the photo for a few more seconds and then tuck it back into the legal pad. I slam the portfolio closed and toss it back onto the coffee table. Why the hell would he still have that photo?

My heart pounds as I debate whether or not to question Liam about the photo, but then I decide to practice the pause.

If I call or text right now, there's no way of knowing what might come flying out of this mouth of mine. Probably better if I wait and confront him in person.

I push myself to my feet and begin straightening the blankets and throw pillows on the couch. I punch a couple of the pillows to fluff them up. I close my eyes and take a big breath in and then exhale and open my eyes. I debate calling off dinner with Annie and Bill tonight but decide to go through with it anyway. Annie would be so disappointed.

My anger gives me the energy to wash floors and scrub toilets like I never have before, and even though my thoughts are frantic, the day flies by. I run to the grocery store and return home to prepare dinner late in the afternoon, but I have to put on some music to quiet my still-racing mind. Liam hasn't texted me all day and I haven't texted him either. I'm desperate to speak to him, but I doubt he'll come home in time to talk before dinner.

I pace in the kitchen while dinner cooks, waiting for Liam to get home. With every sound of a car driving down the street, I spring to the window over the kitchen sink and look out into the driveway to see if it's him. By 5:50 p.m., there's still no Liam and I'm seething with anger.

I'm bent over the open oven, carefully pulling out the baking dish, when I hear someone at the back door. With my free hand, I yank the drawer beside the stove open, pull out a trivet, toss it down onto the counter, and set the steaming dish down on it. I shake the oven mitts off and slap them down on the counter.

I whirl around and face Liam. He's standing with his arms spread wide, holding a bouquet of flowers. My cheeks burn, and before I can stop myself, I bark out, "Where the hell have you been?"

Liam's smile fades, and his arms drop to his sides. "Grace, I told you I would be here as soon as I could."

Liam sets the bunch of flowers on the counter, then wraps his arms around me, knotting his hands behind my back. He leans in close like he's going to kiss me. "I'm sorry. I'm here before six, aren't I?"

I wrench myself out of his embrace, raise a finger, point it at him, then open my mouth to question him about the photo, but before I can say anything, there's a knock at the back door. We both turn and see Annie and Bill in the doorway. I turn away to compose myself, smoothing my hands down my front a few times before turning back around. Liam opens the screen door for them both. Bill hands me a bottle of chilled white wine.

"Thank you." I kiss Bill on the cheek, hoping he won't notice the tears in my eyes or how flushed my cheeks are right now.

Annie looks Liam up and down. "Who is this handsome fella?"

Liam extends his hand to Annie with his usual graceful smile.

Annie turns to me and mouths, "He's cute!"

I force a smile of my own, which I'm sure isn't graceful. Liam's apparently able to compose himself much quicker than I can.

"I really want to thank you for the care you showed my Gracie the other day," Liam says. "I'm glad you stayed with her."

Annie bows, hand on heart. "My pleasure."

"And you, sir. I understand I owe you my gratitude as well, for fixing the broken toilet.

We're lucky to have the two of you next door."

"Happy to help," Bill says.

Even though I can smile at our guests more genuinely now, I'm still boiling with an undercurrent of anger at Liam. My voice almost wobbles when I say, "We're going to eat on the front porch tonight, because of the heat inside. Maybe we'll catch a nice sea breeze."

"Thank you, Jesus," Annie belts out.

Trying to sound chipper, I say, "Bill and Liam, why don't you take the wine and go out front through the living room?"

Liam turns and looks at me again, his brows furrowed. He mouths, "What's wrong?" but I just shove the bottle of wine at him, and he takes it from me finally, the quizzical, innocent look still on his face. Asshole.

The men laugh at some joke and casually make their way to the front porch. I'm certainly ready for a glass of chilled wine, and I bet they are too. The kitchen is hot with tension.

Annie stays behind with me. "Quite a decent grip, huh? Did you see those hands? Jeez! Oh, the things he could do with those hands!" She nudges my side.

I turn away and putter around, checking burners and grabbing plates. Annie tries to help. I try not to seem impatient or flustered.

"Hey, is everything okay?" she asks quietly. "You seem upset." She grips my upper arms to hold me still. "Why don't you take a minute and sit down. You look flushed."

Annie unceremoniously plops me into a kitchen chair. I squeeze my forehead with one hand while Annie opens and slams cupboard doors. She tsks and pulls down a vase from one of the top cabinets, rinsing it off in the sink. She says over her shoulder, "Do you want to tell me what's going on, or not?"

Annie dries the vase with paper towels and arranges the flowers from Liam while she waits for my response. "These are lovely," she murmurs to herself.

I know it's not right to sit here and pout and wallow in my feelings while Annie and Bill are here. I force myself out of the chair and say, "I'm just ready for my life to get back to normal."

I look at the vintage vase but push the arrangement out of the way.

I grab the salad bowl, balance it on my left forearm; my years as a server are paying off now. Next comes the bowl of garlic mashed potatoes, which I place on my wrist and hand. With my right hand, I give Annie the tray of sliced pork and nudge her toward the front porch.

Bill stands when we arrive. Liam remains seated but remembers his manners at the last minute. He stands too and moves toward me to take the salad bowl, but I skirt his reach.

Annie and I set the pretty platters on the table. We all sit, pass the food, and fill our plates.

Annie takes a bite of the potatoes and groans. "Heavenly. Well done, Grace."

"Thank you."

I take a small sip of the wine. I look across the table at Liam as he cuts at his meat. I raise the wine glass to my mouth again and guzzle.

Annie clears her throat. "Tell me the story of how you two met."

I set my empty wine glass on the table and sit in silence, not eating. I cock my head to the side and stare at Liam.

"I guess I'll start?" Liam says.

I raise my eyebrows, and Liam continues: "Well—"

Annie cuts in. "I love a good love story. Start from the very beginning, and don't leave out any details."

Liam begins again: "The first time I saw Grace, she was in the lobby of the renovated mill where we work. A few companies in the building share a common lobby space. You should see the design of this space."

Of course he's going to work architecture into the conversation. I jump in. "Liam had on a blue oxford button-down that day. It looked like he had ironed his shirt perfectly, which should have been my first clue about how anal—"

Annie interrupts again. "If something of mine needs to be ironed, I just toss it in the dryer for a few minutes to fluff it up."

I close my eyes for a long second. I try to picture how everything used to be between me and Liam before the miscarriage, before his non-affair

I open my eyes. Liam clears his throat and says, "I was in the lobby for a quick coffee but had just spilled a huge cup down the front of my shirt. Grace brought me napkins from the counter and tried to help me. After that, we began to talk to each other a lot in the office. A few coffee breaks turned into meeting after work at the local coffee shop. Coffee turned into a few drinks, next came weekend lunches and dinners, and so on. A lot has happened since, but here we are."

I raise my glass to Liam but slit my eyes at him before I take yet another gulp of wine. Bill had refilled my glass, and I thank him then. "Wonderful wine, Bill, really," I tell him between sips.

Annie rolls her eyes at Bill, who's blushing, then looks from me to Liam as she dabs at the corners of her mouth with her napkin. She squeezes my hand under the table but turns her full attention to Liam. She begins to grill him, asking a range of questions about his interests, favorite movies, and whether he enjoys working with Peter. To his credit, he answers every inquiry, no matter how blunt or nosy.

Bill and I chat quietly while Annie yammers on. Bill reminds me of my dad—they both have peaceful personalities—and I begin to feel more at ease. I'm sure all the delicious white wine I've consumed with Bill's help is also helping me relax. I thank Bill again for the bottle, and he blushes once again. He's charming, but like, truly charming. Unlike Liam.

After a long while spent alternately appreciating Bill's quiet chatter, and stewing in anger, mostly to get Annie to stop the interrogation, I announce it's time for dessert. I leave for the kitchen and assume Annie will follow, but she stays to ask Liam more and more questions.

I return with the cobbler and a half gallon of French vanilla ice cream on a tray. I serve everyone generous portions, slapping Liam's into a dish last, then practically tossing the bowl in front of him before sitting down.

Annie moans louder and louder with each bite, throws her head back even. Feeling tipsy, I can't help but laugh at her antics, and as I do, I inhale too sharply, and some cobbler goes down the wrong pipe. I start to cough, and my eyes sting with water. I take a few sips from my wine glass but continue to cough.

Suddenly, Annie pushes her chair back and barrels toward me. I try to tell her I'm fine, really, but I can't stop her. She stands behind me and says, "No one panic. I know the Heimlich maneuver." Annie wraps her arms around my midsection and tries to pull her fist into my sternum, which makes me laugh again, causing me to cough even more. Only to Annie, I'm sure my cough must sound like more choking.

Liam stands and shouts, "Annie, Grace isn't choking! She's laughing. Just look at her!"

His voice is so jarring that we all startle and stare at him. Annie stops her life-saving efforts.

I try to catch my breath. "I'm fine! I'm fine!" I sputter to both Annie and Liam.

Bill, ever the gentleman, hands me a fresh napkin.

Annie lets her arms drop from my middle. She steps back, makes the sign of the cross, and blows a kiss to the sky. "Thank God. I thought you were a goner."

Annie sits back down in her chair and uses her splotched napkin to mop the sweat from her forehead. Liam stares at me for a few moments before he sits back down as well.

Bill lifts his spoon, scrapes the bottom of his bowl, and takes one last bite. I push my own bowl to the side. I have certainly had enough berry cobbler. And enough white wine too, for that matter. I reach for my water glass.

Chitchat is minimal after dessert. Liam only responds when directly spoken to for the rest of the night, though he does shake Bill's hand and kiss Annie on the cheek when they leave.

In the kitchen, I scrape, rinse, and stack the dirty dishes by the sink. I'm not ready to confront Liam yet. Next, I pack away the small portions of leftovers into containers in the fridge.

Liam pecks at the keys of his laptop in the living room while I clean. I wipe the counters and dry my hands on the blue dishcloth. I flick off the overhead lights, tramp toward the living room and then the stairs. "I'm going up," I say in a flat tone in Liam's direction.

Liam turns and sighs. "I'm tired too. I'll come up soon."

He arrives just as I've changed into my pajamas. I fall onto my back on the bed and stare at the ceiling. Liam finally starts to talk again while unbuttoning his shirt. "How do you think it went?"

The anger, the tension, the heat of the kitchen, and the long day have finally gotten to me. Liam strips down to his boxer briefs and hops into bed.

He rolls onto his side and smiles at me, and before I can say anything, he says, "That Annie's ridiculous. I mean, I know she's been good to you, but don't you think she's a little... over-the-top?"

I'm more than a little annoyed by this unkind assessment. I prop myself up on my elbow.

"Seriously?"

Even I can hear the sharp defensive edge in my voice.

"Take it easy." Liam tries to pull me back down to him.

I stiffen under his touch. "You don't even know her."

"Look," he says. "She's fun, but she acts like a nut." This holier-than-thou tone of Liam's surfaces a lot as of late.

"Annie's obnoxious, but she isn't crazy. And she's really been there for me. She was there for me the day I lost the—"

I stop. Tears form in my eyes, and I have a hard time swallowing, my throat still raw from my earlier coughing/laughing fit. "Hey, I am not saying Annie's *crazy*. She's just...a lot."

Liam squeezes my chin. "Relax."

I detest when a man tells me to relax. I scoot to my side of the bed and yank the covers up. Liam wiggles over to me and talks over my shoulder. "Annie's fine. She's just like a cartoon character or something. I'm sorry you took that bit of honesty the wrong way."

I do my best to ignore him and pull the comforter closer to my face while he tries to hug me from behind. Liam throws his arm over me, but just for a moment, because when his phone vibrates on the nightstand, he lunges for it. After a few seconds, I hear him chuckle. Who the hell is texting him, and at this hour? Peter? No—Sophie?

That sick feeling from this morning resurges. Dark, ugly images of the past surface once again, and I try to turn my mind off, but I can't. I sit back up. "I found a picture of you and Sophie today. The one from the Red Sox game."

Liam's smile fades and he sets his phone down on the comforter. "What?"

"The photo from the game you guys went to together."

"Grace, what the hell are you talking about?"

"In your portfolio. There's a photo of you and Sophie in there."

Liam cuts his eyes at me. "What were you doing snooping around in my portfolio?" The word *snooping* makes me furious and the blood behind my ears starts to pound.

"Snooping?"

"Well, you know what I mean. I just don't know why you'd even look in there."

I'm too tired to try to explain, so I say, "I was bored and looked at some of your sketches, and then I saw that picture."

Liam's cheeks burn red. "Grace. I didn't even know that photograph was in there. It must have been in there from a while ago."

My mind flashes to a couple of nights over the past few weeks where I've seen Liam sketching in that portfolio. "Whatever," I say and roll over.

Liam touches my shoulder, and I shake his hand off. "Grace. I swear to you; I didn't know it was still in there."

Still? I want to ask, but don't.

We both sit in silence for a few seconds. Then I turn off my lamp and pull the covers entirely over my head. Liam sighs. Loudly. I place my hands on my stomach, which makes me think about the baby and I want to cry, but instead, I swallow hard a few times to try to tamp down my emotions. Today's been too much of a rollercoaster, and I'm done dealing with all these intense emotions.

I hear Liam set his phone on his nightstand. Sighing, he rolls to his side of the bed. I'm too tired to argue and too sad, so I lie there with my thoughts churning. One thought surfaces over and over again, and it's this: Despite my best intentions, I have very grave doubts that this year in Maine is truly going to "fix" us.

Something, or someone, has to change. And soon.

6

The alarm on my phone goes off at 11:00 a.m. I got up at 5:00 this morning in order to get six hours of work in before getting together with Annie. She's treating me to a pedicure today. After my miserable, self-imposed early shift, I'm ready to take a break from reading about pesticides.

Things have been tense between me and Liam ever since last week. We haven't spoken much. I try to stay away when I know he's going to be home, spending a lot of time out taking walks on the beach. I'm trying to convince myself that what he said was true. I mean, it *is* possible that the photo from the game had been in there for a while. But still, I can't help but wonder.

I shove the kitchen chair back and stand up to stretch. I grab my mug and take one swallow of coffee, which is now cold. I close the lid of my laptop and leave for Annie's.

At Annie's house, I cup my free hand over my forehead to see through the glass door. Chance waits just inside the doorway and cocks his head to the side to look at me. He begins to prance back and forth and wag his tail. Annie turns from the sink and scolds Chance as she dries her hands on a dish towel.

Annie gestures for me to let myself in. When I step inside, I see Bill with his back to me; he's staring out the kitchen window. "Good morning, Annie. Hey, Bill." I wipe my feet on the doormat.

Bill doesn't acknowledge me. I give Annie a look as if to say, "What's up with him?"

Annie swirls her finger around the side of her head in a circular motion and rolls her eyes.

I set my purse down on the counter.

Annie tosses the dish towel in the direction of the kitchen sink and turns to face me.

"How are you feeling today?" She asks, then adds, "Honey, you've had it rough."

For some reason, the tenderness in Annie's voice undoes me. I want to say to her, "You have no idea," but instead, my throat closes, and I force myself to say, "I...I feel...decent. I'm overly emotional today, I guess." What I secretly want to tell Annie, or anyone else who will listen, is that I've been consumed with thoughts about Liam and about how the miscarriage had to have been my fault. I don't drink much (despite the dinner party fiasco), but maybe if I had drunk less, or had exercised less, I wouldn't have lost the baby. Maybe the little bit of lifting I did while packing to come here was just too much.

Also, I can't stop thinking of what life could have been like as a mother. For the past few nights, I've sat on the love seat on the sleeping porch, holding my empty hands over my empty belly. I've even sometimes talked to the baby, apologizing for not keeping them safe. And though I've tried to push her out of my mind, I think about Sophie most often. I picture Liam holding her in his arms and I get upset all over again.

Now, in Annie's cozy kitchen, all of a sudden, my legs feel too heavy, and I lean forward to steady myself on the counter. Annie puts her hand on top of mine, gives my hand a squeeze, then gathers her purse and car keys off the counter.

Bill merely continues to stare trancelike out the window. I clear my throat to try to push my emotions back down, and the noises I make finally catch Bill's attention. He turns around.

"Oh, hey, Grace. Good to see you."

Bill seems to force himself to smile but doesn't make eye contact with me or Annie. He bends, picks up the discarded dish towel off the floor, and hangs it on the rack on the oven door.

Without looking back at us, Bill walks into the living room and then says, like an afterthought, "Hope you girls have fun today."

Sure, he's quiet, but this aloofness isn't like Bill at all. I look at Annie again, but she only shrugs and says, "I had a super early appointment with my doctor this morning. Maybe he's just tired from getting up to take me."

I stare at Annie, then open my mouth to ask what kind of doctor's appointment she had, but she cuts me off. "You drive. I don't feel like it today. Do you mind?" Annie hands her car keys to me.

"Umm. Okay. Sure." I shift my purse onto my shoulder.

Annie raises her brows as she runs her hand down the tattered strap of my purse.

"Hey, this bag and I have been through a lot together these past seven years. I love that it's made of washable cloth. And I take real comfort in knowing I could crash my car into a ravine and survive out of the contents of this bottomless purse for weeks." I stick my hand in, move things around, and pull out a mangled granola bar, still safe in its wrapper. "See?"

"I don't even know what to say."

With her thumb and pointy finger, Annie plucks the granola bar from my hand and holds it out at arm's length in front of her. She opens the garbage can lid and drops the smushed granola bar into the trash. "Sometimes I wonder about you, Grace. Are you ready?"

"After you, my lady."

Annie snorts then bends to pet Chance on the head. "Now, be good until Mommy gets home."

We're not in the car five minutes when my curiosity gets the better of me. "I know your business isn't any of my business, but is everything okay? Bill seemed really upset."

"Bill worries too much. We're fine. It's *you* I'm worried about. What's going on lately, with *you*?"

I give Annie side-eye but say, "I'm okay. The bleeding slowed down. I'll tell you what, I'm looking forward to having my feet massaged today."

"Now look who wants to change the subject. Grace, you've been through something big. I think you should talk about losing the baby."

Another knot forms in my throat. I really want to confide in her, but somehow, I just can't. I say instead, "I will give you one million dollars to talk to me about anything else."

"Fine. But at some point, you're going to have to talk about what you're going through. No one should have to struggle alone." Annie stops talking, rubs my shoulder for a few seconds, then claps her hands together. "Change of subject. Okay, okay. Here goes. I want to remodel my living room. I'm going to start with the ratty carpet. I want it gone, and I want to replace it with hardwood floors."

As I drive, Annie's plan for the living room grows more detailed. "The old curtains need to come down, and I want to put up blinds instead. Maybe we can shop for those soon. You can help me pick some out."

I turn into the parking lot of the strip mall. Annie points toward the windows of the salon. "Go right to the front."

"We'll never find a spot so close." As I veer off to the left instead, Annie huffs: "I always have great luck. Trust me."

I'd rather not have a disagreement. Not today. I drive to the front of the building. Sure enough, another car backs out and leaves a space right in front, just for us.

"Told you so," Annie says with a grin.

At the reception counter, Annie pushes a bonsai tree to the right and drums her fingernails on the pink tile. An older woman bursts through the saloon-style doors in the back. "Can I help you?" she calls out. The woman squints as she gets closer. She smiles when she recognizes Annie. "Oh, it's you. I don't have my glasses on today. Nice to see you again."

"Great to see you too, Minh. This is my friend Grace."

"So nice to meet you." When Minh shakes my hand, she holds onto my fingers to inspect my nails. She tsks and shakes her head. "I know only pedicures today, but you should come back next week for a manicure. You bite your nails?"

My face burns red as I nod. "Lately, I do."

Annie rubs my back. "I think we're ready to come back there and get going."

"Very well. Right this way."

Minh leads us to a row of luxurious black spa chairs with gold trim. "You pick."

Annie climbs into a lounger, and I plop down into the one next to her. She sets up the massage function with the remote and lets out a loud sigh.

Two younger women arrive and begin to fill the tubs at our feet with soapy water. I kick off my flip-flops. Annie doesn't wait for the tub to fill but just shoves her feet into the water and starts kicking them around. Hot water splashes out of the basin. "Does this feel good, or what!" Annie announces, louder than she should.

The two women smile at each other and giggle. The woman in front of Annie pulls out a white towel and mops at the spill. I slide my feet into my own basin of bubbling water. I sigh too.

I close my eyes as my technician scrubs my feet. It feels so good that I could fall right asleep in this massage chair. I'm so grateful for the woman's expert touch, and the chance to relax for once. I try but fail to block out Annie's voice as she instructs her technician.

Next my tech begins exfoliating my feet: first with a pumice stone, and then a metal file.

I'm super ticklish but try not to squirm too much.

"Easy on those heels," Annie yelps. "Last time, you almost hit bone."

The woman working on Annie's feet gives my nail tech a bemused look, and the two of them begin a conversation in Vietnamese, laughing the whole time.

Annie turns to me, and says behind her hand, but certainly loud enough for them to hear, "They're talking about me right now. I just know it."

She leans forward to peer at her nail tech. "You're talking about me, aren't you? About what a pain in the ass I am?"

Her pedicurist grins up at her mischievously. "Who us? Never, Annie, never," she says with an elaborate pantomime, pointing back and forth between herself and her colleague, and then the two women try to suppress their laughter as they go back to working on our feet.

Annie rolls her eyes and leans back in her chair with a huff but then looks my way and gives me a wink along with a slight smirk.

She closes her eyes and lets her shoulders drop in an obvious attempt to relax, but in true Annie form, after only a minute, she pops her eyes open and grabs my arm. "Let me ask you something. The one rule is that you have to answer with whatever first comes to mind."

"Okay," I say, "shoot."

"You swear on your life you'll be honest?"

"Yes, Annie, I promise."

"Okay. Ready?"

"Yes!"

"Here goes. How are things *really* going with Liam?"

"Terrible," I blurt.

"Interesting." Annie once again drums her nails, this time on the pleather armrest.

My cheeks burn. "Why would you ask me that question?"

Annie leans toward me. "I don't know Liam all that well, but I feel like I get to know you more and more every day. I don't hear you talk about him all that much, and dinner felt tense the other night."

I shrug. "I mean, overall, Liam's good to me."

My mind flashes to the photo. "I just feel like his career comes before me and everything else. And he certainly doesn't understand how to talk to me about the baby."

I get a chill and prickly goosebumps. That happens a lot when I say the word "baby" lately.

"Sweetie," Annie says, "Liam *appears* to be a really great guy. He does. Maybe a little stiff and set in his ways. But if he isn't right for you, then maybe you need to cut him loose. If both you and I have learned anything these past couple of weeks, it's that life is short. Don't waste your time on someone or something you aren't passionate about. The right person could be right there, but you may not be able to see him because you're busy trying to make this relationship work with Liam." Annie nods and gives my arm a squeeze, her long nails digging into my skin.

"Since before we even left Portsmouth, I've worked harder than Liam to fix us. Then the baby happened, and on top of all that mess, I'm still pissed about his coworker." I bite my lip.

Annie yanks her right foot out of the water and uses it to propel herself even closer to me.

"Wait wait wait. What happened with Liam's coworker?"

"In Exeter, Liam spent an awful lot of time with a particular woman from his office. This...Sophie woman. A group of us would go out sometimes on Friday nights, and Sophie would always be there. She's nice enough, but the two of them looked at each other in a way that didn't sit right with me. And they had all these stupid little private jokes. I let it go, though, because he swore they had a *good friendship* only.

Annie purses her lips and gives me a look.

"Oh yes. They even went to a sponsored company outing at a Red Sox game down at Fenway once. I was busy and couldn't go and wanted him to have a good time with his work friends... but...when Liam went to the game with Sophie, without me, I think they crossed a line. I found a photo of them yacking it up at the game tucked one of his notebooks the other day."

Annie crosses her arms. "Go on."

"I mean, they never slept together. That I know of. Liam swears not, but I don't know. Liam seemed to like to spend time with Sophie more than me, and he always laughed more with her. After they went to that game, I told Liam I was sick of whatever they had together. Even if it's just a *good friendship*. Right after, Liam got the job here. Now we're here, and Sophie's there."

"Does he still talk to her?"

"He says no, but I don't know if I believe him. Liam always claims the many text messages he receives late at night are from Peter or his mom or a guy friend. Either way, lately, our entire relationship feels...phony. I don't know why I continue to hold on. Why don't I have the guts to end it?"

Annie takes a big breath in through her nose and lets it out slowly through her mouth.

"Sometimes, you just have to wear these things out. You'll know when to say goodbye."

My eyes well with tears.

"Besides, if things *don't* work out, you and I can take a ride to visit this Miss Sophie, and I can give her a piece of my mind." Annie makes two fists in front of her face. "I may not look like much, but I'm pretty tough."

I have to smile at her now. "Okay, Rocky Balboa. I'll keep your boxing skills in mind."

The woman at my feet pulls out an assortment of gel polish colors. I point my left big toe at a shimmery teal. Annie's tech retrieves a bottle of bright red lacquer and begins painting Annie's toenails.

Annie clutches my armrest again. The pleather creaks a little at her touch. "Now," she says, "are you ready to talk about the baby?"

I shake my head and swallow hard.

Annie squeezes my hand. "Okay, then. I won't force it. To be continued, I guess." Annie moans and groans as the massage chair does its work.

The woman at my feet smiles up at me, and I smile back. I tell her I love the color then close my eyes again and allow myself to enjoy the mechanical rollers moving up and down my back. Too soon, my relaxing pedicure is complete as my tech carefully glides my flip-flops back onto my feet.

Annie and I walk back to the counter to settle our bill. Annie glares at me when she sees me dig around in my bag for my wallet. She pulls a credit card from her own wallet and tosses it onto the counter along with a loyalty punch card. "You can add extra gratuity this time around, Minh, for having to take this troublemaker over here," Annie jokes.

Minh rings us up, smiles broadly as she hands Annie a receipt. She says to me, "Now, you come back and get that full manicure soon, okay? We'll make your nails neat and pretty. Put extra coats of polish on, so you'll stop biting them."

I smile and nod.

"See you in two weeks," Annie says to Minh. She turns to me. "Ready?"

"Ready, Freddy."

"Good, because now I have to get home and bleach my mustache."

"Oh my god," I say disapprovingly, but I have to laugh.

When we get back to Annie's house, I secure my purse higher on my shoulder as I lean in to hug her. Annie gives me a quick squeeze and stands back but looks at me and then past me, like she's just remembered something vitally important.

"Wait here a second, will you?" Annie walks down the hallway and opens a closet door. She ducks in and I can hear her digging around. As I wait, I watch Bill mowing the lawn through the window. Annie charges back down the hall toward me and slaps me in the stomach with a brand-new Coach purse, the tags still on it. Maroon with tan trim. It's gorgeous, and I love it.

My eyes well, yet again. "For me?" I sputter.

"Jesus, can't you ever just say *thank you?* You look like a bag lady with that Linus Van Pelt blanket for a purse you drag around. I'm doing you and everyone else on the planet a favor."

"Linus Van Who?"

"The dirty kid from *Charlie Brown*, the one who drags around his holey blanket everywhere he goes."

Other than the bouquet of flowers from Liam, this purse from Annie happens to be the first real gift anyone's given me this summer. The inside of the bag has an intricate pattern, and I run my hands over the smooth, silky lining. The pockets on the inside zip snugly, which means no more free-floating ChapStick or car keys. I won't even have to fumble for my phone anymore because the interior is so spaciously compartmentalized. Maybe now I'll actually get to answer it before it goes to voicemail.

"Thank you." I stoop to kiss Annie's cheek.

"Forget about it." Annie starts to go into the kitchen but then stops herself. "Do you want to come shopping with me sometime soon?" she says quietly. Her eyes glint a bit when she looks at me again. "I want to start to get ready for Thanksgiving."

"Annie, Thanksgiving's still three months away."

"Yes, I'm aware, but I can plan ahead, can't I? I want to buy the nonperishables at least, and maybe get some premade bread rolls and prepped veggies stored in the freezer."

"Okay," I say, but I am still confused. The weird urgency in Annie's voice makes me wonder what's really going on with her. Still, Annie knows I'm struggling with the miscarriage, but she doesn't make me talk about the baby. I decide to reciprocate, to not pressure Annie to talk about whatever is going on with her either. For now.

7

Yesterday afternoon, after my spa date with Annie, I got a lot of work done, and I even had a chance to write last night. Today's also off to a good start, workwise. The clock reads 8:45 a.m., and I've already annotated ten articles. As I click on the next assignment, I hear a noise at the back screen door. I look up, and Annie's there. She barges into the kitchen. "You obviously don't have much going on here today. Let's go to the beach."

"Umm. Okay, sure...but the weather's turning–"

"Oh, for god's sake," Annie blurts. "It's cooler out now, Grace, but I think we'll survive. I'll take Chance home and pack us lunch."

A bathing suit and towel top my mental list as I climb the stairs and enter my bedroom. I'm halfway through the mystery novel on my nightstand, but I don't pack it. Annie will talk too much for reading. Hmmm...what else do I need? Whatever I happen to forget, Annie will have extra, I'm sure.

We arrive on the beach within twenty minutes. Annie carries a big polka-dotted tote bag, a collapsed canvas chair, a striped umbrella, and an ice-blue lunch cooler. I carry my beach bag, a wide-brimmed sun hat, and another chair, but I also manage to wrestle her canvas chair from under her arm.

Annie and I haul our gear close to the shore. On our way down the beach, I had stopped to read the daily tide chart by the pier. It's high tide right now, so we won't have to worry about the tide coming back in and soaking our stuff.

Annie wears a flowy ankle-length skirt, a long-sleeved men's dress shirt (Bill's, I presume), a floppy straw hat, and oversized sunglasses that cover most of her face. And yet, with all of this apparel on, she still prepares to apply sunblock.

I eye the bright orange bottle. "Do you truly think that's necessary?"

"Let me tell you," Annie declares to the ocean air, "I will not leave this world a hot mess. I refuse to be one of those wrinkled old bitches with age spots everywhere. No more nasty sun for me, no way. Nut-uh."

"You are too much." I pull my shirt over my head and adjust my bikini top while Annie applies SPF 100 on all her exposed skin and leaves a thick, noticeable smear on her nose. She wipes the leftover cream on her hands onto her beach towel. I pull out a bottle of spray lotion and give my whole body a spritz. Annie sputters in my aerosol fumes but takes a cigarette out of her purse, lights it, and takes a long, slow inhale.

"You know, Annie—" I start to say, but she shushes me as she exhales her smoke.

"I know, I know already. Jeez. Bill is always on my case about it. I know I need to quit, okay? I've cut down." Annie sounds annoyed. I decide I'd better back down. After one more drag, Annie grinds the ash end of the cigarette into the sand. "Happy now?" she snaps.

I grin at her. She sticks out her tongue at me. I keep grinning as I turn my face to the sun.

We settle into our chairs and sit in silence for a few minutes. The waves rush in and out. When seagulls swoop overhead, Annie tsks as she watches them. The birds break the quiet.

"How are things with Liam?"

My stomach rolls. "I wish I knew."

The photograph flashes through my mind. Annie says nothing but no longer leans back in her chair. She slides her sunglasses down to the tip of her nose. Annie's piercing eyes bore into mine over the top of her glasses.

"Can I ask you something? How do you know if you're in love? I mean, like with you and Bill, when did you know? At what moment did you fall head over heels in love with your husband?"

She snorts and rolls her eyes. "Honey, if you need passion, get your ass onto the internet and order yourself one of those gadgets. Those toys will help you find your passion."

"Annie! Oh my god!" I smack her hand.

"What? Women have needs that men can't fulfill," she says.

I can't help but giggle. I take a moment to recover then continue. "Didn't you ever feel uncontrollable passion for Bill? Didn't your heart beat even faster when you saw him at the end of the day? Didn't you ever wait with anticipation by the door, because you just couldn't wait for him to get home?"

Annie turns away from me and gazes at the water for a long time. "I suppose when we first got together, yeah, I had a passion for him. But passionate sex isn't what gets you through. What gets you through is the real stuff. When you can't see your way out of a very dark place, you at least know that when he gets home, everything will be better because he's there to listen and nod and hold your hand." Annie pauses then says, "You know, Bill *is* home, to me. True love means that no matter where you go, and no matter what you go through, if he's there, you will always feel like you're safe. You're home."

Annie turns back, and this time she takes off her sunglasses entirely to stare at me. "Do you get me? What I'm saying? He should be your best *friend* first, before and above anything else. You should feel like he holds your soul right in the palm of his hand. Home. Home is what you want."

I nod, but I feel like I can't breathe. Annie pats my hand. "You don't have to make any decisions today, though. Today, let's just enjoy the scenery."

I sit back and swallow hard to keep the tears at bay.

For the rest of the morning, Annie and I chat, walk, and wade in up to our calves when we get too hot. The weather has been unseasonably warm until recently, but the frigid ocean temperatures still bite the skin. Around lunchtime, Annie hands me my sandwich. Even through the cellophane, I can see that she's created a masterpiece. Bacon and lettuce peek out from between the neat cut in the ciabatta roll.

I unwrap the sandwich and take a healthy bite. Juice from the ripe tomato slice runs down my index finger. I can't help but moan. "Annie Whitney, this is probably the best sandwich I've ever had. In my entire life. I mean it."

I lick the crumbs from the corners of my mouth. I know I should stop shoving food into my face before I give myself the hiccups, but I don't. I can't. It's that good. Again, I sink my teeth into the perfect BLT. I realize then I've not been eating much these days—and that maybe my appetite is starting to return.

Annie just laughs as she pulls out a snack-sized bag of sour cream and onion chips and tosses them into my lap.

"I'm going to finish this sandwich first," I say. "I don't want any other competing flavors in my mouth right now. What is in this sandwich anyway, cocaine?"

Annie laughs again. "Bacon and mayo make anything taste like heaven."

While I scarf my entire sandwich, Annie eats only half of hers before rewrapping the remains in the cellophane. I move onto the chips, licking the salt off my fingers when I am done.

Annie is starting to rub off on me, for sure. "Delicious," I tell her. "Thank you, again."

"You're more than welcome." She leans back in her chair to rest, and I do the same. We're "full, fat, and happy," as my mother used to say. We sip flavored seltzer and just relax together.

The wind picks up as the day wears on. The slight breeze is just enough to make the climbing heat bearable. The sand feels so wonderfully warm under my feet, better than the spa pedicure even. Children's laughter mixes with percussive waves crashing against the shore.

Someone nearby plays rap music on their phone.

I realize I need to take a quick trip to the bathroom. "Annie, I have to pee. Do you need to go?"

She scoffs, points to the water. "Everyone goes in the ocean. Don't waste your time at the pier bathrooms. They're gross. Go right there instead."

"I'm going to take my chances and use the *actual* bathroom

if you don't mind. Be back in a few."

I laugh off her continued protests and walk in the direction of the pier.

"Suit yourself!" Annie hollers from her canvas chair.

Annie was right, as usual. The pier restrooms *are* gross. They stink. The trash bins overflow. I hold my breath and do my business as fast as I can.

When I return to our spot, Annie is sleeping in her chair, mouth open. I should've brought that novel, after all. Instead, I settle in and watch kids play. A woman who looks to be my age helps her baby to her feet and wipes the sand off the white ruffle on the bum of the baby's swimsuit. The baby reaches for her mom's hands and the mom picks her up. They skip down to the water. The baby's arms flail as the mom bends and dips the baby's toes in and out the clear, cold water. The baby squeals at the shock, then smiles into her mother's face.

I swallow hard, shift in my chair, and focus on a different section of the beach. Two girls ride the waves on boogie boards, and they make me think of Say. We spent a lot of time together at the beach when we grew up. The two girls even look like we used to, all sun-kissed and beach-curled. I make a mental note to text Say as soon as I get home. I bury my feet and calves in the warm, warm sand. I ease my head onto the back of the chair and close my eyes.

Annie jolts awake about fifteen minutes later. "Oh, sorry. I never take naps."

"Can we go for a swim? I've got the sweats over here."

Annie gives me a stern look. "I'll watch you from the shore."

"Come on, please?"

"I'll just stick my feet in."

"Deal." I know I'll be able to convince her to get in at some point today. The sun's hot, even if the water's cold.

Annie takes off her hat, her shirt, and her skirt before we stroll down the short slope left behind after the tide went out even farther. The hem of her ruched swim skirt flaps in the breeze.

She pulls on her thick black shoulder straps to adjust her bosom.

I snort and tell her, "Come on. Let's get that body moving now so you'll warm up in the water faster." As we march toward the shoreline, I link Annie's arm in mine.

When we get to the water's edge, Annie steps in and cries out. I see goosebumps rise all up and down her arms.

I have to laugh. "Come on, Annie," I coax. "Let's go! You'll get used to the temperature. Think of it as a polar plunge!"

Annie shakes her head. "Nut-uh," she repeats.

I laugh and respond with, "Suit yourself."

I wade to my knees and splash some water on my goosebumps. The water feels absolutely icy, but I will my body to adjust to the temperature. When I feel brave enough, I plunge and swim, allowing the briny sea foam to wash over me with every wave. The water numbs my body, but floating out here alone is nice—amazing, even. For the first time in weeks, nothing hurts.

I close my eyes as the sun warms my face, neck, and shoulders. The rest of my body enjoys its total lack of feeling and warmth. The water rocks me, and I just let the ocean hold me.

When I open my eyes again, Annie waves at me from the

shore with one hand, shielding her eyes from the sun with the other. She looks a little worried, honestly, but I can't imagine why.

"Get out here, you wimp!" I shout. "You'll get used to it!"

"Have you lost your mind?" Annie hovers on shore for a few moments longer, but then she gives in. "Fine. But if I die, I'm gonna kill you!" Annie yells when she steps knee-deep. She holds her arms in the air—in an attempt to keep them dry.

The deeper the water gets, the higher she raises her arms. Her arms stay up, and when a wave comes, she tries to hop over it. When she finally gets to me, she scoops two handfuls of water and throws them into my face. "Take that!"

I sputter and splash back. I giggle, grab Annie's arm to pull her out farther. "Come on." I rub my hand over Annie's forearm where I can still feel the prickly goosebumps. Suddenly, I stop tugging and let go of her. "Actually, let's just float here."

"Yeah. I think I am out far enough, thank you very much."

We lie back and float around in the water for a while without talking. We're both frozen, but we're having so much fun that we stay where we are. We're very quiet until Annie remembers, "I haven't done this since Kelly was little. Bill and I bought her one of those cute boogie boards. Kelly loved it so much that I ran to the beach shop and bought one for myself. We used to play on them together for hours."

By now, we've drifted out quite far. The waves continue to lull us back into silence, which is rare for Annie.

"Grace," she says finally, "I love you, but my whole body feels like a popsicle. Let's go back in, please." She clutches her hands as if in prayer and pouts.

"Who can resist such a face?"

Annie gets winded as we swim to shore. I haul her closer to me to help her. Because I'm taller, I'm better able to keep my footing. The closer to shore we get, the more Annie struggles. Out of the water, our feet sink and suck into the wet sand left behind by the receding tide. Annie wheezes. By the time we reach our beach chairs, Annie's doubled over. She hacks and hacks. I hand Annie my dry towel, with which she wipes both her face and mouth. Her terrible coughing eventually subsides. She steadies herself on the arm of her chair and admits, "Whew, that episode was a doozy."

"You okay?" I ask.

Annie winks at me. "I haven't had that much fun in a long, long time."

Annie plunks down into her beach chair. She reaches into her beach bag and yanks out her purse. She pulls out a pack of smokes but stops herself when she looks over at me.

I scowl.

"Fine!" She shoves the cigarettes back into the purse, tosses the purse into the beach bag. Smoking seems to be such a touchy subject lately. Maybe Bill is really giving her hell over her unhealthy addiction.

In lieu of smoking, she digs around in the bag and produces a baggie of Canada mints. Annie rattles the pink candies at me.

"Annie, I swear you're a hundred years old. Who even eats those things? I thought my grandmother was the only one left in the world who ate those candies. Like chewing on chalk."

Annie pops two mints in her mouth. "Suit yourself."

We spend the rest of the afternoon lolling in the sun. Whenever I start to doze off, Annie slaps my arm before I can fully fall asleep. She regales me with stories of her courtship with

Bill.

After a long time, the rectangular shadow of the pier crosses my thighs.

"We should go," Annie says. She huffs as she stands.

"Sand," I mutter as we pack. "The worst part about the beach, am I right? Everything ends up damp and coated in sand."

Most people have already left for the day. A few stray toys, half-buried in the sand, litter the beach as we walk back. I take Annie's beach chair from her, and she doesn't protest this time. Both chairs slap at the back of my thighs with each step. When we get to the edge of the beach, Annie bends down and finds a sand dollar.

"How do you do that?" I ask her. "I always want one, but I can never find one."

"You have to know where to look." Annie slips the off-white shell into her beach bag.

When I get home, I go upstairs to take a shower. I throw all of my sandy clothes and beach towel in a wet heap on the bathroom floor. I'll scoop that pile up and do some laundry later, but not until tomorrow. As I kick the stack out of my way, I see a small but lurid smear of red on the corner of my towel.

Marvelous. Just what I need. I'm still spotting. I had pushed what happened to the baby out of my head for a few hours, but here's another reminder in my face. I think about the baby, and I think about Liam and then I get that dizzy feeling again. I don't want to think right now. Or feel. But I know at some point, I'll have to face those feelings. Things can't go on like this forever.

8

Even though Thanksgiving Day won't be here for almost two and a half months, today is the day we go to the grocery store together to pick out the nonperishable ingredients necessary for the feast. Annie wants canned green beans, a couple of boxes of instant stuffing, and jellied cranberry sauce. Just the thought of that horrid stuff sliding out in one solid chunk and landing in a bowl with that terrible sucking sound is enough to make me want to gag.

I know there are more items on the list, but that's all I can remember from what Annie rattled off in the car on the way here. We're at the entrance to the grocery store by 9:00 a.m. Parked right up front, per usual. Chance zipping around in the back seat of Annie's car, per usual.

"You know, let's get two carts. Done faster. Let's be quick, for Chance's sake. Meet me at checkout in twenty." Annie pulls a chicken-scratched list from her purse, rips the crumpled paper in two and hands me the bottom half. She yanks a metal cart out of the interlocked row and takes off before I can agree to the new plan. I sigh, grab a plastic basket, hook it over my forearm, and step into the too-bright store. It's too early for sprinting into stores and speedshopping. *Slow your roll,* I want to call out after her, but she's long gone.

I know Annie wants me to start on her list, but I want some apples. I've had pie on my mind since our first day in Maine, and besides, fresh apple pie is (reasonably) healthy comfort food. Apple pie also happens to be one of Liam's favorites. I've tried for years to perfect my mother's crumb-topped recipe. Tart, juicy Granny Smith apples work the best. With all that's happened since we got to Maine, my mom's apple pie would taste just like home. Butter, brown sugar, spices. I *need* pie. Today. I won't wait until Thanksgiving for pie.

I beeline toward the display of shiny, waxy apples, and peel a plastic produce bag off a roll above my head. I shake the bag open, select five plump, firm apples—with no spots or bruises—then knot the bag closed. I'm about to move on to the baking aisle for flour and vanilla when I see a man ahead of me. I observe as he struggles to hold back an unending avalanche of oranges. I place my bag of apples in my basket and set both on the just-mopped tile floor. I weave around a yellow sign that reads "Wet Floor" and ask, "Can I help?"

"That would be great." He glances over at me for only a brief moment then concentrates again on the falling fruit.

I help place the oranges in a manageable stack that does not seem about to tumble over. The man bends at the waist and picks up the ones already on the floor. He straightens himself with a little satisfied grunt. "Thank you. You saved me there."

Those eyes. Wow. Now I can't help but stare at this handsome man. I try to keep my mouth from flopping open. He's got shaggy blond hair, and his tan skin contrasts nicely with his white tee shirt. He locks his vivid blue eyes onto mine.

"Matthew," he says as he extends his hand. I take his warm hand into mine and shake.

"I'm Grace."

"This may be an odd question but, do you live around here?"

He picks up his own basket off the floor. Normally, a question like this from a complete stranger would put me on high alert, but Matthew has such a kind voice.

"Sort of? I'm here, well, we're here for the year. We have this rental place." I stop.

"Wait—TMI." I grimace.

He laughs, but again, not unkindly.

I just met him, but I feel like a silly teenager around this guy. My face flushes. I'm not sure I've ever stood this close to such a good-looking man. I need to get myself together here.

Matthew chuckles again. "Let me start over. What I should have asked was if you knew of a local farm or butcher. I'm here to see my folks, and they want fresh chicken for a barbeque. I forgot to ask if they had a preference on where I bought the chicken. Odd request, right?"

Even given his deep, soft voice, I am relieved to know he's not asking for my address so that he can follow me home and murder me. "Oh, okay. Well, I know of some local farms, but I don't know if they sell fresh chicken. I can ask my friend Annie. She'd know. She's right down that aisle." I point with my index finger.

"Do you mind?"

"Not at all."

"After you." Matthew motions for me to step ahead of him, which I do, but not before I somehow manage to nearly trip over my own flip-flop while retrieving my basket. Matthew touches the tip of my elbow to help straighten me. I stand taller and smooth down the front of my khaki shorts with my free hand.

"Sorry about that."

I'm not sure why I'm apologizing. I flex my toes to pull my flimsy flip-flops more securely into place.

Matthew and I walk toward the baking aisle without talking. Muzak plays from the overhead speakers. Our shoes squeak against the wet tile floor. My feet make additional soft clopping noises with each step. I'm overheated, and the air conditioning makes my skin prickle. As we turn the final corner to go down the baking aisle, I see Annie in mid-conversation with a woman in front of her. Even though her back is to us, I can still hear every word she is saying.

"Listen. I'm telling you. You don't want to have to take all that time frigging around with all of those ingredients. Get this instead." Annie hands the woman a box of quick-bread mix. "Sold! Thanks!" The woman nods, tosses the box into her cart, and continues down the aisle. Annie turns and faces the rows of mixes in front of her. I watch her place her reading glasses back on the tip of her nose. She studies the narrow side of one box and mouths the words as she reads through the list of ingredients.

I get within a foot of her, but she doesn't look up. "Annie, do you know where you can get fresh chicken?"

Annie continues to consider the box in her hand as she scolds me. "Grace! What the hell? We're not shopping for live chickens. Do you see live chickens anywhere on your half of the list?"

"Annie, I...."

Matthew steps forward. "She's asking for me."

Annie looks up and opens her mouth to speak but loses her words. She slides her reading glasses off her face and lets them dangle from the hot pink cord around her neck. She stares Matthew up and down. "Woah, is it hot in here, or is it just you?"

Matthew laughs and extends his hand.

Gallant again, I note. I blush, again.

"My name's Matthew. Pleased to meet you."

Annie drops the quick-mix box into her cart to take his hand in hers. She keeps a firm grip as she continues to gawk.

"I'm here to see my folks, and they want fresh chicken for a barbecue. Do you know of any place local?"

Annie lets go, finally. She clears her throat but speaks with her eyes locked on Matthew.

"Well, I know of a farm about fifteen minutes from here. Grace and I have been there before. She could go with you, to show you the way. Grace, I'm talking about that cute place that sells the raspberry pastry we like." Annie gives me a nudge. A shove, in fact.

I resist, but she continues to push me forward. I give in and take a step toward Matthew, but just to make her stop.

Annie announces, "That settles it. Grace will go with you, and you can drop her off on your way back through."

Matthew smiles. "I'd love that. But what do you think, Grace?"

Even the icy air conditioning can't appease the flood of sweat under my arms now. The slick moisture trickles down my rib cage on both sides. "I guess, sure, I could go. I mean, don't I have to help you here, Annie?" I widen my eyes and shake the torn grocery list.

"Oh honey, I'm more than all set here."

She snatches the paper from me with those long fingernails of hers. "You go. You go with Matthew and find him some chicken. Go on, now." Annie shoos me with her arms.

Heat crawls up my neck and my face. I take Annie's keys from my pocket and drop them into her open palm.

"We'll check in with each other later." She winks at me.

I give her a stiff smile that's all teeth. "Sounds like a plan," I grit out.

My heart thumps harder and harder as Matthew and I move toward the front of the store. I almost forgot I need to pay for my apples, and he needs to pay for his oranges. Matthew goes to the checkout one aisle over from me. I can hardly manage to properly swipe my card through the reader in my lane. The first time, I swipe the card upside down. Then backward. Or whatever. Then I take a breath and get it to work.

The cashier bags the already-bagged apples in a slightly larger plastic bag. She ties the looped handles into a loose knot. Finally, she hands me the printed receipt. "Have a good day."

I wait by the drinking fountain near the sliding doors for Matthew. I shift the apples from one hand to the other so I can take turns wiping my sweaty palms down the front of the thighs of my shorts.

Matthew strolls up moments later, even before I gather myself, and says, "Sure you've still got the time for this little detour?"

I nod. "I can get my work done this afternoon." I run my hand through my hair and tuck a bunch behind my ear.

Matthew again gestures for me to go ahead of him.

He's too nice, I think. *Way* too *nice, maybe.*

We step together through the swoosh of the electric doors and into the shady parking lot. The weather's a lot cooler today, actually, though you wouldn't think so to look at me. I'm a hot mess.

As we approach Annie's vehicle, I see Chance there, still happily ensconced in the back seat, all four windows cracked. And now, licked, from what I can tell by the gooey smudges. I peer in through the rear window. Chance barks, and his tail thumps against the seat. I want to lean in and rub his nose, but instead, I follow Matthew to the trunk of his Volvo, parked just one spot over from us. It's an older model, navy blue, with dents in the dull fender. Not fancy, but steady. Used, but nice.

Matthew loads his groceries into the trunk, then does the same with my apples. When our hands brush in the exchange, I almost chicken out. I mean, am I actually going on an impromptu *date* with a stranger, as in—a man who isn't Liam? Is *this* a date?

Matthew walks to the passenger side, unlocks it, then opens my door for me. He holds it wide open with raised eyebrows and a cutely crinkled forehead. I shrug and follow his lead, slide into the front seat, and arrange my purse on my lap. Matthew makes sure I am buckled before he closes my door.

Then he jumps in on his side and starts the car. He buckles his seatbelt too, braces his arm on my headrest as he backs out of the parking space. As we pass, Chance ogles me through the rear windshield of Annie's car. I swear he looks judgmental in that way only a poodle can. Matthew shifts the car into drive. *No turning back now.*

He adjusts the temperature controls. Heavenly cool air blasts from the dashboard's vents.

"Tell me if you get too cold."

"Will do." Hot and sticky, I lift and settle the seatbelt more comfortably across my chest.

I hope I don't smell like an animal.

At the edge of the parking lot, Matthew stops and waits. Looks over at me. Waits more.

After a few moments, he laughs. "Which way?" he asks. I swear his eyes do sparkle.

In all my bewilderment—of meeting the way-too-sexy Matthew over apples and oranges, of Annie's strange insistence that I ride off in a strange car with said sexy stranger—I'd forgotten he isn't from around here. "Um...left." I scooch back so Matthew can see past me. He signals, looks right and left twice, then pulls out onto Main Street.

He drives on. Steers with his left hand, rests his right on the gear knob, close to my knee. Doesn't talk much. I gaze out the window, worry again about Chance in the car. Did Annie finish her list quickly? *What was Annie thinking? Why am I here?* I sweat even more, even with the AC still on high. I suddenly blurt, "So, where do you live? Normally."

Matthew grins. "I'm from Pennsylvania," he says. "My folks retired here a few years ago. I visit as often as I can, but I'm in the middle of a second degree in architecture."

The word *architecture* sinks like lead into my belly. I think of Liam again. Really think of him, this time. Picture him at work. In the kitchen, on his laptop, late at night. I shift the slats of the air vent to get more coolness to hit my face.

"I spent my first career as an elementary physical education teacher," Matthew explains. "I loved the kids, but the district politics just became too much. Too many decisions passed down from people who had never taught a day in their lives. That's enough about me, though. What brings you here?" he asks me without taking his eyes off the road. He's nice...*and* safe.

"Well..." I hedge. I want to tell Matthew why I'm in Maine, but all of a sudden, I decide to leave Liam out of the story. *Fuck it.* "I work for a media research company. I don't need to be in the office in person every day. Plus, I write some of my own stories, and you can't find a more perfect setting for writing."

"This town does seem a great place to write. I'd love to hear more about your stories."

Matthew's comment makes me blush. Again. "I've got something in the works right now, but I'm not sure where the piece is going. It's a journal, but it's also a real story, of sorts. I guess. I don't really know what I'm writing yet. It just feels...good. You know...feels right. Somehow."

"Well, I'm sure you'll find your way. Although sometimes it's better not to know how it's going to end, right? Isn't that what all the good writers say? You keep writing to see what the characters will do next?"

"Yeah. Something like that." I pluck at the collar of my shirt to get some extra air moving around in there.

Matthew glances over. "I meant what I said earlier. Adjust the air conditioning or whatever you need."

I shrug again, like I did at the trunk, and he turns the AC blower up a notch for me. I have to smile. He smiles back, but with his eyes *still* on the road. I like the little crinkles at the corners of his eyes.

At the end of Main Street, I tell Matthew to make yet another left. The ocean fades from our view, and we drive out through the winding road by the marsh. Matthew cracks his window.

"I hope you're okay with a little outside air. Maybe it's weird, but I love the smell of the marsh."

As if on cue, the sultry smell of low tide in the flats seeps in through the window. I take a deep breath in through my nose. Matthew hums along to the song now playing low on the radio, and then we make more small talk, which feels less and less forced as we drive on. We talk about books, music, and parents. I tell him about the pie I'm about to make. "Mmm," he says, and I shiver.

I continue to leave Liam out of the conversation, and I am as vague as I can be about the rental house. At one point, when I lean on the middle armrest, my forearm brushes his. I recoil and shrink back into my seat space. "I'm sorry," I say.

"You're fine. Just get comfortable." He takes his hand off the gear shift, pats the armrest.

I place the very edge of my left elbow back onto the shared armrest, careful not to let our skin touch. I look to my right out the window. I see a silver truck in the side mirror behind us and think about Liam. And I think about the baby. And then I decide to do something I've never done before: ignore all of it. I sit up straighter in the seat and clear my throat. "What a great day," I say with a grin. Matthew looks over at me and smiles. The way he looks at me makes my stomach do a little flip.

9

Finally, we arrive at the farm. If the drive from the grocery store seemed rather long, time has truly stopped here. No modern conveniences, no free Wi-Fi with your coffee. An antique red truck with wooden paneling sits parked at the property's entrance. On a pole stuck into the bed of the old truck, a patriotically striped flag with the word *OPEN* in blocked black lettering flaps in the breeze. Annie loves this place for all its hokey quaintness. So do I.

We turn onto the dirt road lined by giant maple trees. The leaves will turn colors soon. Part of me can't wait for fall here. Fall in Maine is wonderful. In my head, I thank Annie for kick-starting my feel-good holiday mood. I'm not sure if I'll ever thank her for foisting me upon a stranger, however, no matter how hot he may be.

Matthew drives slowly, but the rear tires still kick up clouds of dirt behind us. He rolls up his window as he eases the car into a spot close to the barn. No official parking spaces here; people just park their vehicles in a wonky row along the field where they grow the pumpkins.

"Look at this place," Matthew says as he opens my door. He admires the great big barn, notices the rope swing hanging from the inside beam. "Golly," he exclaims, which tickles me. Metal toy tractors lay scattered here and there on the lawn.

To the right of the barn sits another dated building with grayed wooden siding, reminiscent of an old country store. Which it is, I guess. We take in the scene together: White rocking chairs grace the front porch, faded Fourth of July bunting drapes itself under the many windows, and tables spill over with yellow squash and green peppers. We pick our way through the minefield of toy tractors toward the store's entrance.

Nervous again, now that we're out of the cocoon of the car, I start to ramble. "Annie says that this place gets packed in late fall. People come here from all over to have lunch, pick apples, and haul their kids around in the Radio Flyers. Or to buy their Halloween pumpkins. You know."

"I do." Matthew picks up a basil plant from a wooden crate by the door and sniffs it. "So fresh," he whispers, almost to himself, as he sets the pot back down. I shiver again at his low, rumbling voice.

Then he pulls open the screen door, which creaks quaintly, just as I'd remembered. He steps one foot through the frame and pushes open the large interior wooden door. He looks like a street cop directing traffic, both arms spread wide as he props open the doors for me. He motions with his head for me to enter first. I step in sideways to make sure my body won't swipe against his. All I need is to accidentally rub my boobs on this guy. The way this day is going so far, I'll be surprised if I *don't* trip and fall chest-forward onto him.

Inside the cozy store, the smell of fresh-baked sourdough bread overwhelms me. Just to the side of the front door, all manner of pies cools on a tall wrought iron baker's rack. A glass case displays dozens of fresh donuts. I see labels for chocolate, pumpkin spice, and plain, all dusted in delicate powdered sugar. Like the red truck at the outside entrance, the donut case must be antique as well. A small black chalkboard with a handwritten sign advertising an ATM hangs by the register for those without cash. The cash machine in the corner seems out of place here.

Matthew follows me around as I browse the shelves. The ladies who work here come from the same family, I inform Matthew. I've seen a couple of them on earlier visits, and none of them wear a drop of makeup, they are that naturally beautiful. They all have these wonderful, sun-soaked faces, with wrinkles from their work on the farm in all elements and seasons.

"I appreciate and admire their wrinkles," I confess. "Do you know what I mean?"

Matthew laughs but says, "I do, I do."

I like the laugh lines around his mouth, too, I realize.

One of the farm sisters appears from behind the counter with a tray of loaves of pale, uncooked bread. She blows upward to remove a wisp of bangs from her forehead. She sets the tray down on top of the black stove in the corner. An "AGA," I think they call it. After a quick nod to us, the woman pulls open the door to the old cookstove. She bends, loading the tray into the glowing heat. She finishes with a single precise kick to the door with the toe of her barn boot. She wipes her hands on the thighs of her overalls and slips behind the counter once again.

I watch her disappear, then turn my attention back to Matthew. "Annie and I have been here before, for the fruit pastries. We've had their sandwiches a few times as well."

"I love this place." He looks up at the exposed beams along the ceiling while I approach a shelf lined with checkered fabric. I hear him inquire about fresh chicken. I pick up a canning jar and inspect it. Raspberry jam. I don't see the price, and I really don't need any jam or jelly, so I set the pint jar back down and go to the counter where Matthew waits.

He asks me, "Want a quick cup of coffee?"

"I'd like that a lot." My stomach flutters, but I ignore it. It's just coffee. This isn't a *date*, after all.

Matthew scans the display case, looks at the woman behind the counter. "How about two apple cider donuts, two chocolate donuts, and two coffees." Matthew swivels around to look at me again. "I'm sorry. I shouldn't have ordered for you." A flash of red rises on his cheeks. "I just got so excited. It all looks so good. Would you like something different?"

"Nah, I like what you picked. You've got good taste." I smile, but I'm not sure whether or not I've just set womenfolk back a hundred years by letting a man order for me. Though I don't know him well, Matthew doesn't come across as a typical chauvinist. He seems genuinely kind, friendly, and chivalrous. So far, anyway. I dig around in my purse to find my wallet.

Matthew holds up his hand when he sees my money appear. "If you'll allow me, I'd like to pay today. To thank you for coming out here with me."

"Okay," I say as I slip my wallet back into my purse.

He plucks a worn brown leather billfold from his back pocket, flips it open, and hands one of the sisters a credit card. At that exact moment, I see him notice the large sign that says, "Cash Only." A sheepish smirk spreads across his face, but he simply shrugs as he looks at me.

"I don't have any cash on me. Hang on a second, while I use the ATM?"

"You know what? I've got cash. Let me pay." I pull my wallet back out of my purse, retrieve a crinkled twenty, and hand it to the patient gal behind the counter.

"Thank you, Grace. I'll pay next time."

My stomach lurches. I'm on a not-date with a stranger who's already talking about a "next time." What is happening here? I feel a little unsteady on my feet again. I fumble and drop some of my change when the cashier tries to hand it to me. Coins ping against the counter and bounce onto the floor.

"Let me help you." Matthew bends and scoops up the pennies and dimes, then puts the cool coins in my hand. His fingers feel hot against my palm. His hand is so, so warm. I thank him, too profusely. He smiles. I smile. I blush and avert my gaze. *Stop flirting, Grace. Oh Annie, Imma gonna* murder *you later today.*

The woman plucks our donuts from the case with a sheet of waxed paper, arranges the sugared rings into pretty piles on two dessert plates. She crumples and expertly tosses the used square of waxed paper into a tall trash can behind her. Back at the register, she rips off a piece of receipt roll, retrieves a pen tucked behind her ear. She jots something down and hands Matthew the curling slip of paper. I glance over to see she's written the store's number. "Tell your mom to come in anytime next week for that chicken."

"Will do." Matthew folds the paper in half and tucks it into his back pocket.

Every part of me wants to run out to the barn and call Annie on my cell. By now, I don't know if I want to berate her or praise her. I can't decide which, so I spin around and scan the room for a place to sit. I spot a small round wooden table wedged into the far corner. I tap Matthew's arm. "I'll go grab us a seat."

"Perfect. I'll get the coffee."

I slide into a chair against the wall. Once seated, I don't know what to do with my hands. I pick at some invisible lint on the front of my shirt. I cross my ankles, clasp my hands in my lap. I fidget with my nonexistent lint some more.

Matthew joins me, finally, and sets down the tray with the donuts and coffee. "I take mine black. Didn't know how you take yours?" He scatters a pile of thimble-sized half-and-half containers and pink Sweet'N Low packets on the table in front of me. I think of friggin' Annie and her artificial sweetener addiction. The cane sugar is in an old-style diner canister on the table, but I don't need either. The donuts will be sweet enough.

"I take my coffee black too." I blush.

"Let's get this out of your way then." He pushes the pile to the side, takes the open chair, and scoots himself an inch or so closer to me. The legs scrape against the polished cement floor.

He passes me my donuts. "These look delicious," he says, and I nod my thanks to him.

Matthew rubs his palms together as he contemplates his food. I think of Annie again, how she, too, savors her sweets. I watch his face as he takes his first bite. He closes his eyes as he tips back in his chair so far he must lift the front legs off the floor. He opens his eyes to meet mine when he leans forward again. He covers his mouth with the back of his fist. Blushes, but faintly. "Oh man," he admits, "that has to be the best thing I've eaten in a long time. And they're still soft and warm," he says around another bite.

Sugar falls like the first snow off his donut, leaving a dappled trail down the front of his shirt. I'm about to wipe the mess off of Matthew's chest, but I pull my hand back just before getting too close.

He doesn't seem to notice my awkward movements. I break my first donut into pieces so as not to end up with sugar all down the front of my shirt too, but the sticky sugar just ends up on my fingers instead. I probably shouldn't in front of a near stranger, but I lick clean each of my fingers anyway. As the sweetness dissolves in my mouth, I can't help but let out the smallest of moans.

"So good, right?" Matthew chuckles as he takes another bite of donut.

We eat, sip our coffee, and talk for a while. I realize Matthew hasn't mentioned a girlfriend or a wife. He does have a dog named Skippy, a black-and-white border collie back home in Pennsylvania. "He's a great dog. Loves to run."

We're almost done eating when I hear the creak of the screen door and in walks a man in a sleek gray suit, which certainly sets him apart in this quaint country setting. *Wait, where do I know this guy from?* Spider chills race up my back when I realize the man in the doorway is Peter Thorndike, Liam's current boss.

Shit. What if Liam's here with him? Even though I'm sitting, the hard floor feels unbalanced under my feet. I reposition my hips in my chair to steady myself. I'd met Peter only once when he had me and Liam over to tour the site when we first moved here. Peter will probably recognize me if he glances our way.

Peter struts to the counter and orders a dozen donuts in his booming voice. I prop an elbow on the table and shield my forehead with a lifted hand as casually as possible. I peek over just as Peter pulls a folded wad of cash from his back pocket, removes a gaudy money clip, and thumbs through the many bills. He tugs loose a few and tosses the cash onto the counter.

Matthew stands, blocking my view of Peter at the counter. "I'm going to grab a few more napkins and a refill. Would you like more coffee?"

"I'm all set, thanks." Matthew moves away, opening my view again. The woman hands Peter some change. He trickles a few coins into the tip jar and pockets the rest. He picks up the white bakery box and walks toward the door but stops when he sees me in the corner.

Shit shit shit. Fuck. Damn.

Peter scrunches his eyebrows as if he needs a moment to register who I am. When he realizes he knows me, he sidles toward the table, free hand extended.

"Liam's girlfriend, right?" he asks with a politician's smile. Giant bleached teeth shine down on me. A wave of old-fashioned Old Spice hits my nose.

I stand to greet him. "It's Grace. Great to see you. How are you?" I feel my face flush with heat for the hundredth time today. I shake Peter's hand but grope behind me for the side of the tiny table with my other hand to bolster myself.

"I'm well, thanks. Liam's a gem with that remodel. I just had a meeting down in Portland. Thought I'd stop by on my way back through and get the guys something to eat."

"How kind of you." I look over as Matthew helps himself to more coffee across the room. I hope he takes his time. What am

I going to do if he comes back over here?

"Well, I'd best get back. Those guys have been working hard all morning, and I'd like to see the progress. Great to see you again...." He searches for my name even though I just said it.

"Grace."

"Ah, yes. Grace. Now I remember." Peter gives me the up-and-down, eyes half-lidded.

"Really great to *see* you again, *Grace*." The way he hisses my name makes me almost recoil.

I'd love to slug this guy in his jaw, but he's still Liam's boss. I have to play nice. "Good to see you. Take care now," I call out through gritted teeth as Peter leaves.

My knees feel like they might buckle, so I sit back down. I try not to breathe too heavily, so I take a sip of my coffee instead. The mug shakes in my hands as I bring it toward my mouth.

The lukewarm coffee slides queasily down my throat, and I nearly choke.

As Matthew returns, he's clearly concentrating on not spilling his overfilled refill. Somehow, he manages to get to our table without a dribble. He doesn't sit yet, but nods toward the door instead. "A friend of yours?"

"Just an acquaintance." I let out a long, slow sigh now that Peter is gone.

Matthew sets his mug down. When he scoots his chair close again, he accidentally bumps into our little café table. His coffee sloshes over the rim. He reaches for a napkin and says, "Tell me more about you?"

I tell him what I can, and he listens. The more I talk, the more he laughs. Matthew soaks me in, and I love that someone actually wants to hear what I have to say. He doesn't take his eyes off mine once, even when he sips his coffee. We chat as other customers come and go.

When the conversation lulls—but comfortably—about thirty minutes later, Matthew pulls his cell phone from his pocket and taps the screen. "I don't want to seem rude, but I do need to check the time." He glances down, then turns the phone to show me a pic of his dog with a piece of frayed rope in his mouth.

"Aww, so cute!"

Matthew smiles as he looks at the phone again. "Grace, I wish I could stay here all day, but I should get back to see my folks."

"No worries, I should go too. Get some work done."

Matthew takes a last sip of coffee. We stand at the same time, but he takes the lead and gathers the dishes, carries them over to a bin on top of the trash, and places them into the plastic tub. I hover behind him—probably too closely—as I wait to throw away our dirty napkins. When he turns and bumps into me, he mumbles, "Excuse me," just as I say, "My bad," and we both laugh. He holds my gaze and this time, we both blush.

He laughs again and says, "Let's get you home."

I nod as he guides us toward the door. I'm way too hot and sweaty, yet again, but I also feel kind of tired. Pesky hormones, I guess. I could use a long nap, after all this stress and anxiety and...excitement.

Matthew holds open the doors for me in the same traffic-cop manner as we step out into the bright sunshine. My exit is more graceful than my entrance. Even all hot and bothered, I still feel much more relaxed with Matthew now. I let my hip brush against his thigh. He's super tall too, I note. Belatedly. Earlier, I must've been mesmerized by his baby blues.

On the way to the car, Matthew stops in front of the open barn doors. "Wait...can I just take five more minutes of your time?"

"Sure. Why not?" I shrug. "For what, though?" I raise a suspicious brow.

Matthew grins, takes my hand, and pulls me gently into the cool shadows of the red barn.

Once inside, I let go of his hand as I look around.

Bales of hay line the outer walls in neatly graduated stacks. A green tractor sits squat and idle in the open entryway on the opposite side. The breeze whistles through the middle of the barn.

Matthew looks down and shuffles around some loose straw on the floor with his foot. "Look at this place," he repeats. I half wish he'd say *golly* again. Matthew tugs at the ropes that attach the swing to an upper support beam. "May I give you a push?"

Everything in my head tells me to say, "No thank you."

I shake my head, try to gather my wits. I should tell Matthew I need to go. I should say, "I don't know you. I live with someone. I can't believe I even got into your car today." I'm fully prepared to recite all those phrases but "Yes please" blurts out of my mouth instead.

"Come on over," he says.

The sanded seat feels cold on my backside when I slide onto the swing. Matthew moves behind me then puts his hands on the ropes. I feel his shirt brush against mine.

"Hang on," he says.

I run both sweaty hands up the ropes and grip tightly.

Matthew pulls me back higher and higher—then lets me loose to fly into the air.

I go giddy, like a little kid again. I pump my legs until I'm well into the rafters.

Matthew gives me a couple more strong pushes before he comes around in front of me and watches me swing. He crosses his arms and grins. I laugh, and my whole face feels like it's on fire.

I eventually drag my feet through the dusty straw to slow myself down. I ask if he'd like a turn.

"No thanks. I prefer to watch you."

My stomach lurches, and my lungs seize in a somersault. Matthew offers his hand to help me off the swing, and I take it. I hold on a little longer than I should.

He glances toward the swing one last time. "I want to have a swing like that someday when I have kids."

The muscles in my body tighten like ripcords. My breath gets caught in my throat, and I swallow hard to try to push the pain down.

Matthew, still intent on the barn swing, doesn't notice my sudden distress. "Well, I bet you're ready to get back," he says into the rafters as he further inspects the thick lengths of rope.

"Yes," I croak, and he turns to me. I see the concern on his face, but he can't know why I'd want to cry in this barn. On this glorious day, with him. "The dust," I croak again. I make an exaggerated show of coughing. He laughs and pats my back. I swipe at my eyes when he turns to walk back to the car.

Now I keep my arms stiff against my sides so as not to "accidentally" brush against Matthew again. I start to feel very weird about holding onto his hand longer than I should have.

At the car, Matthew opens the passenger door for me and waits until I'm fully in and buckled before closing the door. I admire the honest consistency of his chivalry despite myself.

Back out on the road, we chat easily again, but neither of us mentions a significant other.

We both are avoiding the topic altogether, or so it seems to me.

I start to talk less and less as we get closer to town. "Everything okay?" Matthew asks. "You seem quiet all of a sudden. Did I say something wrong?"

"No, no. You didn't. I'm fine. Just a little tired, I guess." I smile but continue to look directly forward through my side of the windshield.

When we turn onto my street, I half expect Annie to be on her porch, like a parent waiting for a teen girl to come home. Annie's not on my porch either, but I feel like she must be at her window. Probably peeking through the crack in the curtains.

Matthew parks then walks around to my door while I rummage inside my purse for my keys. He offers his hand once more to help me out of the vehicle. This time, Matthew holds on a little longer than *he* should. I let go and turn toward the porch.

Matthew gathers my apples from his trunk then carries the bag up the porch steps for me. "I had fun this morning. Thanks for your time and your company. You're a great tour guide." He hands me the apples, an open, pure look on his face. *Genuine gratitude*, I realize.

I am struck anew by how handsome he is—and kind. And nice. But not *too* nice. The sick, sludgy feeling that's been in my stomach since he mentioned wanting to be a father vanishes, only to be replaced by excited jitters. Good jitters. Hopeful jitters.

"I had fun too," I say. "Great to meet you.... Hope your parents like the fresh chicken...."

Matthew grunts quietly but stares at his feet. I wish he'd look at me. Smile again, this one last time.

We just stand there. I want to say something more, but really, I just...can't.

Finally, the house phone rings—shrilly, even from so far away on the front porch.

"I should get that," I say. "It's probably Annie." I point with my thumb toward the door over my shoulder.

He nods. "Nice to meet you, Grace. Thanks again for your help today. I'm here a few more days. Maybe I'll see you around?"

"Yes...I'd like that."

I can't help but blush one more damn time. I think I set a new record for blushes today.

Matthew pivots on his heel and clomps down the front steps. I struggle to fit my key in the lock. The ringing continues as I shut the door behind me. I toss my keys, purse, and even the apples onto the floor. I kick off my flip-flops and run to the kitchen to answer the phone.

"I want every juicy detail. Don't leave a thing out."

"Well, first of all, lady...." I am set to deliver Annie a blistering lecture, but at that very moment, I hear a familiar noise at the back door: Liam's home. My pulse thumps in my temples. Did he pass Matthew out front?

"Annie, I have to go."

"Wait. What?"

"Liam's here. Gotta go."

"Interesting. How very, very fascinating," Annie says with a cackle.

"Talk to you later."

I hang up the phone and prepare myself for the blistering lecture Liam's about to give *me*. Peter must have told Liam I was with a strange man today at the farm. Or worse yet, he's about to ask about that same strange man who just brought me home in his car.

Liam actually doesn't speak of either when he enters the kitchen. He looks at me and lets his shoulders droop. "I've had a long day already, and it's not even lunchtime. Peter wants to change some fixtures at the last minute. I need to revise the master bathroom design. I came home to work in peace." Liam flops his laptop case onto the counter, then clunks down his travel mug.

I'm annoyed that Liam doesn't bother to ask about me or my morning, but I'm also, obviously, relieved. No new "discussion" on the horizon. Another emotion adds itself to the mix as well. I feel...cheerful?...for the first time in a long time. Is that it? A casual morning with Matthew has made me...happy? I can hardly trust the feeling anymore.

I remember the bag of apples by the front door. I go back into the kitchen to set them on the counter by the sink.

Liam eyes the shiny Granny Smiths through the clear plastic bag. "Are those for a pie?"

"Yes, they are," I say.

"Your mom's recipe?"

I nod. Swallow some spit.

He grins. "You're the best."

10

Liam and I are seated by the window at Frieda's, a quaint restaurant on Main Street. This place is a mix of everything: bar, booths, and cozy two-tops next to the floor-length windows by the entrance. I look around and admire the exposed brick walls, the dark oak expanse of the bar, and the steampunk lighting fixtures. I like it here by the tall windows, where I can take in all the little details, but I should try to focus on Liam tonight, since I can't remember the last time we went on a date. Not that I could classify this as a date. I didn't feel like cooking tonight, and Liam actually made it home in time for dinner on the one night I didn't cook anything. Plus, we could probably use this time together if there's going to be any chance of making this work. I take Liam's hands in mine and smile right at him. "I'm glad we're having dinner together."

As I search Liam's face for a reaction, his phone vibrates against the wooden table. I grip his hands to ask him not to answer the call. Liam pulls his hands away and snatches up the phone. He looks at the screen. "Babe, I've got to take this."

My heart, very strangely, stops beating—but I can't say why. I want to cry too, but the idea makes me feel ridiculous.

Liam pushes his chair back and with his long legs, strides

away from the table. My blood begins to pulse in my ears. I'm so pissed, I could spit. I'm angry, not hurt, I realize. I always cry when I'm angry. So stupid.

The waiter, a short, balding man, approaches and asks if I would like anything. "I'd like to order my food, but my boyfriend would rather see me starve to death first."

The waiter hides a smile with his hand. "Why don't I come back then," he says as he sets a basket on the table. "Maybe this fresh bread will hold you over. There's honey and cinnamon butter in there too."

"Dear lord, that sounds good."

"It is. Believe me." The waiter pats his stomach. "I'll check back. Enjoy."

"Thank you." Before the waiter even steps away, I fold back the black cloth napkin that covers the bread. Heat rises and steams my fingers. I take a piece, hold it hot in my hands.

Liam's now in my direct line of vision through the window. He laughs into the phone.

The fuck is he laughing at? I rip the slice into two pieces.

I use my knife to scoop a glob of butter from the white ramekin situated inside the bread basket. I slather the bread and shove a bite into my mouth before the butter has a chance to melt and drip. Sweet heaven hits my tongue.

I take another buttered bite and can't help but grunt at its goodness. An elderly couple at the next table looks over at me. They both chuckle. I point to the bread basket. "So good. You have no idea."

They nod then go back to their quiet conversation over held hands. I watch them, looking for clues now that they've caught my attention. How long must they have been together?

One of the women breaks her grip long enough to rub her wife's cheek, then squeezes both her hands again. The two exchange intimate, adoring looks. Must be nice. I sit up straighter in my chair, avert my eyes, and glance out the window at the darkening sky. I study the other pedestrians on the sidewalk—a dad and his two young daughters—and think of Matthew.

I run my fingers up and down my water glass then press the glass to my neck and forehead. The condensation leaves cold water droplets on my face. I put the glass down and pat my wet face with my napkin. I reach for another piece of bread, and cram it into my mouth, forgetting the butter this time. I swallow as best I can with a fat dough ball stuck in my throat. I cough, and the older ladies look over at me again.

I smile, remembering my manners. I dab at the corners of my mouth with my napkin. I glance up and see Liam. Still on the phone. Still smiling. Still laughing. I should text Annie and tell her how my date is going. I'm sure she'd have plenty to say. I reach into the basket again, tear off a crusty corner of a small slice, drag it through the butter, pop it into my mouth, and try to chew.

To distract myself, I dig into my purse, find my ChapStick, and run it over my dry lips. Next, I pull out my phone and send Say a text. After that, I open my notes app to type in the words "real cinnamon and honey butter on warm white bread." I'll have to look for a recipe to duplicate the mouth-watering spread when I get home later. Or I'll work this scene into a story at some point. The bread's that good, I decide. I set my phone down on the table to look out the window yet again. Liam pulls his phone away from his ear but puts it back after running a casual hand through his hair. *That's it.* I throw my napkin onto the table.

Outside, Liam's back is to me. I clear my throat. Loudly. Liam turns. I clench my teeth and motion for him to hang up. Liam lifts his finger as if to tell me to wait. Heat spreads through my every limb, and I start to shake. A scream begins to mount inside my head, and I have to tell myself to go back inside the restaurant before I lose my shit. I swing the door open and storm back to our table.

When Liam finally does return to the dinner table, to resume our *date*, I've eaten all the bread and butter, I've already downed my first glass of red wine, and I'm about to order another. Or a whiskey. Anything.

Liam sits. "Sorry about that." He sets down his phone, unfurls his folded napkin, places it in his lap, and opens the menu instead of looking at me.

My foot bounces on the floor as if it doesn't belong to my body. I have to force myself to speak softly. "Unbelievable. You're something else. You know that?"

Liam lowers the menu. "Grace," he hisses, "what's your problem? I got a call. I took it, and now I'm here. Let's eat. Why do you have to make such a big deal out of everything?"

"Oh, I don't know, Liam. Why would I be upset? Could it be because once again, you've ignored me for half an hour to have a conversation about work?" My voice rises despite myself. "Or maybe I'm pissed because you ignored me to do whatever *that* was." I rattle the menu in my hands, raise it so high that I can't see Liam anymore.

The nice bald waiter appears at our table yet again. "Did you need just a few more minutes to decide?" he asks Liam.

Before Liam answers, I blurt out, "Nope. I decided ten minutes ago. I'll have the eggplant parmesan with green salad, vinaigrette dressing on the side, please." I slap my menu on the table, cock my head, and stare at Liam.

The waiter grimaces, repositions his pen on the small pad in his hand. "And for you, sir?"

Liam glares at me before he shifts his eyes back to the menu. "I'm just now looking at the menu for the first time."

"I take it you'd like me to come back, sir?"

"You know what? Just give me the prosciutto plate."

Now comes Liam's turn to slap his menu down on the table. A wave of angry air hits my face in its wake.

"Very good, sir." The waiter retreats. Liam's phone vibrates again. I give him a look that says pick it up, asshole. I dare you.

"Grace, do you even know what it feels like to have someone like Peter on your ass all day long? If I don't get right back to him, he pitches a hissy fit. When Peter asks a question, he wants an answer. Now. Period."

"I didn't know you and Peter liked to laugh so much on the phone together. Sounded a little less perfunctory to me."

"Oh, so *that's* what's going on." Liam folds his arms across his chest. "When will you let that go? That whole mess was over months ago. I said I was sorry. What else do I have to do?"

My mouth gets even drier. "I don't know anymore. I've had a rough couple of weeks, and all I'm asking for is a bit of your undivided attention. I don't think I'm expecting too much." I widen my eyes.

"Here," Liam snarks, "I'll turn off all notifications until after the food arrives." He makes a big show of adjusting the settings on his phone. "Happy now?"

I smile sweetly. "You're too kind." Almost without thinking, I raise the first two fingers of my left hand to my mouth to bite my ragged nails. A bad habit. An *angry* habit.

Liam winces and turns away, no doubt thoroughly disgusted by my poor table manners.

I need to talk to Annie. I shift my whole body in my seat to survey the dining area again. I see another cute but younger couple seated at the bar. The man rubs circles on the woman's lower back. She leans over and puts her head on his shoulder. They laugh. I bite harder until I taste cuticle blood. I won't look at Liam. He can suck it.

We sit in stony silence. Peripherally, I see Liam turn his head a few degrees toward me. Hear him clear his throat. He lifts the drink menu and scans the single page with intense interest. I decide to go to the bathroom without saying a word. Liam does not speak or stand when I leave the table.

I splash handfuls of cold water onto my face. In the mirror, water drips from my chin. I press at the stress lines that have formed between my brows. I dry my face with a scratchy towel then toss the paper into the wastebasket beside the sink.

When I get back to the table, I sit without comment. Another server, a stout woman with fiery red hair, arrives with a serving tray balanced on her shoulder. "Eggplant and prosciutto?"

I nod. I don't blame our bald waiter: I'd send someone else over to deliver the food too. I'm sure he needs a break from Liam. From me too, probably. I sigh. So do I—need a break, from both of us.

Thankfully, the food smells fantastic, especially the fresh oregano. The redhead places our plates in front of us. I shake out my napkin again and drape it over my lap. I pour the herbed dressing onto my salad. Next, I cut my eggplant then take a small bite.

I look over again at the couple at the bar. She feeds him a tiny square of vanilla cake with her spoon. My chest feels heavy. Disney movies ruined me as a child, I guess. I'd give anything for that kind of unabashed affection—the kind that makes you want to feed each other and share all you have with one another.

Before I begin to eat in earnest, I close my eyes, take another deep belly breath, and tell myself to be the bigger person here. I cut the next bite of eggplant, balance it on my fork, and offer it to Liam.

Liam waves away my peace offering. "Nah. I'm good."

Liam focuses on his food and does not offer me even a tiny tidbit from his prosciutto plate. Not even a sliver of the cantaloupe, which he hates. Not even one measly green olive. I stab at my salad, stuff lettuce into my cheeks.

We eat, mostly, in silence. At one point, Liam does ask how I'm feeling, but I know he doesn't care.

I can barely look at him. "I'm fine, Liam."

"Well, I mean, because of—"

"I said, *I'm fine.*"

"Whatever, Grace." Liam keeps eating.

As soon as I finish, I cross my fork and knife on my plate. Liam reaches for his phone, clicks off silent mode, sets the device screen-side-up on the table. To his credit, he doesn't text anyone. He just scrolls through his messages. Liam smiles and chuckles at the last text. I glance at the screen and see some emoji I can't quite make out from my side of the table. The hair on the back of my neck stands on end. Peter Thorndike doesn't strike me as the type to use cutesy emojis.

I flop my napkin onto my dirty plate. Then I pull my own phone out of my purse and start to scroll through my new texts. Say has sent a quick, cheery hello during this dinner from hell.

The original waiter brings the check to the table. "I hope you enjoyed your food, and I hope you have a great night. Please take the check to the front when you're ready."

I smile. "Thank you. Everything was just...delicious."

Liam plucks the check off the table. He huffs and walks to the cashier to pay the bill. I stand quickly too, tucking my phone into my purse. I notice that the younger couple has already gone home. So has the older couple from the adjacent two-top at the streetside windows. How long have we been here? Feels like forever.

I step outside to wait at the curb. Moonlight reflects off the hoods of the cars parked on the street. I look up: has to be a full moon—or very close to it. I love nights like this one; when the moonlight shines so bright, you could almost read the newspaper by it.

Liam emerges from the restaurant. He's returning his wallet to his back pocket as he comes toward me, and I think of Matthew doing the same earlier today. How he couldn't pay but wasn't a jerk about it. About anything, actually.

"Liam, could we walk along the beach on the way home? Tonight's the full moon. I think I could use some ocean air."

"Babe, can't we just go home? I'm exhausted."

"The shore isn't that far out of the way. It would only take a few extra minutes and would mean a lot to me. Please?"

"I'm too beat."

"Lovely," I say and push ahead of Liam. I can hear the waves. I look between the beach houses to see the full moon's light dancing on the water. A romantic sight like this usually fills me with joy, but tonight, it only adds to my anger. How hard would it have been to go two blocks over and walk the beach to get home?

I increase my pace to a stiff clip. I stop briefly only once to look over my shoulder. Liam meanders behind while he stares at his phone; the light from the screen glows in his eyes. *Prick.*

We're back to the house faster than I'd expected. I thud up the front porch steps, and Liam trudges in after me, locking the door behind him. He unbuttons his nice shirt and drapes it over the chair by the door. Then he goes upstairs—I assume he wants to change into his sweatpants.

I need to make myself some tea to calm down.

I hear Liam come back down the stairs as I take the mug of hot water out of the microwave and set it on the kitchen counter and dunk the square herbal tea bag with my fingers.

It burns a bit. I watch as Liam sits on the couch and opens his laptop. I lift the mug to my mouth. I know I can't take a sip yet because it will be too hot, but I let the warm steam crawl up my nose and forehead with my eyes closed. I inhale the warmth.

As I savor the welcome heat, I decide I'll go up to bed with my tea instead of standing here in the kitchen watching Liam work away yet again. I don't say goodnight as I pass him.

Upstairs, I switch on my dim reading lamp. I slip off my

jeans, remove my bra through my shirtsleeves, peel back the cool sheets and down comforter, and slide in. To hell with getting my real pj's on tonight.

I punch and prop the pillows behind my head, staring at the ceiling. I could call Say. I have a lot to tell her. I haven't told anyone else about the baby yet. Say does quite a lot of networking, though, and I'm sure she's out on the town right now at some upscale bar in Manhattan.

I scroll my phone's contacts, hit the entry labeled "Home."

After only two rings, I hear a familiar voice. "Hello?"

"Hey, Dad, can I talk to Mom?"

"Sure, hold on a sec, sweetie. Everything okay? It's late."

"I'm fine, Dad. I promise."

"Okay then. Here's your mother."

My dad's not much of a talker, especially over the phone, so he and I don't bother with the pretense of small talk. I hear a shuffle on the other end, then another concerned "Hello?"

Just the sound of my mom's voice makes me weepy for some reason. I rub my eyes, hesitate before I get out a crackled, "Hey, Mom."

Tears threaten to spill, and my throat constricts. I don't—can't—say anything more.

"Oh, honey...what's wrong?" Mom waits silently, patiently, for me to answer her.

I manage to find my voice again: "I don't know, Ma. What's it all about, Alfie?"

This old movie line belongs, originally, to my mom, but it somehow has also become mine over the years—a generational gift. One of many, I guess.

"What's the matter, sweetheart?" she asks again.

I sit up, blow across the top of my mug of tea, put it to my mouth, finally, and let one still-too-hot drop touch my lips. I wince and set the mug back on the nightstand. "I don't know. Things with Liam aren't...great. His job always comes first. I feel like I'm second to everything in his life. I just want Liam to want to spend time with me. You know. The usual."

My mom remains quiet on her end. I want to tell her about the baby, but I don't know *how* to tell her.

"Take your time, honey. I've got all the time in the world for you."

"Everything just feels like a lot sometimes, you know?" I pick up the mug once again, allow a little more of the steeped tea into my mouth. The temperature is better now. Just about right.

"I do know," Mom says.

I prop the phone in the crook of my neck, open the small drawer of the nightstand, rummage around, and find a crumpled tissue. I manage to both blot my eyes and not spill my tea.

"You know, dear, I have times like these with your father too. When we go to weddings and he won't dance with me, I always think that I'll marry a dancer in my next life. But you know what, if I left your father and traded him in for a newer model, that dancer would have something else about him that I wouldn't like. Love isn't always perfect, but I do know one thing for sure. Don't ever settle for something that makes you truly unhappy. Don't sell yourself short. Your dad and I like Liam, but *you* need to like, and love, him. You need to like and love lots of little things about him. You need to be able to throw all of those little things into a pile and stand back and see if that pile is big enough for you. He should be enough for you, and even a little bit more than enough. Have you tried making a list?"

A list is my mother's first go-to solution for any problem, big or small.

"Mom...." I start to groan aloud, but deep down, I know we're too alike. A list could probably really help me right now. But what would be the columns? Liam versus...being alone? Liam versus...Matthew?

As if she, too, can read my mind, my mom says, "Just some pros and cons, darling. Sometimes you have to see the facts right in front of your face, in big, bold letters."

My mother's right. As always. I groan, for real this time. "Fine. I'll start a list. Tonight. As soon as we hang up."

"Remember, that pile of pros should be big and bold, Gracie. You deserve the best."

"I'll work on it. I promise."

"Your father and I love you very much."

"Love you more than my luggage." Another line stolen from a movie and passed back and forth over the years.

"Okay, darling. Call me anytime if you need to talk. Bye, dear."

I set my tea down to grope around in the nightstand again. I locate my yellow notepad then dig around some more for a pencil. I squish flat the pillows behind my head, bring my knees closer to my chest, and balance the notepad on my thighs. I draw a thick black line down the middle of the sheet of yellow paper. I scrawl a big plus on one side of the paper and a large negative sign on the other. I put the pencil to the paper and begin to write.

11

Liam comes to bed an hour or so later. I debate playing dead so that I don't have to interact with him, but instead, I sit up and reach for my laptop on the nightstand. "Liam. I've been working on a short story. Do you want to hear about it?"

"Sure," he says, as he undresses and climbs into bed and lies on his side facing away from me.

I begin to tell him what I've been working on but stop midsentence to see if he's paying attention. He grunts out an "mm-hmm" to make it seem like he's interested. I know he hasn't heard a word. In my head I count to see how long it will be before he speaks to me or looks in my direction. I make it to seventy-Mississippi, then give up. I open my laptop and write for a while. After a half hour or so, Liam clicks off the lamp on his side of the bed. He mumbles goodnight, then falls silent. He snores within minutes. Must be nice.

I settle myself back into bed and try to sleep but fail. Maybe something warm and heavy in my belly will help me sleep? I pull on some jeans and head downstairs.

Down in the kitchen, I rummage through the fridge. Nothing appeals to me. I lift a block of cheese, inspect it, then put it back on the shelf. Maybe some toast. I snag the loaf of wheat bread from the counter, stick a slice into the toaster, and push the lever down.

A thud on the porch rattles me. I strain my eyes but don't see any shady men in ski masks ready to break in. Probably raccoons. I tiptoe to the back door to turn on the porch light. When I flick the switch, light floods the silhouette of Annie with a bottle of wine in one hand and two glasses in the other. "Jesus! Annie!" I utter, and she nearly drops everything she's holding.

When I unlock and prop open the back door, Annie hisses, "Are you trying to kill me?"

"Hey, you're the one creeping out there. You're lucky you didn't get a baseball bat to the kneecaps, sister."

"I can't sleep, and I saw the kitchen light...." Annie gives me her best pout.

Moths flock to the porch light and make little winged shadows on Annie's face. "Well, come on in then."

Annie barges in and pours herself a glass of wine. My toast pops up. I nab the hot bread, toss it back and forth in my hands, then pull the crust off when it cools enough to eat.

Annie blinks at me. "What are you, five? How can you waste perfectly good crust like that? The crust is the best part!"

I toss the leftover crust at Annie. "Why don't you mind ya business over there, killer."

"Jeez. Somebody's moody. Why don't you have a drink with me and calm your ass down." Annie fills the second glass. "Now tell me everything"

I swallow some toast. "Hey, not too much for me."

"You're young. You can handle it."

Annie pours even more into my glass, and I slump into a

chair next to her. I tell her that I talked to Say on the phone the other day and it made me feel better. "Grace, did you tell her about the baby?" She lays her hand on my wrist.

I take a long steady sip. "Not yet."

"Are you ever going to?"

I slide my arm away. "Can we maybe talk about this some other time?"

"Sure, sweetie. I'm sorry I brought it up. Let's talk about other fun stuff."

We talk and drink, and Annie gets louder the later it gets and the more wine she consumes. I alternate between sips of wine and shushing Annie. I don't want to have to deal with Liam tonight. I look over at the clock. Annie notices and says, "Hey, I have an idea. Let's go down to Patty's for a drink."

"Annie Whitney, you've lost your mind," I declare. "I just got done telling you that I'm not going to drink much tonight."

"Life is short. We need to live it up while we can. It's Friday night. Go get your purse."

I roll my empty wine glass on its base against the table. Annie bats her eyelashes at me and makes whimpering noises like Chance.

"Fine. I'll go. But this is going to be a quick jaunt, okay? Promise?"

Annie starts clapping. I stop her hands and whisper, "Let me go on record and say this is your worst idea yet. But I'll do it just to get your loud ass out of the house."

I should probably leave Liam a note. Nah. He won't even notice I'm gone.

"Works for me!" Annie swipes the half-empty wine bottle

from the table. I fetch my purse off the counter, and Annie pushes me out the door. Out on the porch, Annie insists we take the wine with us on the walk, but I won't let her. "That wine stays here," I say and set the open bottle down on the top step. "You've had enough. I've had enough."

"Fine." Annie sticks her tongue out. I take Annie by the arm and help her down the stairs and onto the street. A few people pass us along the way and of course, Annie tries to engage in conversation with all of them. Most of them smile politely but walk on by.

We stop in front of a bar on Main Street. Annie cracks a smile. "Ready for some fun?"

I sigh. "If you say so."

Loud music grows louder when Annie opens the door to usher me inside. "Oooooh, that's right!" she cackles. "It's karaoke tonight!"

Annie drags me by the arm, staggers to the bar, and attempts to haul the poor bartender over the counter by his shirt collar. Annie kisses the man on the forehead. "Jake!" she yells into his face.

Jake laughs, catches his balance behind the bar. "Annie!" he shouts back. "Been awhile! What'll it be? On the house." He's fit, this guy, somewhere in his fifties.

Annie grins. "In that case—gin and tonic. No, wait, make that two. Strong. My friend and I are going to find a seat."

"Annie," I protest.

I turn to Jake. "I'll have a club soda."

"Suit yourself," Annie says with a huff, but then she gives me puppy dog eyes and bats her eyelashes.

"Oh, for god's sake. Fine. Gin and tonic for me, too, I guess."

Annie claps and grins.

We find a table near the stage. I look around at the décor: a pirate statue by the bar, stacked lobster traps and buoys along the walls.

Jake himself arrives with our drinks not a minute later. "Introduce me to this pretty lady," Jake says to Annie.

I shake his hand. "I'm Grace. Annie's temporary neighbor."

Jake nods and turns toward the bar. "You ladies holler if you need anything, okay?"

I sip my drink. I'm starting to think that Annie had a few drinks before she got to my place because I already hear a distinct drag to her words. We chat and people-watch. Annie shares a few stories about some of the locals and before I know it, my drink is done. Just as I push my empty glass away from me, Jake shows up with four shots on a tray.

"Oh, my dear lord, Annie. What have you done?"

Annie winks at me and grabs the drinks off the tray. Sets two in front of me and two in front of her.

"Ladies and gentlemen of the jury, I want to say whatever ensues from this point forward will be entirely Annie Whitney's fault."

Annie is rubbing her hands together. I pluck one of the shot glasses off the table with my thumb and forefinger and then sniff the contents. "Oh, Annie, no," I say, setting the glass back down.

Annie shoves the drink at me. "Tequila, baby!"

I raise my glass in her direction. "To terrible choices."

"Yes. Here's to terrible choices."

I take the contents of my glass down in one swig, and then I wince, stick my tongue out, and shake my hands in front of me.

Annie gulps, slams her glass down, and immediately guzzles the second shot.

"Oh man," I say but follow suit.

Within minutes, Annie is swaying back and forth, snapping her fingers in the air and clapping along with the music. I sit back and smile. She's having such a good time.

A few songs later, I'm starting to feel more than a little tipsy. The latest song ends and then Annie shakes her head side to side. "Life is short. It's go-time!"

She jumps up and almost falls over her chair.

"Easy, easy," I say as I steady her.

She hurries toward the karaoke machine, beckons me over with her pointy fingernail. She hops on stage just as the last act wraps. I follow, finally just pleasantly tipsy enough that I don't even protest.

Annie swipes through the machine's selections like she's on a dating app. "Bingo!" she shouts.

I look over her shoulder and bark a laugh. Patsy Cline. Her selection is one my mother used to sing all the time when I was little. I don't even need the lyrics.

The song begins. Annie and I pretend to struggle over the mic, but I let her win. By the time we hit the chorus, we're both shaking our asses. A sloppy gaggle of local drunks cheers for us. For the next verse, Annie rests on a tall stool and hands me the mic. I take the lead.

I belt the words with my eyes closed. When I open my eyes again at the chorus, I stop singing and nearly drop the mic. Matthew stands in the doorway. What in the actual fuck?

Annie snatches the mic to finish out the song from her little perch. I stand beside her and mumble along. My throat is too tight to sing.

Matthew scans the room, sees me. He does a double take, looking as surprised to see me as I am to see him. He waves and takes off his coat, then hangs it on the rack by the door. I bite my bottom lip to conceal a smile.

The music finally fades, and our sloshed fans give us a standing ovation. Annie wraps her arm around my shoulder and forces me into a bow. She touches her toes with her free hand, then yanks me back up with her. Stars wink in front of my eyes, and I don't dare look at Matthew.

Annie starts to take another bow, and I duck from beneath her arm.

I turn my back to the room for a second to collect myself. I've only sung karaoke once before back in college. Of course Matthew would show up exactly when I'm doing something so dorky. He's going to think I'm such a weirdo.

I leave Annie to her adoring fans and jog toward Matthew, who still stands, albeit casually, by the entrance. Almost to him, I trip over the rug by the front door and fall forward. I don't fall into his arms like in a rom-com. Instead, my forehead smacks the side of a big metal garbage can as I crash down.

"Wow. Well." Matthew bends to hoist me up with both hands. "Are you okay?"

"I'm great!" Once I'm steady, I run my fingers over the lump on my forehead. Even in my inebriated state, I predict a nasty bruise. My face burns. "What are you doing here?" I blurt. "I mean, thank you. How are you?"

Matthew laughs. He looks me over and says, "Let's get you a

seat, maybe get some ice on that head."

"Good idea." I follow him but crane my neck to check on Annie.

Across the room, Annie allows a bearded man to escort her off the stage. He walks her to our table, where she slumps forward and puts her head down on her arms. Annie hasn't even noticed Matthew.

I move behind Annie to rub her shoulders. She moans, then giggles. Matthew takes one long look at us and walks away, but soon returns with two white mugs. One holds ice, the other black coffee. I thank Matthew, then sit again, right next to Annie, to hold the chilled mug of ice to my forehead. Annie doesn't stir.

Matthew shrugs, fetches a third chair. "Fun night?"

I smile. "We've had a blast. But I have to tell you, I'm a little embarrassed. I'm no karaoke queen. I swear I've only ever done karaoke one other time in my entire life. But I love this woman, and I'd do anything for her." I rest my head on Annie's shoulder. She grunts.

"Well then, you're a good friend. You two actually sounded pretty good up there."

"Yeah, I'm thinking of changing careers," I try to joke. "Maybe even take our show on the road." I laugh, but when I do, my whole forehead throbs. I wince, and Matthew frowns in sympathy. He pushes Annie's coffee mug toward me, and I take a slow sip. Then another.

"Better?" he asks, but before I can answer, a rich, deep voice fills the room. The bearded man has chosen a Sinatra song, and he's good. Really good. We give him our full attention. When the song ends, the place erupts. I realize then that Annie has fallen asleep, but before I can even get my phone out of my purse to call Bill, he's there, standing next to our table.

"How'd you know where to find us?" I ask.

Bill angles his chin toward the bar. "Jake and I go way back. He called the house and said Annie might need a ride home." Bill nudges his wife. "Wakey wakey, old girl."

Annie lifts her head and gazes at Bill. Her eyes nearly cross with the effort.

"I'm so sorry, Bill. I didn't mean to let her get this drunk."

"Oh honey, Annie had a good time, I can tell. She needed a break, I think. Distractions are good." Bill pats my wrist then introduces himself to Matthew. The men shake hello.

Distractions?

Matthew stands. "Can I give you a hand?"

Bill sighs. "That would be nice."

Annie snaps back to life when the men help her to her feet. "One more song," she slurs.

"Not tonight, honey. Another time, I promise."

Outside, the cool air refreshes me. I realize then my stomach had gone a little queasy in the bar. I guess my pounding head had taken precedence. But I feel much better now, out here under the stars. Pretty soon, I bet it will be too cold to stand outside on a clear night like tonight.

The men load Annie into the front seat. Bill fastens the seatbelt across Annie's lap just as her head slumps forward. "Hop in, Grace, I'll give you a ride home," he says over his shoulder.

"Thanks, but I think I'll walk. I could use the fresh air."

Bill unrolls Annie's window, closes her door. I bend down to tell her goodnight. At the sound of my voice, Annie revives once again. She locks her crossed eyes on mine. "I love you," she whispers. "I love you like a daughter."

"I know, Annie, I love you too." I pat her cheek.

She points at my nose. "We've got that thing tomorrow."

I'd almost forgotten we'd made plans to attend a local craft fair. "Yes, tomorrow. I'll see you by 8:00 a.m."

Over the top of the car, Bill studies Matthew. Looks at me. "Sure you don't want a ride?"

Matthew says, "I'll see that Grace gets home safe. I promise."

Bill chuckles but scans my face one last time. I start to feel a bit lightheaded. "I'm fine, Bill. I swear."

"Okay. Turn off your porch light when you get home so that I know you are home safely,"

"Will do."

Bill starts the car and steers to the edge of the parking lot. He beeps as he drives away.

I raise my hand to wave, but all sound starts to fade, my vision blurs, and the parking lot itself shimmers.

Matthew steps closer.

My ears ring. "I think I need to sit." I lower myself to the ground. The asphalt feels like slick black ice under my palms.

Matthew kneels down.

I clutch my head, then let it sink between my knees. "What is wrong with me?"

"Just stay down for a minute. This happens all the time with my sister. Low blood pressure, probably."

I take Matthew's advice. I stay down. Breathe deeply. Once more. Gather my strength. I lift my head, and Matthew helps me stand. Again.

"I probably just needed to drink more water today. And less booze." My mouth suddenly feels like a desert. "You know what? I'm starting to feel better already."

"*I'd* feel better if I walked with you, just in case." Matthew takes off his flannel jacket and drapes it over my shoulders like a cape.

"You don't need to," I say. "I'm fine. Just dehydrated. And I live right up the street."

"No dice. I promised Bill."

He raises an eyebrow at me, and I give in. "Okay, take me home, Jeeves."

We walk toward my house, and the moon lights our path. Not too far away, the waves crash against the beach. I wish we were there despite my lingering headache. My head hurts a lot lately, now that I think about it. "Hey, you don't think I have a concussion, do you?"

"No, your symptoms aren't so severe. But you are a little unsteady. Here, let me check your eyes." Matthew pulls his jangling keys from his pocket, clicks on a tiny flashlight attached to the ring. He holds me still by the arm and glances the beam off each of my eyes. "Your pupils look fine."

I wobble when he releases me, a little dazed by the sharp light. Or Matthew's proximity.

Maybe I am just impressed by his first aid skills. Or the fact that he cares.

"Where did you learn—"

"I actually just made all of that up. I have no medical training whatsoever. Now, let's get you home before I invite you on a moonlit walk on the beach and keep you out too late." He grins and offers me his arm.

12

The alarm clock on the nightstand says 8:30, which can't be right. Annie and I had planned to leave by 8:00 to go to the craft fair. The bed is empty, so as usual, Liam must have left for work before I even woke up.

I slog down the stairs and hold the railing the whole way down to steady myself just in case I get lightheaded again. I should be surprised, but I'm not when I see Annie at my kitchen table in a pair of oversized black sunglasses, elbows propped, head in her hands. A glass of clear liquid fizzes in front of her. Annie waves me into the kitchen.

"Here," Annie points to her Alka-Seltzer, "want some?"

"I'm all set, but I think you should take a swig."

"Fine." After a quick sip, Annie says, "We sang last night, didn't we? How was I?"

"You made me proud."

"Good. Should we do this craft show today?"

"You up for it?"

"Yes. But I need to go home and try to make myself look decent first." Annie raises her head to scrutinize me. "You too. You look like you've been hit by a dump truck."

"Well, thank you, and right back at you." I start to laugh but

Annie shushes me reaching for her head. She rubs small circles on her temples.

Seconds later, she lets her arms drop and looks up at me. "Help me get outta this chair, would you?"

Two hours later, Annie and I arrive at the craft fair held in the cafeteria/gym of the local elementary school. I smell fresh baked goods, holiday candle scents, and the warm spices of homemade chili. People of all ages mill about.

Annie moves a little slower than usual, still in her giant sunglasses. She stops at the first table to grill the woman about her organic soaps. I walk away when Annie asks about rashes.

The next crafter offers hand-knit baby sweaters, mittens, and hats with animal ears. Do I have to live in a cave to avoid all of this baby shit? I avert my eyes and plow past to the third table, where black velvet trays of silver jewelry rest atop a white tablecloth. My kind of display.

I pick up an ornate silver ring, admiring the twisted band with a smoky green stone at its center. I love everything about this piece. I find the attached white tag: $200. Well, I love everything about it *except* the price. A fair price for the handiwork, but a little too expensive for me just now. I browse the rest of the trays and talk with the jewelry vendor while holding the ring, just in case I change my mind.

Annie sidles over. "Gorgeous!" she sings out. She snatches the ring from me to inspect it.

"Unbelievable. You're going to get it, right?"

"I want to," I sigh, "but I should be more practical."

"Of course you're going to be *practical*." She drawls the last word and rolls her eyes, replacing the ring on the tray.

Annie looks to her left. “Kate!” she shouts, then rushes behind the next table to embrace the older woman. “Grace, meet Kate. Kate goes to my church.” Annie takes in all of the hand-painted ornaments on the table. “Look at this stuff,” she croons.

“Lovely,” I agree.

While Annie continues to talk to Kate with her arm around her shoulders, I spot an apparently very popular display of pottery just ahead. The crowd lingers and blocks my view. Some shoppers rummage through a cardboard box marked “clearance” placed at the corner of the booth. I weave my way over and then wait my turn to approach the main table.

A mug with a delicate stencil of da Vinci’s Vitruvian Man catches my eye. The mug is a plain cream color, and the light brown sketch contrasts nicely. I’ve been intrigued by the Vitruvian Man’s symmetry and mirror writing since college. I flip the mug over to look at the bottom, and the price sticker says $15.00. That’s in my budget for sure. I set the mug down while fumbling through my purse for cash.

“My son has that figure tattooed on his back,” a woman who’s come up next to me says.

I smile and nod.

She continues, “His father and I initially resisted the idea because he was only eighteen at the time. We thought he would regret it, but so far, I guess not.”

“The Vitruvian Man is a striking image, isn’t it?”

“My son would love one of these.” She leans over the table. “Excuse me,” she taps a fingernail to the mug on the table, “do you have another?”

The potter replies, "One of a kind, I'm afraid."

"Shoot," the woman says.

I know I should do the right thing and let this kind woman buy the mug, but I've already passed on the ring, haven't I?

"Here comes my son now," the woman says.

I count out my money while the potter wraps my purchase in newspaper.

"Hey, Mom," a deep voice calls.

Wait, what? I turn to the right. "Matthew!"

"Grace!"

Matthew's mother looks from me to her son and back again.

At this exact moment, Annie walks over. "I want to buy some earrings for my Kelly. Come give me your opinion." Then she does a double take, pulling her sunglasses down her nose. "Hello!" Annie howls as she kisses Matthew on the cheek. "This guy saved us last night." Annie extends her hand to his mother.

"I'm Annie Whitney. Are you Matthew's mom? You must have done something right. He's a good kid. So handsome too!" Annie squeezes Matthew's biceps.

Matthew chuckles. "Mom, meet Annie and Gracie." I like that he adds the *ie* to the end of my name.

"Pleased to meet you both," his mom says. "I'm still confused, though. How do you all know each other?"

"Long story," Annie says. "Your name?"

"Nancy. We live over on—"

"Lexington! Now I recognize you! I remember the yard sale you had last summer. I bought that big mirror from you, and we talked about your dog. Rupert, right?" Annie slaps my arm. "You should see their dog. He's a sweet old golden retriever."

Of course, Annie remembers all the minute details of a near-perfect stranger's life. "Well, we should have coffee sometime," Annie says. "Here, let me give you my number."

I look at Matthew and shrug. He smiles and shrugs back.

I turn back to the pottery vendor, who's been patient during our introductions, despite the eager crowd at her booth. She hands me a paper bag and a handwritten carbon copy of a receipt, and I thank her profusely. I tuck my purchase inside my purse and take Annie's arm. We need to move out of the way.

Annie plants her feet, then looks at both Nancy and Matthew. "Grace and I were going to get something to eat before we call it a day. Would the two of you like to join us?"

"Terrific," Nancy says.

I want to protest because I'm not sure my stomach can handle food yet, even though it's approaching lunchtime. I glance over and see that the lunch line already extends into the middle of the room.

"Mom, why don't you and Annie go find a seat. We'll bring you some food."

"What a gentleman!" Annie gushes. "I just have to stop by a particular booth and ask a lady a question really quick before we sit down. Nancy, would you like to come with me?"

"I'd love to."

Matthew marks our place in line, and I join him. He nudges my shoulder with his own.

"And how do you feel today?"

"Much better, thanks. I think I was just dehydrated."

"Well, I'm glad you came to the fair."

"Me too."

We chat easily as the line moves forward inch by inch. I spot Annie and Nancy near the picnic-style cafeteria tables. Several have been pulled away from the walls and arranged in neat rows, just like a regular school day. The two women slide down one bench on the same side.

They're talking and laughing, and the sight of them as fast friends tickles me.

At the window finally, we order four bowls of chili with cornbread and bottled water. Matthew carries the tray to the table. Annie helps dole out the food and drink while Matthew and I take our seats on the opposite side.

After only one bite, Annie announces, "This chili needs more salt." She points to her bowl.

"How about I get you some?" Matthew scoots down, starts to lift one leg over the bench to stand. As he maneuvers, his knee bumps into my thigh.

He frowns and says low, "Sorry about that, my bad."

"No worries."

Nancy shoos Matthew from the table. "Don't mind my clumsy son. He gets *that* trait from his father. Did you grow up around here, Grace?"

"I did. But then I moved away. I'm here for a year...."

"Just a year?"

"Yes. I, um—"

"Grace is quite the writer," Annie says, "and this town is the perfect place to come and write for a year, wouldn't you agree?"

"It certainly is," Nancy says with a smile. "What do you write about?"

Matthew returns and sets the salt and pepper down in front

of Annie as he slides back into his seat. His knee brushes against mine, but very gently this time, and rests there once he's settled. I don't move my leg away.

We're all quiet, intent on our food, until Annie blurts: "Woo! Spicy!" She fans at her open mouth with one hand, then chugs from her water bottle with the other.

Nancy nods and sips her water as well. "So, what do you write about, Grace?"

"Mostly, modern life. Families, you know. The piece I'm working on now is more like a journal. Maybe I'll turn it into a novel or something."

"Well, that all sounds fascinating, Grace."

"She is pretty cool, isn't she?" Matthew winks at me.

I smile, tap his knee with mine under the table. He nudges me back.

"Grace, have you tried the cornbread yet? It's to die for!" Annie tosses a wrapped pad of butter at me, which bounces off my chest. "Matthew, Nancy told me earlier all about your new internship at that architecture firm. Seems like you really like it there. Do you think you'll stay there for a while? In Pennsylvania, I mean. I bet your mom would like you to move closer to home, wouldn't you, Nancy?"

Annie kicks me under the table.

Both Matthew and I jump. I kick her back.

"Of course, it would be lovely if he moved up here," Nancy says, "but I also know how important it is to be happy in life. If he is satisfied where he is, then I'm content as well."

Matthew squeezes his mom's hand.

"Amen to that!" Annie barks. "We know how important it is

to be *truly* happy, don't we, Grace?"

I clear my throat. "We sure do." I lock my eyes on Annie's while I lift my buttered square of cornbread and take a huge bite. Annie laughs as yellow crumbs avalanche down my front.

Matthew hands me another napkin.

Annie grins, then asks, "Matthew, darling, how long will you be in town?"

"Until tomorrow, or maybe very early Monday morning. I want to beat the traffic."

Nancy says, "Good idea."

We continue to eat and chat, but at some point, I realize I've lost the plot. I haven't heard much of what anyone's said since Matthew said he's leaving soon. I've also become too quiet because when Matthew stands and offers to clear away our trash, Annie gives me a look. I shrug at her.

As we all move toward the exit, I see a young mother buckling her toddler into a stroller. The mom then snugs a hat with a fox face and ears over the baby's forehead. When I practically stop to stare, the mom smiles, and I try my best to smile back.

Annie links her elbow through mine. "That food isn't sitting right with me. I think we should get going."

I nod, coming back to myself. Even though I don't want to miss more time with Matthew, I do desperately need to get caught up on some work. "Nancy, wonderful to meet you. And you," I turn to Matthew, "don't be a stranger." I offer my hand for a shake, but he pulls me into a hug.

"Aww, me too!" Annie whines, and Matthew frees one arm to snug around her shoulders.

"My favorite local ladies," he says.

Nancy interjects, "Ahem!" and Matthew adds, "Next to Mom, of course."

Nancy rolls her eyes. "Let's get home to watch that game with your dad."

Matthew releases us but catches my eye. "Maybe I'll see you around before I go back."

"I'd like that. A lot." I feel my face flush once more as I watch them walk away.

"Hey. Hey! Earth to Grace." Annie snaps her fingers in front of my eyes. "What's with you today?"

"I want to stop by that jewelry table before we go. Do we have time? Or are you going to explode soon?"

"I'm okay, for a few. Just indigestion. But I also need a nap. Let's take a quick look on our way out, even though I have a bad feeling that gorgeous green ring has been snatched up by now." Annie rubs her belly and burps.

We stroll by the table, and Annie's right—the ring is gone. Oh well, it wasn't meant to be.

Annie and I ride home in near silence. She pulls a large bottle of Tums out of her purse, pops the cap, and shakes a few of the pastel tablets into her palm. "You want?" Annie asks.

"Ew. Worse than Canada mints."

"Suit yourself." Annie shoves a handful of antacids into her mouth. I almost gag as I listen to her chomp.

When I put on the blinker to turn into the driveway, I catch a glimpse of Annie in my peripheral vision. "Hey. You really don't look so hot."

Blotchy and sweaty, she dabs at her head with the arm of her sleeve. "I'll be fine, Grace. Just need to rest."

"I think I should walk you back to your—"

"I said, I'm *fine*!"

I wince at Annie's tone.

"Sorry. That came out all wrong. You know how it is when you don't feel well. I just want to crawl into my bed as soon as possible. I'll catch up with you later, okay?"

"Fair enough."

I linger in my yard as I sneakily watch Annie hobble to her back door. She shouldn't be that sick after one night of drinks. Probably just overdid it. Time to focus on nothing but work for the rest of the day.

13

A key in the front door wakes me. I sit up on the couch, but my head feels sodden like I'm deep underwater.

Liam enters, his laptop case tucked under one arm. "Hey, babe," he says. He kicks off his shoes, unwinds his scarf, hangs his jacket, and then stands beside me.

I sit up, feeling very disoriented. "What time is it?"

I grope around on the couch and uncover my laptop, now tipped at an angle in a heap of blankets. "Must have dozed off," I say with a yawn and stretch.

Liam steps closer. Rubs my cheek, his knuckles icy cold. The weather has finally turned, I guess. "Did you remember that Peter invited us over for dinner tonight?"

"Shit. I totally forgot."

I start to protest when Liam says, "You *did* say you'd go."

"I know. I just forgot."

I want Liam to change his mind and say I don't have to go. He doesn't. I sigh. "Fine. I guess I'll get ready."

"Great. Why don't you go hop in the shower and I'll join you in a few."

I drop my shoulders and turn my face away to hide my cringe. "Sure," I say.

Liam takes his phone from his pants pocket and walks toward the kitchen. I push myself off the couch and slog up the stairs.

A few minutes into my blissfully hot shower, I hear Liam enter the bathroom. I peek out through the curtain and see that he's already undressed. Jesus Christ. We haven't been intimate since well before the miscarriage, and now he wants romantic shower sex?

Except, it isn't romantic. Liam presses against me without preamble. I act enthusiastic, trying to hurry the act along.

Liam washes up after and then pecks me on the lips before he leaves to shave at the sink.

I linger in the shower.

I take my sweet time doing my makeup and hair. Liam hollers my name up the stairs every few minutes. I ignore him. He can wait.

I open the closet doors to survey my choices. I flip through the hangers and yank off a black fit-and-flare dress with a lower neckline. With opaque tights and black booties, my ensemble strikes a nice balance for an evening with the boyfriend's boss.

We arrive at Peter's house at around 7:00. I like group dinners, but I hate the fussy kind of dinner party we're attending tonight. Since I will hardly know anyone, my plan is to keep Liam close. He pushes the doorbell with a gloved finger.

A moment later, Peter greets us with his shiny white teeth. "Liam! Grace!" He ushers us into the foyer. "Grace, let me introduce you to my wife."

Peter's wife, Carol, is gorgeous, as predicted. She's in her mid-fifties but doesn't have a wrinkle on her face. Her blonde hair cascades down her shoulders. She's wearing a shimmery silver blouse that hurts my eyes. She grabs my hand. "Great to finally meet you."

My stomach clenches as I suddenly remember that day at the farm when I last saw Peter. Surely, he'll mention it next, just as a quick, casual point of reference. I need to change the direction of this conversation, and fast.

"What a charming home you have." I look around to feign appreciation while I count the many other guests I can see over Peter's shoulder. They mill about the open plan dining and living area. About twenty of them, and I don't know a soul. Why did I let Liam drag me here, especially given how we've barely talked lately? And now I have to be charming for strangers?

Carol offers to make me a drink.

"No, thank you," I say.

Liam squeezes my wrist. I know he wants me to play the grateful guest. "On second thought, why not? A white wine, if you have it?"

Carol departs while Liam and Peter continue to chat. I smile and nod appropriately until a waiter approaches with a tray of assorted appetizers. I take a stuffed mushroom cap to be polite but simply tuck it inside a cocktail napkin. Soon enough, Peter turns us toward the larger group, and the interminable mingling begins.

Liam leaves my side to dart in and out of the crowd—schmoozing, no doubt. I stay in one place near a wall, sip my wine, and make small talk with those who engage me. Everyone's pleasant enough, but the evening drags on and on.

At one point, I excuse myself back to the foyer. I pull my

phone from my coat pocket to check the time. Only thirty minutes have passed since we arrived.

Just as I return, Peter announces that he'd like to give us all the grand tour before we eat dinner to show off all the work Liam's done so far with the remodel.

The bulk of us follow Peter up the stairs. Everyone offers glowing compliments. I hate to admit it, but Liam's incredibly good at what he does. The completed renovations look both cozy and classy. Liam's added wall-to-wall bookshelves in the home office, reading nooks in the bedrooms with soft lighting. The new master bath, his most extensive redesign thus far, now features a whirlpool tub in front of large windows that face the ocean. We end the tour at a set of double glass doors that lead to a widow's walk—Liam's next project. He needs to refurbish it for safety, so we can't explore further. Peter tells us about the custom-made iron railings on order.

Back downstairs in the dining room, the table has been meticulously set for the meal.

Then I see something I really don't like—personalized name cards at every setting.

"Excuse me, everyone." Peter picks up a wine glass and taps its side with a fork. "As you can see, Carol has assigned your seats. No cheating!" Peter laughs and his guests chuckle along as they begin to locate their names and chairs.

I glare at Liam. He shrugs.

I scan the table. *Great.* I've been seated just to the right of the head of the table, next to Peter. Is it too late to pretend to be ill?

Peter pulls out my chair for me. "Wonderful," he says. "Let's get to know each other better, Grace."

His tone triggers my fight-or-flight reflex. I smile and sit, then stare at the assorted cutlery in front of me. Peter leans in and whispers, "Start from the outside and work your way in." The smell of red wine on his breath makes my stomach lurch.

I force another smile even though I want to tell him where he can stick his own fork. No—what I want to do more than anything else at this very moment is to start with the most prominent fork and stab myself in the thigh as a surefire way to get the hell out of here. Instead, I thank Peter.

Peter talks my ear off about his house, his investments, and how much the people love him in this town. I nod every ten seconds or so to make him think I'm listening. Now and then, he asks me a question, but when I start to answer, he interrupts, launching into another story about his life. Peter finishes half a bottle of red wine well before the third course of braised vegetables arrives. As I nibble, I think about how Annie would act if she were here. She'd outtalk Peter by a mile. I use my napkin to dab my lips to hide my grin.

An economics professor named Daphne sits to my right in a sleek pantsuit. I overhear her lament at this semester's students and their intellectual inferiority. She's so tipsy already that she continues to bring her long-empty wine glass to her mouth. Without warning, Daphne shifts toward me. "And what do you do for a living, Grace?"

I'm too tired to explain my job in detail. "I work for a media research company. I also like to write in my spare time."

"What do you mean, *you write?*" Daphne grabs the arm of the man next to her and says, too loudly, "She's a writer."

All conversation stops, and all eyes turn to me. I squirm in my seat.

"Go on. Tell us all about your writing," Daphne demands.

I take a sip of water. "Well, I usually write short stories—"

Daphne clasps her hands and says, "How precious." When she smiles at me, I notice the gaudy orange lipstick smeared on her front teeth. I'm not about to tell her.

People around the table nod at me and wait, unlike Daphne, for me to continue. I can't find one decent word in my head.

Peter interjects, "She's writing the next *great* novel from what Liam tells me." He leans over, squeezes my knee under the table, and only winks when I swivel my leg out of his reach.

The fuck was that?

Through the next course, some kind of fish, I try to focus on my plate. I can barely eat or drink. I only look up from my untouched food to locate Liam from time to time. He's at the far end of the table, thoroughly enjoying himself. He's rubbing elbows with Rebecca, Peter's daughter. When I fail to catch Liam's eye, hoping to send him clear signals of distress, I study the two of them instead. They seem comfortable together, and Rebecca is certainly beautiful. Tall and blonde and polished, like her mother, except her makeup might be even more flawless—practically professionally done arched brows, long lashes, winged eyeliner, lush lips. I have to wonder again—why am I here?

Peter makes a big production when he himself carves and serves the next course, a tremendous hunk of meat. He shares the story of hunting this poor deer, then brings the last two sliced servings to the table, mine and his, as he resumes his seat. He watches me cut the meat and move the small bites around on my plate. "Not a fan of venison?"

I sigh then and pat my belly. "Full already, I guess."

Peter laughs and puts a hand on my shoulder. The hair on my neck rises as he lets his touch linger. I shift away, but Peter seems unfazed as he returns to the deer on his plate.

The venison is followed by a small fresh salad, then assorted fruits, cheeses, and desserts.

When Peter rises again to graciously help pour coffee and tea, I make a quick exit.

I escape to the powder room off the foyer. After I flush, I wash my hands for a full sixty seconds in soapy hot water to let the warmth settle my nerves. I hear a light knock, and I know I have to go back to the party or look rude. I dry my hands on the softest, fluffiest white towel I have ever felt. When I swing the door open, Liam stands in front of me.

"Thanks for coming with me tonight." He kisses me on the cheek. "Ready to mix more?"

I can't believe these are the first words he's said to me in hours. "No, I am not," I hiss. "That boss of yours has got his hands all over me. Not that you'd notice. You look pretty busy down at your end of the table."

"What?"

"Peter! He kept touching me. My knee, my shoulder. He even winked!"

"I'm sure he was just being friendly."

"Liam, you can't be serious? I'm mortified, and that man gives me the creeps. I want to leave."

Liam glances over his shoulder and shushes me. "Babe, relax. We'll leave after coffee, I promise."

He tries to kiss my cheek again, and I recoil. My whole body starts to shake with anger, but I'm mostly angry with myself. This one is on me. I've put up with this shit for way too long. I push past Liam toward the dining room. I raise my voice to announce: "Thank you so much, everyone. Dinner was delightful."

Peter walks toward me. "You haven't even had your coffee yet."

"Thank you, but we need to get going. Maybe next time." I take Liam's arm and spin us back toward the foyer. Peter follows.

As we gather our coats, Liam shakes Peter's hand and thanks him for the "spectacular evening." Peter leans in to hug me, but I stiffen my arm at the elbow and extend my hand for a shake. Peter simply uses the gesture to pull me closer. He whispers in my ear, "I hope you had a good time, too. By the way, you looked gorgeous tonight." He snakes a hand around my waist.

I pull away from Peter so quickly I almost stumble. I lock eyes with Liam, who gives me a weird look but helps me into my coat. Liam couldn't have heard Peter, but he knows I'm pissed now. Liam nods at Peter but says nothing in my defense. I yank open the front door and march toward Liam's truck. Liam's not far behind, and he beeps open my door with the key fob.

We ride home in stony silence for the first few minutes. "Grace, I work for him," Liam finally concedes. "I need this. *We* need this. I'm sorry. I didn't know what to do."

I continue to stare forward.

"But yes," Liam continues, "I see now that he's a little too touchy-feely."

I hold my breath, afraid of what I might say, and stare at his profile, lit green by the dash. "Grace..." he begins, but I turn away, holding up a hand.

Through the windshield, the dark asphalt looks too shiny, maybe even icy. "Just focus on the road," I tell him.

"Fine," he says. "We'll talk at home." He switches on the radio.

At the house, I jump out of the truck. A brief, bitter wind makes my teeth chatter even as I rush inside. I keep my coat on, and head straight for the kitchen for a mug of tea. Liam comes in a moment later, and I hear him lock the front door and close the living room curtains. He seems to be battening down the hatches, delaying, which makes my anger finally boil over.

"You're one hell of a boyfriend," I shout from the kitchen.

Liam walks in and just stares at me. He forgot to take off his shoes at the door.

I meet his gaze and lower my voice. "You were so busy with Rebecca that you didn't even notice how your boss was practically molesting me at the head of the table."

"Grace, don't overreact—"

"Overreact?" I'm shouting again. "Don't you see? Once again, you focused on another woman while you ignored me."

"Grace, we've been through this so many times. Too many, if you ask me. Nothing happened back in Portsmouth. What I had with Sophie was just a harmless flirtation that went a little too far. I stopped it before anything too physical happened."

"Oh, how thoughtful of you."

"And as far as Peter goes, he's harmless, really. He's just one of those guys."

"What the hell does that mean?"

"You know. Just a guy. Having a little fun."

"Oh, when you put your hands all over an unwilling woman, that's fun? Sounds like a great time to me." A lump forms in my throat. I need to cry, but I can't.

Liam sighs. He slumps into a kitchen chair and unlaces his shoes, head down. "You know what? I'm tired. I'm tired of your constant hypersensitivity. The past few weeks have been hard on me too, you know. I lost a lot of time at work after the miscarriage because I had to take care of you."

I suck in my breath, bare my teeth like a rabid animal.

Liam lifts his head and widens his eyes at my expression. "Grace, you know what I mean."

When I don't respond, he says, "Whatever. Forget it." He stalks to the stairs and doesn't look back. I hear the sharp squeaks of the second-story floorboards as he prepares for bed.

I need to leave.

Annie's backyard is all aglow in the dark night. They've lit their gas firepit, and multicolored lights line the back fence. I stop when I see Annie and Bill out there together. Annie reclines in a lounge chair piled with blankets, and Bill's in a camp chair beside her. Light laughter passes between them. Bill leans over and kisses his wife on the lips.

Even spitting mad, I can't help but smile at the pure sweetness of this moment. I also can't help but wonder if I'll ever find what Annie and Bill have. I gaze at them for a moment longer, but I need to sneak away before they see me. I don't want to intrude, but I have zero desire to go back into the rental house with Liam. Instead, I stroll across the street toward town.

Main Street twinkles with gold and silver lights. All the shopkeepers have decorated and backlit their big display windows for the holiday season. My anger dwindles as I walk and absorb the simple, festive mood of the town. I inhale and smell salty air and seaweed, maybe a hint of snow yet to fall.

A bit further down the street, I see a man gazing into a shop window, just as I've been doing. It can't be, but I know it must be Matthew. Who else?

14

"Hey!" I say when I reach him. Matthew startles but cracks a huge smile when he recognizes me. "That's so weird. I was just thinking about you. What are you doing out so late?"

"Just like a movie," I say out loud before I can stop myself.

"What's that?"

"Nothing. I just can't believe it's really you." I poke his shoulder. He pokes me back.

Matthew cups his hands and blows into them. "When I come to town, I sometimes stroll around at night. My folks go to bed at 8:00, and I get bored. I can't ever find anything on the television to watch."

"I hear you. I always watch the same old movies over and over again." I shiver. "God. The weather changes fast around here."

"Care for a hot chocolate?"

"Absolutely."

We duck into the Tap & Fin, a cute little bar and bistro, but maybe, at first glance, a touch too fussy for this town, with its marble-topped bar and high-backed barstools. Still, even if a little fancy, soft background music, paired with low lighting, makes this place feel inviting on a chilly night.

Matthew asks, "Bar or booth?"

"Whatever you want," I say, even though I prefer the bar.

"The bar it is."

When we shed our coats, Matthew notices my dress. "All dressed up and no place to go?"

"Something like that," I say.

The bartender, a younger woman probably in her mid-twenties, greets us. You can tell right away from her cheery smile that she loves her job.

"What can I get you folks?"

"What do you have for dessert?" Matthew asks.

"Chocolate cake, lemon cake with berries...." She goes on from there, but I don't listen after I hear "lemon cake." Something light and fresh after all the heavy food at Peter's house would be great.

Matthew says, "You choose. We'll split."

I laugh. "It all sounds wonderful. You pick."

Matthew grins. "Okay...the lemon cake. And two hot chocolates."

The bartender says, "You've got it," and hustles off to fill our order. Matthew looks over at me. "You did still want a hot chocolate, right?"

I nod.

"I don't want to order for you again, like I did at the farm."

"No worries, I promise."

The bartender returns with two oversized mugs. "Would you like whipped cream?"

Matthew shrugs but I say, "Yes, please," for both of us.

"Good choice," the bartender and Matthew reply in unison.

The bartender giggles. She turns and pulls an aluminum can from a glass-front fridge behind her. She squirts giant dollops into our mugs, then hands us two spoons. We dig into our drinks like ice cream sundaes and fall into a comfortable silence.

The television behind the bar broadcasts an earlier football game, and I gaze at the screen, even though I don't follow sports. I sip my drink and look around and realize Matthew and I are the only patrons in the bar now. The silence grows a little too long, and I'm about to try to talk some nonsense about football when Matthew spins his barstool to face me.

"Grace, I need to tell you something. I have a girlfriend. Well, I *had* a girlfriend. We've dated off and on for years, but I ended it for good a few months ago. I found her so intellectually stimulating, and she was always kind, but we didn't connect here." Matthew points to his chest. "Well, we did, but just as friends."

I nod, waiting for him to continue.

"I know my parents want me to get married, but I'm not sure I can marry someone unless they check off all the boxes. What do you think? Should I go for someone who scores a two out of three?"

"Nope. Call me a hopeless romantic, but that last item on the list, the heart, seems most important. If you don't feel it there, what's the point?"

"You think so?" Matthew stares at me.

I sigh. "I hope so," I say, and the honest, open look on his face makes me confess as well.

"I'm with someone too. Except I can't stand him sometimes." I stop. "I shouldn't say it that way. He's not a monster. We're just two different people...and we want different lives."

"I'm sure he's got some good qualities?"

"He does, but the relationship's been over in my mind for a while. I don't know why I can't rip that Band-Aid off."

Just then, another couple sits down near us. Matthew and I smile hello, both grateful for the distraction, I think. The man orders an Allagash White, and the woman notices our hot chocolates and orders one for herself but asks the bartender to add a shot of Kahlúa.

The couple tells the bartender that they're visiting family here in Maine. They live in Texas and have left their three young kids with his parents for their date night. I can't help but eavesdrop. The bartender chimes in, "I'm from Minnesota. Came here for a girl." Then she looks at us. "Are you two from here?" My entire body tingles at that question. She thinks we're a couple, and we don't correct her.

"Pennsylvania," Matthew answers. He puts his hand on my upper back, then slides his fingertips back and forth. I play along, smile at everyone, and try not to melt.

A server from the kitchen delivers our slice of lemon cake. I pluck a raspberry from the plate and run it through the drizzled sauce, then pop the plump berry into my mouth. Matthew grins and hands me a fork. I take the first bite of cake, widen my eyes at its deliciousness.

Matthew takes the fork from my hand and helps himself, then cuts another bite and passes the fork back to me. His other hand now rests atop the back of my barstool, his forearm warm against my shoulders.

As we eat and chat, the other couple joins our conversation. "Any kids?" the man asks.

"Not yet," Matthew says.

My breath catches in my throat, but I cover it with a cough. Matthew pats my back again, and I feel just fine.

"Good," the man says. "You should wait until you're really ready." The man's wife hits him on the arm. "What? I'm kidding." He stops laughing and mouths, "Not kidding."

I make eye contact with the wife. She smiles at me but rolls her eyes at her husband.

"The kids are with my folks," the man continues, "and we've already called to check in twice. Our goal: Stay out until at least midnight tonight. We don't even know what to do with ourselves." He puts his arm around her, and they kiss on the lips.

Matthew and I avert our eyes only to look at each other. "Do you mind if I order a beer?" he asks.

"Be my guest."

Two beers later, Matthew scootches his stool even closer to mine. We're both "touchyfeely" now, laughing and joking, and I can smell the beer on Matthew's breath. I flash back to how this evening began but force both Liam and Peter from my mind.

The bartender arrives with two shots of whiskey on a small tray.

"What's this?" Matthew asks.

"From us," the husband answers. "To you. Feel free just to be a young couple in love tonight. No kids attached. Enjoy it while it lasts. Salud!"

The husband raises his glass. Matthew raises his shot and hands me the other one. "Salud," Matthew says to the man and downs his shot. I sip mine and enjoy the slow burn as its heat blooms in my chest.

We all four sit content at the bar. The chatter dies down again, and soon, the husband points to the clock on the wall, which says 12:15 a.m. He turns to Matthew and shouts, "We made it!"

The bartender laughs. "You want a photo?"

The wife says, "Hell yeah. First successful date night in six months!" She hands the bartender her phone, and then husband and wife ham it up for the camera: kissing, hugging, pretending to take more shots.

"Now, you two," the man says.

I look at Matthew, and he says, "Fair enough."

I stand to retrieve my phone and fumble in my deep coat pocket until I find it. Matthew pulls me tight next to him, still seated, his arm around my waist. He's tall enough that our heads still align, and we smile into the flash.

When I resume my seat, Matthew says, "Let's have a look." He leans over, studies the snapshot. "It's a keeper."

"Yes, it is," I say. "Should I text it to you?" My heart starts to thump, but way too hard. What if Liam looks at my phone? I should explain myself in advance—but what would I say? I left him home very late at night? That I met a friend for dessert. Sounds like a lie, even though it isn't.

"Hey, are you okay?" Matthew asks.

I meet his eyes, manage a half smile. "I should...probably get back home."

"Of course. It's late."

Beside us, the married couple are yawning, asking for their bill.

"Ours too," I say. "This one's on me," I tell Matthew, then

reach for my purse.

I stop. *Shit.* I left everything at the house. "Would you believe me if I told you I forgot my wallet at home?"

"I would, and I still owe you for the farm, anyway."

"But you bought the chili," I protest.

He shrugs and hands the bartender a credit card. She runs the tab, and he signs the bill.

I watch him with narrow eyes.

"What, you wanted to do the dishes?"

I slug his arm, and he catches my fist, holds it a beat too long until the husband nudges his opposite shoulder. The couple wishes us goodnight, then walks out of the bar, entangled. We stand to wave them off, bundling ourselves into our coats. Matthew leads me outside with his hand at the small of my back.

On the sidewalk, Matthew says, "I'm parked over there." He points to the right.

"I'm that way." I point to the left.

"Can I give you a lift?"

"No, I'm good."

"You sure?"

"I'll be fine."

"Well."

"Well," I repeat.

We look at each other.

"Good luck to you," Matthew says.

"You too," I respond automatically. "Goodnight."

"Goodnight, Gracie."

I make it about twenty feet before I turn around, open my mouth to speak, and see that Matthew's done the same. He laughs as he walks back toward me.

"Let me just say one more thing before I go. This guy of yours is the lucky one. I hope you know how great you are."

He stares at me until I nod. "Good," he says, then turns to leave again. I want to tell him that he's great too, that we had a great night...and I don't want it to end. *Don't go,* I want to say, but I just watch him disappear. Then, I look both ways, cross the street, and go home. To Liam.

15

Liam announces, "We need to talk," the moment I step into the kitchen the next morning.

I stifle a yawn as I fold myself into a chair at the table. I rest my head on my raised knees.

"About what?"

"You need to apologize."

"I'm sorry, did I wake you when I came in late last night?"

"Wait. You went out? After I went to bed?" Liam scowls.

"Let's talk later, when I'm actually awake?"

Liam hands me a cup of hot coffee. "Get yourself together, Grace. We need to talk about last night, and then you should go over with me to apologize to Peter."

Suddenly, I'm wide awake. I clutch my cup, so I won't throw it at Liam.

He continues: "You left in such a huff last night. I'm sure Peter thought we were being rude."

My mouth pops open. "You want *me* to apologize to Peter? Never."

"Grace, he's one of our company's biggest clients."

I stand and move closer to Liam at the counter. I place an index finger on his sternum and push. Hard. "If anyone should apologize, it should be *him*. And *you* should apologize next. To *me*. You just stood there and did nothing."

"Grace—"

"You know what, Liam, I did go out last night. Without you. I had drinks and dessert. With someone else."

There, I told him. Liam raises his eyebrows.

I shrug. "But nothing happened, of course. I just met this nice guy at the supermarket with Annie and I helped him find chicken. I ran into him again last night, walking downtown." I sit again, limbs heavy. Sip my coffee.

"Go on," Liam says.

"His name is Matthew, and he's been nothing but kind. He listens. In fact, I told him about you and me, and you know what? He thinks you're lucky to have me."

Now Liam's face turns red. "Let me get this straight. You went out last night and talked about me and our private relationship with a *stranger*? Where did you even go? What time did you leave?"

"I told you. I went for a walk, ran into him by chance, and ended up at a bar."

Liam's eyes bulge, and I don't care. I've never seen him this angry, and I just...don't...care.

I look him straight in his enormous eyes and say, "I won't lie. I enjoy his company. You're always so consumed with work. I have to fight for your attention. All the time. Even when I'm unwell, you worry more about your work than you do about me."

Liam takes a step toward me. "You know what? I think losing the baby was a sign. You know, I wasn't sure if I wanted to have kids with you anyway. Besides, you were only what, four months along? I don't get why you're still upset."

My body goes rigid, and lightning bolts race down my arms. "Not sure if you want to have kids? With me? Fuck you, Liam."

He flinches, but I don't back down. I stand and tighten the belt of my robe. "You need to find another place to stay for a while. I need a break."

"A break?" he squeaks.

I raise my hands to my head and clutch at my hair. "Yup. Pack a bag and get out."

I march past him, but he grabs my arm. "Grace, come on."

I yank away and veer toward the stairs.

Liam follows me. "Grace, you can't be serious."

I stop, face him. "I'll go somewhere for the day, and when I get back, I want you gone. I need you to just leave me alone for a while. I feel like I'm going crazy."

I'm practically vibrating. He stares at me for a long moment, then throws up his hands and stomps away.

Upstairs, I shower and throw on warm activewear. My hands are still shaking when I pull on my socks and sneakers.

Downstairs, Liam's gone. I pass straight through the kitchen and right out the back door to Annie's house.

Annie answers with a large glass of water in her hand. "Just let me take my vitamins," she says. In her kitchen, she washes down a handful of assorted pills with the water, then refills her glass and downs it again. She grins at me. "You look ready for a walk." Today, Annie's wearing her winter-green jogging suit.

"Annie, I need to talk to you."

"What's the matter, sweetheart?"

My throat tightens, but I manage to tell her everything that's happened. She scowls when I talk about Peter and Liam's nonresponse to Peter. When I end with a description of this morning's blowout, she hooks her arm through mine and tucks me close to her. I realize she's been uncharacteristically patient while I told my story. But now—she has all the questions:

"What now? Will Liam move out for good, or will you? If you leave, where will you go?" Annie scowls again but with worry this time, I think, instead of anger.

"I told Liam *he* needs to leave for a while."

"Smart girl." Annie heaves a big sigh like she's been holding her breath.

She takes me into her arms and gives me a warm hug for a long time. "You're going to be okay, Gracie. I promise."

After another minute, I stand back. She wipes tears off my cheeks. "Annie Whitney. You're a great friend, you know that?"

"You're a good girl too," Annie says.

"I think I'm going to take a ride. I need to get away from here for a few hours. Give Liam some time to pack a bag."

"Understandable," Annie says patting me on the arm. "Take all the time you need."

I lean in and hug her once again. "I love you, Annie."

"Love you too, kiddo. Call me later, okay? Let me know when you've made it home safe."

"Will do."

I step outside and turn toward my place, but my stomach fills with that sick, anxious feeling again when I think about Liam. Instead of entering the house, I simply reach inside the front door, grab my purse off the hook, and hop into my car.

I speed down the highway to a town on the coast known for its small shops. The place I'm interested in isn't a shop per se but rather a yellow house Annie had mentioned, where the owners sell antique furniture year-round out of their tumbledown barn. The GPS struggles to find an exact match, but Annie had said to drive a few miles down Route 1 and that I'll know it when I see it. Whatever the hell that means.

A half hour later, I can see Annie's right—the place is unmistakable. I put on my blinker and pull into the dirt driveway. The sprawling old house has faded yellow wooden siding and four chimneys. Gray shutters hang limply at most windows. The large warehouse of a barn leans to the left, doors open wide to the crisp day. The owners have moved much of their inventory onto the lawn, probably for shoppers like me taking advantage of the nice weekend weather.

An older man in overalls and a flannel shirt comes out of the house to greet me from his front porch. He holds a small green apple and a paring knife. "Do you need help," he calls out, "or do you want to just look around?"

"I'll look around, thanks."

"Holler if you need anything." He smiles and sits on his stoop with his snack.

I browse the claw-foot tubs and vanities, the bureaus and headboards, the side tables, and the draped patchwork quilts. I circle back to a rocking chair painted a robin's-egg blue. The color has worn off the seat, but otherwise, this chair is in good condition. I sit down, rock back and forth in the grass. Mind made up, I approach the house, but the man's gone back inside.

I knock but get no response. "Hello!" I shout and knock a

bit harder.

I hear footsteps on floorboards, and the man swings open the door. "Hey there. Sorry about that. Just feeding the fire and making some tea. Nice day, but chilly, eh? Would you like a cup?"

"I'm all set, thank you." I point toward the lawn. "How much for the blue rocking chair?"

"Oh, I'd say, for you, twenty is a fair price. That there belonged to my Jenny. She rocked all four of our babies in that."

My stomach rolls, and I swallow hard before I speak again. "Sir, I'd have to pay you more than twenty dollars. A lot of history in that chair."

"I know it, but it's time for that old rocker to find a new home. I've marked things down in my ledger, you see, to get rid of them." He rattles the doorframe with a gnarled knuckle, then rests his hand on the scarred wood. "Time to get rid of this old place, too, I suppose."

I look at his arthritic hand, then back to his face. I don't know what to say.

"Cancer," he tells me. "My Jenny's been gone two years. The kids say I need to sell the place, but I don't know. I want to stay, just a little longer."

I begin to say, "I'm so sorry..." but he waves me back toward the lawn.

He smiles and says, "Let's get you sorted." He carries the chair for me and even wedges it snugly into the back seat. "Looks secure," he says, "but take it slow, okay?"

I hand him a crumpled twenty from my purse. He tucks the bill into the bib of his overalls. I thank him, and he says, "Come back soon. Who knows, the whole place may be on the market then, and I plan to sell cheap!"

I laugh and say, "I'll keep that in mind."

I stay out most of the day. I find the more traditional shops in town, take a late lunch break, and meander my way home the long way on windy roads. I'm eager to show Annie my new purchase, but I realize she's probably just sat down to dinner. Her house looks dark and quiet, and I hope Bill took her out for a romantic evening.

When I pull in, Liam's truck sits in the driveway. Great. Leave it to him to be here clearing out his things still. Probably went and worked all day first. I glance over and see a car I don't recognize parked on the street. Probably someone visiting the neighbors on the other side. I sigh. Time to face Liam and finish this day.

I wiggle the rocking chair out of the car and carry it to the house. Just inside the front door sit two pieces of Liam's luggage. I stop when I hear a somewhat familiar voice. Everything in my body tenses up. I know that voice from somewhere. It takes only a moment to register.

That voice belongs to Sophie.

I set the rocking chair down and walk slowly toward the kitchen.

Liam stands when he sees me, nearly knocking the chair over as he stands. "Grace, I didn't expect you back so soon."

I run my hands through my hair. "So, I see."

Sophie nods at me, then turns to Liam. "I should wait outside."

My heart thumps in my chest. I give her a broad smile and

say, "Good idea."

Blood pounds behind my ears, and rage burns up my cheeks. She ducks her head and walks past me.

"Grace—" Liam begins to say, but something on the table catches my eye. I tilt my head and squint, and what I see takes my breath away. It's a sonogram photo. My mouth goes dry.

Liam grabs the photo and snatches it up, but it's too late. I've already seen it.

Tears come to my eyes, and I let them fall. It feels like the floor is tilting beneath me. My throat closes up, and my chest feels tight. I grab the back of a chair to steady myself. "You son of a bitch."

Liam reaches a hand toward me, but I shove it away. "Don't touch me."

I point at him and continue. "Don't you ever touch me ever again."

"Grace, I...."

I cut him off. "Enough. Not another word."

My voice trembles, and tears continue to run down my cheeks.

"I didn't know. I swear. She told me we needed to talk in person, so I gave her the address, and I thought she'd be gone by the time you got back. I'm just as shocked as you are."

I guffaw. "No. There's no way in hell you can be as shocked as I am at this very moment, buddy."

My voice rises. "How could you? How could you do this to me? How could you do this to us?"

Scenes from the bloody miscarriage flash in my mind. I begin to sob as everything hits me all at once. My hand goes to my mouth. He *did* sleep with Sophie, and now she's pregnant. And Liam's going to have a baby. And our baby is dead. It's all too much.

Liam stands with his mouth hanging open. He takes a step toward me. "Grace."

"Get out!" I scream. "Get the hell out of here and leave me alone."

I point to the front door. "Go!"

Liam shakes his head, trudges toward the living room, then returns. "I'm sorry," he says with his head hanging down. He doesn't even try to look at me.

"Just go," I say, jaw clenched.

I step into the half bath, wad up some toilet paper, then blow my nose and wipe my face. I stare at myself in the mirror. My face is puffy and blotchy. I look so very tired. I hold my breath and don't let it out until I hear the front door close behind Liam.

I lock the door with a satisfying clunk. From the living room window, I watch Liam's taillights flare red then disappear down the road. The tears return. I need to talk to Annie.

16

I jog over to Annie's back door, prop the screen with my backside, and then give the inner door a good rap. Unlocked and unlatched, the door inches open, so I stick my head inside and start to call out, "Hello, hello—"

I freeze when I see Annie and Bill at the kitchen table. They sit with a woman I've never seen before. The woman holds a computer tablet in her hands. All three stop talking and stare at me.

I step inside, but just to excuse myself. "Sorry, I didn't know—"

Annie rocks the tabletop as she launches to her feet. She takes my arm as if to guide me back out the door.

"Oh, this must be your daughter?" the strange woman asks as she scrolls her screen. She looks up at me. "Kelly?"

Annie stops pushing me but keeps hold of my upper arm. "Well, no, this is Grace. Grace, meet Nicole," she says.

The woman stands, takes off her glasses, and sets the tablet down. She walks over to me and takes both of my hands in hers. "Nice to meet you, Grace. I'm Annie's hospice nurse."

The floor begins to tilt beneath my feet like I'm on The Gravitron at the fair. "I'm sorry," I repeat, "you are...."

Nicole studies Annie's face, but Annie looks away.

I wrench out of Annie's grip. I look at Nicole again. "I'm sorry, you're what?"

Nicole's lips part, but nothing comes out. Now I glare at Annie. "Is this...some kind of joke?"

Annie steps away from me toward the table. "Grace, please, sit down."

"Why the hell is she here?" I shout without meaning to. Heat scorches my face and my ears.

Annie twists toward Bill, then looks back at me. She clears her throat and then takes a breath. "Grace, I have lung cancer. Stage 4."

I put my hands to my mouth. Annie's lips still move, but I can't hear anything she says because it's as if someone has turned off the volume on my life. Then Nicole's lips move too, but her words won't register.

Suddenly, Bill's rubbing my back. Tears come, and I can't stop them. I cry against Bill, and he holds me, shushes me.

I start to hear static, and then certain words break through. I have to cover my ears with my hands. "I just don't understand. How long have you known? Why didn't you tell me?"

"Let me explain," Annie pleads.

"I have to go."

"Grace, wait–"

I turn and bolt out of the house.

Back home, I stand in the middle of my own kitchen. Then I pace. Then I slap my hand against my left ear to try to get the ringing to stop. I should call someone, but I don't know who to call. I have to go. I have to get the hell out of here.

Out on the street, I start to jog, slowly at first, but then I run much faster than I should. My calves burn, and my thighs twitch. When my feet hit the beach, I fall forward and get a mouthful of sand. I spit, stand again, and race ahead until my rib cage seizes. Then I have to lie down.

I lower myself onto the sand and rest there awhile until I notice that the damp has seeped through my clothes. I sit up, shaking, and try to breathe but can't. I blow my nose on one sleeve of my sweatshirt, wipe my eyes with the other.

Out on the waves, a lobster boat cuts its motor. The sky is clouding over. A woman in orange coveralls handles her traps, tosses some too-small catches back into the ocean. I watch her work until she's finished the chore and speeds away. Then I get up, dust off, and walk home.

I collapse onto the couch in my wet clothes and stare at the wall. Soon, I hear footsteps on the front porch and see Bill peek into a window. He sees me and lets himself in. I don't get up, just move a leg. He sits down on the other end of the couch.

"Annie didn't want to tell you. She figured you'd be gone in a few months, and you wouldn't have to give it any thought."

"Any thought? Not give *it* any thought?"

He grimaces, and I lower my voice.

"How long have you two known?"

Bill laces his hands together as he stares at the floor. "A few months."

I stand and wrap a throw blanket around my shoulders. I debate whether to sit again, but I feel rude, looming over Bill in the living room. He looks up at me, and then I sit next to him, close enough for our shoulders to touch.

We sit still together in the silence. Outside, the wind muffles against the house.

After a long time, Bills says, "Annie hopes you'll understand. She didn't want to see you get hurt." He pats my knee. "Annie loves you, you know. Like family. We both do."

I can't speak, so I just nod.

Bill stands stiffly and walks to the front door. He stops with his hand on the doorknob and turns back to me. "You'll lock up behind me, right?"

I want to say, "Okay, Dad," but stop myself. I just nod again.

He nods back and leaves almost as quietly as he'd come in.

I stay bundled and slumped on the couch for too long. I should work to occupy my mind, but I know I won't be able to concentrate. What's that saying? *Move a muscle, change a thought?* I'd like to change all the thoughts in my head right now—erase all of them, but I know I can't. It's time to move this body of mine.

I pop off the couch and head for the backyard. The other day I noticed that the Hosta plants out front have flattened out and gotten mushy. Time to cut them back for the year.

I flip on the outside lights and find some rusty hedge shears and soil-stained gloves in the garden shed out back. Out front, I try not to look at Annie's house for fear of...I don't know what. *Focus*, I tell myself.

I kneel on the damp grass and begin with some modest hacks at the wilted stems. The yellowed leaves fall away easily, even with the dull shears. Once I've pruned a couple of plants, I begin to make a pile of the dead foliage behind me. I find my rhythm as I work my way down the Hosta beds. My muscles start to warm and loosen with the activity, but my whole-body tenses again when I hear movement next door.

My face flushes red-hot. I stare at my porch, holding my breath. I don't know if I'm ready to face Annie, and I'm not sure she's ready to face me either. I hear feet shuffling in Annie's driveway, and then the footsteps stop behind me.

I pivot slowly on one knee. Annie stands several feet away. She uses one hand to hold her purse in place on her shoulder and dangles her keys from the other. I want to stand but feel frozen to the ground. I look up at her, and a sudden breeze whips my hair across my face. The stray strands anger me, and I push to my feet.

Annie grimaces but takes a step closer. "I want to apologize, Grace, for not saying something sooner." Her eyes look tired, her face pale. "I didn't want to drag you into this mess. Who would want to be a part of this shit show?" She shakes her keys with a harsh jangle.

I want to throttle her, but instead, I say, "We could have at least talked about it."

"What's there to talk about? I'm done. Game over."

I open my mouth to disagree, but Annie blurts out, "And before you ask, I won't do any of that chemo or radiation bullshit. The cancer's spread everywhere already. The doctor says chemo might give me a little more time, but I'm all set. I don't need to spend my final days hooked up to machines that will make me lose my gorgeous mane." Annie grins and fluffs her hair.

I force a tight smile, and her face brightens a little more. She starts to gush details at me like a broken dam, and the buzzing starts in my ears again. I can barely follow her words, but in the back of my mind, other details click into place. The remodeled living room with hardwood floors will make it easier to wheel around a hospital bed. The larger bay windows that face the ocean will allow for a better view of her last sunsets. Annie remodeled her living room so that she would be able to be comfortable in her final moments. She'll be able to look out at the beach until her dying day. Those last two words make my heart seize, and my chest goes numb.

Annie shakes my arm, snapping me back to reality. "Are you listening to me? We have to move forward. Business as usual."

"Okay, okay," I snap. I meet her gaze, try to focus my attention on her. She holds my arm and my eyes. I know she's asking me to see her again without the cancer, but for the first time, I truly notice the effects of her illness. She's had less spark in her mood of late, but I don't know why I hadn't noticed the ashy skin of her cheeks nor the blue-and-purple circles around her eyes.

Annie lets go of me and looks down at her watch. "We can talk more about this later. I have to meet with some of the church ladies to finish our planning for the Thanksgiving food drive."

My mouth's gone dry. I swallow. Lick my lips. I search for something useful to say, but Annie stops me with a final pat on my shoulder.

"Grace, I really am sorry. The last thing I wanted to do was upset you."

"I know," I say.

"Love you, kiddo."

"Love you too." I pull Annie in and give her a soft squeeze. "Drive safe."

"Will do."

I finish tending to the Hostas and clean up my mess. The day seems too long already, and it's only early evening. I need to occupy myself, at least until Annie gets home. Maybe take a drive? Better yet, maybe Matthew's still in town? At the craft fair, Nancy said they lived on Lexington. I should be able to find the house if his car is still there. And didn't Annie say something about a dog, who might be in the yard? Shit. If only I were like Annie and could remember small details. What the hell kind of dog did she say they had? I shake my head—my brain just won't work today. I remember then I'm still dressed in ratty sweats, and now they're also very dirty sweats from the yard work. I tell myself I'll give up this cockamamie scheme to go find Matthew while I get cleaned up, but I don't believe myself.

Seagulls swoop into the pinks and oranges of the early evening sky as I drive. Cold, fresh air swirls in when I roll down the window. When Lexington Street comes into view, I start to mumble under my breath. *Bad idea, bad idea, bad idea. And, what will you do if he* is *there, Grace?*

But then I'm on Lexington. "Fuck it," I say aloud. I scan house after house, but I don't see any vehicles with Pennsylvania plates. Or any dogs, not that a random dog could help me right now. The street's not that long, a quarter mile at most. When I get to the end, I turn around to do one last sweep on my way home. My heart sinks when I hit Main Street again, but this jaunt *was* a stupid idea, after all. Suddenly, I feel very out of place. And embarrassed.

My stomach grumbles. *Go home, Grace. Get some food in you, and then try to do some damn work,* I scold myself. But as I approach the rental house, I see something that makes my skin tingle: a navy-blue Volvo in my driveway. I speed up.

17

"I got caught up helping Mom with some projects today, so I stuck around instead of leaving this morning. And then, well, I just...wanted to see you before I left," Matthew admits.

The sun is setting, the sky a dusky pink, as we stand in my yard.

"Do you want to hear something weird? I just drove over to Lexington. I thought you might be gone, but I needed someone to talk to."

"Who, Nancy?" he jokes.

I smile and take hold of Matthew's hand. He doesn't resist, so I lead him to the porch steps, and we sit. He's quiet; I'm quiet. I want to tell him everything, but the words won't come.

Matthew waits, then puts a hand on my shoulder. He squeezes gently. "It's okay," he says. "Take your—"

"It's Annie," I blurt. "The prognosis isn't good." I hold my breath. No more tears today, I promise myself.

"Oh, Gracie, I'm so sorry."

"Lung cancer. She's refusing treatment. But that's not the worst part. She didn't even tell me, and she's known for months." My voice rises. "Who knows if she would have *ever* told me? I just happened to go over when someone from hospice was there.

Now she's only got months left. And I'm pissed."

Matthew tucks me into his side.

"And then there's everything with Liam."

"With...Liam?"

"I caught him with someone else. And there's a baby." I shake my head. "I wanted him gone anyway, so we're taking a break. Likely a permanent one. Now that I know the real him."

"Whoa. Wow. Umm. That's a lot. For sure."

He reaches inside the neck of his shirt under his open coat to scratch his chest. I spot a tuft of curly gray hair at his collar. There was a time I would have looked away, but now, with Liam gone and with everything else, I don't avert my eyes. Part of me wants him to know that with just one small gesture of encouragement, I would be all over him. But when I see a few remnants of the wilted Hosta on the grass, I think of Annie again. I put my head into my hands, trying to keep my thoughts in one place.

Matthew starts to rub my back.

I raise my head and catch his eyes. He stops trying to comfort me and just waits for me to speak again. "I'm sorry to put all this on you."

"Grace—"

"Really. You don't need all this drama."

"Hey," he shrugs, "like I said, it's a lot. But I'm here for you. If you want me to be."

I nod and then glance away but can't quite hide my smile. "I know you have a long drive back, but would you like to come in for a cup of tea?"

"Well, yes. I would. Yes."

In the kitchen, I fill the kettle and pull the boxes of tea from the cupboard. "I bet you could use a snack too."

Matthew grips the handle of the fridge. "May I?"

"Yes, please. I am actually sort of starving."

Matthew finds a bag of green grapes, rinses two bunches in the sink, sets them on a paper towel to drip-dry. Next, he slices some cheese, and I hand him a roll of crackers from the pantry.

He arranges everything on a plate to take to the table. I finish making the tea and we sit together.

I pluck a grape from its stem and pop it into my mouth. "You know, now that I think about it, maybe it's a good thing that Liam's gone. I'll have more time for Annie."

My whole-body aches. When I start to rub my neck, Matthew stands and takes over. He moves down and kneads away the tightness between my shoulder blades too. I moan, and he chuckles. When he massages my neck again, I reach up and still his hands. "Would you like to sit in the living room with me?" I ask.

He steps back, then helps me out of my chair.

Matthew sits in the middle of the couch. I sit too, but cross-legged, facing him, my back to an armrest. "So, what should I do?"

"Do you mean what should you do...with me...right now?"

"Aren't you funny." I swat at his leg.

"You mean about Annie? Or Liam?"

"I mean about everything."

"Well, you and Annie are so close. I can't imagine what you must be feeling."

"I just don't know what's happening."

Matthew simply nods.

"I mean, I haven't even known Annie that long, but I honestly can't imagine my life without her." I turn away, biting the inside of my cheek.

Matthew takes my hand, holds it atop his thigh. "If there is any gift in any of this, it's that you'll get to say goodbye to Annie as many times as you want. You know the timeline, well, the rough timeline, so you've got the time to tell her you love her a thousand times if you want to."

I rub his thigh. "You're right. I know that some people lose friends or family suddenly and don't get the chance to say goodbye. I should be grateful."

"I'm not saying you have to feel *grateful*. I just think that in shitty situations like this one, you've got to look for the good, or else you'll go crazy."

"True." I pick up Matthew's hand, massage his palm. He relaxes into my touch. I take my time, then make my way up and down each finger.

Finally, I say, "I just thought my year in Maine was going to look one way, and now my life is going in a whole different direction."

Matthew cocks his head again, narrows his eyes. "Is that a bad thing? Despite the obvious horrible stuff, I mean."

I hesitate, then meet his eyes. "No," I say. I interlace my fingers with his and smile.

"Come here." Matthew stands, lifts me to my feet. He looks at me, rubs his thumb across my cheek. I close my eyes, but I can still feel him leaning into me. He puts his lips so close to mine that I hardly dare exhale. He waits. And waits. And then I feel Matthew's soft lips on mine. We kiss for a long time before he pulls back.

Without taking his eyes off mine, he places one hand on my lower back, then my hand on his shoulder. He brings me close, begins to sway back and forth. I wrap both arms around his neck and rest my head on his shoulder. We rock side to side for a bit, and then we fall into a rhythm, our feet in sync. Even with our bodies pressed together, I can't help but shiver, which Matthew feels and somehow tucks me closer into his body.

I close my eyes again, allowing myself to sink into the moment. Matthew raises my hand and gives me a twirl. He guides me back into his arms so that he's behind me. He leans down and rests his cheek against my ear. I spin around to face him.

We're both gentle at first, but the more we kiss, the more I need him. I need to feel his skin on mine. I whisper, "I want you."

Matthew inhales, then puts his hands all over me. I clutch at his clothes, tug at his waist in an attempt to untuck his shirt. He catches my hands but drops his gaze to my mouth again.

"Grace, we don't have to.... We can just talk."

I shake my head. Matthew steps back, looks me up and down. His eyes linger longest on my face. When I can't take it anymore, I rush toward him. Matthew finds the crook of my neck and nuzzles me there.

He glides his fingertips up and down my spine as we kiss. I take time to kiss his cheeks, his forehead, that little vee of exposed skin at his collar. I look up at him when I bring both hands to the buttons of his shirt. "May I?"

Matthew doesn't break my stare as I slip the little buttons free. I get about halfway down when he says, "Let me help," then drags his shirt over his head by the back of the collar. I trace the smooth skin along the top of his belt, then fumble, unable to unhook the buckle. He helps me then too, and his jeans drop to the floor. Matthew stands before me, almost naked, in his boxers and socks, tugging at the bottom of my shirt. I strip down to my underwear.

With each touch of our bodies, my muscles warm and loosen. I massage his shoulders, his arms, his chest, his hips. Matthew groans and sits back down on the couch, pulls me down onto him. I straddle his lap, sinking my knees into the couch, then lean into him for another long, long kiss. My hair falls all around us and tickles my face, gets snagged by his five-o'clock shadow. I sit straighter, gather my curls on top of my head, hold them in a messy bun, and look down at him. He lowers my arms, slips off my bra.

I put my lips right against his parted mouth and whisper, "Please."

Afterward, we spoon on the couch, wrapped in throw blankets. Matthew is on his side behind me, propped on one elbow. "I'm so glad I've met you," he says into my hair.

I turn halfway onto my back to meet his eyes. "Same," I say.

"You know, if you ever need to get away from everything for a weekend, I'd love to see you. Or we could get together when I come back next time. I like to keep an eye on my parents."

"I think I'll stay close to home for the time being. For Annie, you know."

Matthew slants his arm across my chest, holds me tighter. Within a couple of minutes, Matthew begins to breathe heavily, and I can tell he's starting to doze. I try not to move so as not to disturb him. Just when I think he's actually asleep, he says, "Grace, I'm so comfortable that I could stay right here with you all night."

I snuggle into him. "I know you have to get back. I'll give you ten more minutes."

Matthew laughs, covers my shoulder with the corner of a blanket. "So, what are you up to tomorrow?"

"Well," I sit up, "I'll check on Annie in the morning, then do some work. I think...it would be good for me to write later in the afternoon, if I can."

Matthew sits up too. "Tell me about what you're writing these days."

"I've written a couple of short stories, but they need revision. And I've been journaling. A lot."

"I'd love to read some of your fiction when it's ready."

"Sure, when it's ready."

He gives me a soft kiss at my temple. "Deal."

I ask Matthew about his internship.

"I love the design for the museum we're working on now. There's a lot of glass. I love the light."

"Tell me more," I say.

Matthew goes into great detail about the project. He makes frames in the air with his hands as he speaks. "It'll be done next fall. You should come check it out."

"Maybe I will...if you ever get home to finish your work."

Matthew grins but says, "I really wish I could stay."

"Me too," I say.

When Matthew stands, I catch a glimpse of a tattoo on his back. "Hang on a second." I stand behind him, trace the outline of the Vitruvian Man with my fingers. "You won't believe this, but I love this image. Always have. In fact, I have a new mug with this design on it. I got it at the craft fair. Your mom wanted one too, actually, but there was only the one left."

"Really? That's too funny." He starts to get dressed. "Sometimes I forget that tattoo's even back there."

"Well, your mom hasn't forgotten."

Matthew laughs again, then hands me his phone from his coat pocket. "Put in your number?"

"Only if you text me when you get home."

"Deal."

Matthew and I embrace for a long time and then he kisses me on the forehead and stares into my eyes.

"Promise you'll text when you get home so that I know you've made it home safely."

"It's going to be late. After midnight at least."

"I don't care. I probably won't sleep much tonight anyway."

Matthew holds my chin. "Take care, okay?"

He gives me one more kiss then turns and leaves out the front door. I watch him drive away until his taillights disappear completely. I slide my back down the front door and slink to the floor. I take a deep breath and then blow it out. "What a day. Holy shit."

I sit there on the cold floor and run the events of the past twenty-four hours through my head. My body feels beyond exhausted. Eventually, I pull myself to my feet and head for the stairs. I say aloud, "This is definitely not how I thought my summer in Maine was going to go."

I shake my head and climb the stairs.

In the bedroom, I pick up my cell phone. I know I should at least try to get some work done, but what I want to do is get away for a while to sort through all of my feelings. A trip to see Say is just what I need.

18

When the morning train approaches the platform, I secure my laptop bag on my shoulder and clutch the handle of my carry-on. I tap my phone's screen. Eleven o'clock. Right on time. Annie and I talked yesterday, and she agreed that some time away would do me some good.

A rush of air hits me as the train comes to a full stop. The doors open; I step into the car and onto the blue carpet. I look around. *Shit.* There's only one vacant seat, *way* in the way back. Everyone else had the bright idea to board in Portland. I thought if I got on further down the line, at one of the lesser-known stops, I would get my pick of seat. Like everything else in my life, I should have known.

I take my seat and put my earbuds in. To pass the time, I read articles and annotate, and every so often, I picture Matthew on the train with me. I'd be more than okay if he crossed the invisible border between us on the armrest to hold my hand.

I work some more, then fade in and out of sleep for a couple of hours. I open my eyes just a crack every now and then to see where we are. The buildings get taller and taller, and the farther south we travel, the less green I see.

When the train pulls into the station, I stand and stretch.

I'm so excited to see Say that I can't help but smile. I step off the train, and a blast of warm air hits my face, as does the smell of burnt rubber and mildew. Grand Central never changes. I stop to look up at the iconic gold clock.

Four o'clock. Right on time.

New York City feels more urgent than any other place on the planet. The ability to hail a cab has never been my forte, but I step to the edge of the curb and try anyway. Only when I visit Say do I get to practice, and the process takes me too long every damn time. Say's office is only about thirteen blocks from Midtown Manhattan.

After a long few minutes, a yellow cab stops. Before I can get in, a red fire truck comes screaming down the street. Horns blare, and a few vehicles attempt to get out of the way. I stuff my belongings into my cab, slide them across the back seat as I hop in. "And hey, how are you today?" I ask after I tell the driver the address.

The cab driver doesn't speak many words, just mostly grunts. Okay, the poor guy probably just wants to work in peace.

We stop at a light, and I look over and see an older man with a long beard on the corner. He wears a woman's formal evening gown, and he holds the handle of a pram. A tie-dyed poodle with green-and-purple fur perches inside. The two look as regal as ever. Makes me wonder what Chance is up to right now. Maybe I should buy Annie a new-fangled stroller to push Chance around in. She'd be the talk of the town.

After a series of loud honks and quiet curses from the driver, we pull up in front of Say's office building. I pay the man in cash, and he mumbles something terse. Grunts again. I tell him to keep the change.

Say works in a building so tall it hurts my neck to look up at it, but I throw my head back and gawk at its impressive height every time I visit. The façade is all windows.

Inside, a silver fountain flows in the center of the lobby, surrounded by black-and-white marble floors. New York is funny: one moment, you're on a noisy, busy street, but once indoors, you're in a sleek, shushed lobby. A stern security guard sits behind a shiny, granite-topped desk.

He nods my way and returns to his newspaper.

My sneakers squeak on the polished floor, and the sharp sound echoes off the walls. I push the elevator's call button; when it rumbles to a stop in front of me and the doors open, I shove in with all my gear in tow.

Quiet music chimes overhead. The walls are all mirrors; I can see myself at every angle. The lone passenger, I lean in to inspect my teeth. This elevator is one of those new ones that travels, practically silently, at what seems like the speed of light. I feel queasy, put my hand on my stomach, and the familiar gesture makes me even more nauseous. My head feels hot now. I pull at the neckline of my jean jacket.

I take a big, fresh gulp of air when the doors open on Say's floor.

When I get to the reception area, the administrative assistant shifts her high-tech headset off of one ear. "Can I help you?" I've never met this particular gal before, I realize.

"I'm here to see Say—I mean, Sarah Miles."

"Your name?"

"Grace."

"Grace...." The administrative assistant smiles and waits for a last name, which I do not provide.

"Just Grace," I reiterate.

The receptionist tucks a blonde lock behind her ear, readjusts her headpiece, and pushes a button or two on the phone on the desk. "Hey, Sarah, *Just Grace* is here to see you." She grins up at me now. Nice sarcasm. I like this one.

A few seconds later, not too far down the hall, an office door opens. "Hello, Just Grace," Say announces in a low, serious voice.

"Hello, *Sarah,*" I say back in the same deep tone.

She studies me while I study her, up and down. When my eyes graze over her obviously expensive shoes, I give a low whistle, almost a catcall, and we both burst into laughter.

"Get over here, girl!" Say runs at me with arms flung wide.

She picks me up and squeezes me, and I see the receptionist smirk over her shoulder. Not unkind, but definitely sassy.

Say sets me down with a theatrical "Oof!" She laughs and smiles into my eyes with hers. "Come on back," she says. "I just need to wrap up a few things." She snatches the handle of my suitcase from me. "Let me help you," she insists, then wheels my wonky carry-on down the tile floor toward her door, but it doesn't act up for her like it does for me. Say's like some superpowered, big-city super-human who takes no flack, not even from a broken suitcase.

Say parks my luggage by her desk then crushes me into a hug once more. We both sit, and Say grabs my hands in hers. "So, what do you want to do while you're in town?"

"Food. That's my first priority. I'm ready to chew my arm off after that long train ride."

The sassy secretary interrupts through the speakerphone on the desk. "Sarah, I hate to bother you, but a Mr. Flynn would like to chat with you."

Say stands again, lets out a long sigh. Jogs in place for a few seconds and rolls her eyes. Shakes her head. Stops her tantrum. "Sure, put him right through. Grace, give me just one minute." Say plops down into her black leather office chair, which squeaks. She punches a large button on the phone, holds the receiver to her ear, and says hello.

I stand by the window to afford her a little privacy. No matter how many times I see it, the spectacular view from Say's office still stuns me, but especially right now, at the end of the workday. I've never seen the city skyline's staggered buildings with that particular dusky light settling across the horizon behind them. The evening sky over Staten Island is now cast in a purplish orange. I turn back to her. "Look at this sunset," I mouth.

"I know!" she mouths back.

Say talks on and on while I explore her decadent office once again. I run my hands over all the smooth surfaces, the towering built-ins full of books, magazines, and trade catalogs of color swatches. When I pick up a small framed photo, my hand goes over my heart. The photo is of the two of us in our Wonder Woman Underoos. We wear beach towels as capes. We can't be more than six or so in the faded photo. New questions race through my mind: Would my baby have looked like me at that age? Would they have had that giant gap between their front teeth, like I had in the photo? Would they have had my personality, including my anxieties? Worn Underoos with their best friend?

Say quietly snaps her fingers at me, holds her palm over the receiver, and whispers,

"Sorry, sorry. I didn't think this call would take so long."

I shake my head to clear my thoughts, grateful for Say and her ability to bring me back to reality, literally, with the snap of her fingers. I whisper back, "No problem," but I clutch my ribs as if starving. Say has to camouflage her giggle.

I march over to the desk and kneel beside Say, who now murmurs encouragements into the phone. I start to rummage through her desk drawers. Say opens the bottom drawer. Bingo: Assorted crunchy granola bars and two bags of peanut M&M's.

I snag a sweet and salty peanut butter bar, plunk down in the chair across from Say's desk, and put my feet on the glass top. Say guffaws, apologizes to her client, shifts back to her serious business voice. She debates about color design and uses specialized technical jargon like "banding" and "inlays." I don't understand any of what's coming out of her mouth. I wave to get Say's attention. I mouth the word *banding* with air quotes. Next, I mime straightening a necktie. Say points her finger and tells me to be good with her eyes.

When I rip into the green wrapper, little clusters of oats and nuts sprinkle on my chest. "Damn it," I mutter, and Say looks up at me, concerned. I half smile and sweep the crumbs off my jacket.

Moments later, Say ends the call. "I'm so sorry."

"No big deal big wheel," I say through a mouth full of granola. I toss the wrapper at the trash can, but it bounces off the rim and lands on the floor. Crumbs scatter across the carpet.

"Real classy, Grace."

I giggle and crouch to sweep up my mess with my bare hands. Most of the debris burrows deeper into the carpet.

Say watches me struggle for a minute and then informs me, "We have cleaners, Grace. They have these powerful machines that suck up spills. Like magic." Say gives me jazz hands, and I have to laugh again. "Let's get out of here."

"Sounds good." When I stand, all the blood rushes to my head, and I stagger a little. "Woah. Are you okay?"

"I'm fine." I steady myself on the corner of the desk.

"Let's get some food in you before you pass out on me." Say gathers papers and her iPad off her desk and shoves everything into a brown leather messenger bag. "Ready, Freddy?"

My head rush is gone. "Ready."

Say dons her bag crossover style and hijacks my luggage again.

"You don't have to do that for me, you know. I'm not some delicate flower."

"For once in your life, let someone take care of *you* for a change. I want you to be able to relax while you're here, okay?"

I sigh. "Fine. Since you want to help so much, take this too." I offer her my laptop case.

Say reaches for the computer bag, but I snatch it back. "Will. You. Just. Stop. I can carry at least one item myself. You would carry it for me, though, wouldn't you?"

"Anytime." Say squeezes my hand.

We stroll down the hall to the elevator, where Say makes faces at me in the mirrors. Another Say trait that will never change.

Outside on the busy sidewalk, the streetlights are already lit. Say hails a cab in fewer than ten seconds. How does she do that?

She guides me into the back seat, then jumps in next to me, with all our bags piled on our laps.

After we get comfortable, the first question Say asks is about Liam.

I hesitate before I answer.

"Okay, here we go again. What's going on now." Say throws both hands into the air.

I push her arms back down. "Just listen, will you?" I try to give Say a good picture of everything that's been going on with the Liam situation.

Say slugs me in the arm repeatedly the more I share and punctuates her jabs with a series of "Holy shits," and "Jesus H. Christs." While she listens, Say pulls a travel tube of lotion from her bag and begins to moisturize. Except, she's squeezed out way too much, so she deposits the excess onto the back of my hand. The reassuring smell of lavender fills the cab. But when I get to the part about Sophie and the baby, she stops everything and yells, "Are you fucking kidding me?"

When I eventually stop talking, Say declares, "Fuck that guy. That Liam is an actual piece of shit. Holy fuck. I'm too stunned to even know what to say."

We sit in silence for a moment. "It's stupid shit just like that makes me want to stay single," she says, "I find life much easier that way."

Say's had boyfriends here and there. In truth, they've all been more like pleasant acquaintances due to her independent nature. I secretly envy her nonchalance.

Nevertheless, I open my mouth to give Say my speech, one she's heard a thousand times, about my views on relationships.

She grabs my wrist to cut me off. "I know, I know. You want the moon and the stars and all that fairy-tale shit."

"Say!" I protest. I snatch my wrist away, but I know she's right. I am utterly hopeless.

But then I tell her all about Matthew. I tell her about the barn swing, the main-street bar, the lemon cake, the dance in the living room, all of it, not leaving out any details.

Say takes both my scented hands in hers. "I'm so happy for you, Gracie. Truly. The guy sounds pretty amazing."

I nod and start to speak but Say interrupts again: "I can't wait to get more of a chance to brainwash you about modern relationships after I get a few drinks in you. What do you want to eat?"

"Anything. That granola bar took the edge off, but I'm still pretty hangry."

"Me too." Say draws her hands up like bear claws and growls at me.

The cab jerks to a stop in front of Say's apartment building. We're both thrown forward. We grab for the headrests at the same time, glance at each other, then try to stifle our laughter.

I'll wait to tell her about Annie. And *my* baby.

Inside her building, the elevator looks uncannily identical to the one at Say's work. Say, as predicted, makes more silly faces at our reflections. "Wouldn't you swear this elevator *mirrors* the one at my office? Get it?" She nudges her elbow into my ribs.

"I can't with you today. Your dad jokes are the literal worst."

I lose my stomach again when the elevator surges upward. I wonder if I should tell Say about the baby now? Annie? I reach for my belly but stop myself, clutch Say's arm instead.

"Hey, Say?"

"Yeah, sweetie?" She looks over at me, then cocks her head. Tears burn in my eyes, clouding my vision.

Say tucks me closer to her. "Hey, what's the matter?"

I hide my face in her shoulder, take a breath. She smells like boutique organic shampoo. I try to gather myself: *This is your time away. Put all of that stuff out of mind for now, and just enjoy tonight.*

I raise my head. Blink a few times. "Nothing's wrong. I'm just really happy to see you. That's all."

19

Say stops outside Number 16B, fishes a key from her bag. Inside, she says, "I need to clean up before we go out. I probably stink like a barnyard."

"You do," I lie with a grin. "Wait, that's probably me who smells like a goat, after being on that train all day."

"We could both use a good hose down, I'm sure." Say kicks off her heels and flicks a light switch by the door.

In the entryway, I take a nice long look. I love cozy beach cottages, but I also love this high-rise apartment. The cathedral ceilings and exposed-brick walls make me envious every time I visit. All the furniture has crisp edges, made of either real wood or buffed metal. Nothing made of cheap wicker or molded plastic. No shabby chic here, which makes for a nice change of setting.

Say interrupts my gawking: "You want something before we get ready? Let's go see what we've got."

I follow Say into the galley kitchen. The surfaces shine so clean that the space seems unused. A shallow bowl on the counter cradles three shriveled pears. Say goes to the stainless-steel refrigerator, swings the door wide, drums her nails on the top edge of the door. The fridge holds nothing except a pricey bottle of white wine, a half-eaten block of hard cheese, some take-out containers, and a few cans of seltzer water.

"As enticing as that all looks," I say with a swirl of my index finger, "I think I'll wait."

"I do need to get to the market. I've just been busy. We'll order an appetizer as soon as we get to the restaurant."

"I'll survive."

"Well, let's get a move on," Say slams the fridge door closed, "before you turn on me."

We primp and gossip like we're teenagers again. Say showers while I sit on the toilet lid and file my jagged nails. I've been trying to bite them less and to take care of them better lately.

Steam billows from the sides of the shower curtain as we chat. A few minutes later, Say turns off the shower, then reaches out for a towel and pulls it back behind the curtain. When she steps out onto the bathmat wrapped in her towel, I stand to move out of her way.

"My turn. I want to kill all the staph infection germs I probably encountered on the train."

"You go, girl. I'll put your stuff in my bedroom." Say slaps my rear as she saunters out of the bathroom.

The decorative metal loops ring across the pole as I enter the shower. When I turn the knob to *H*, perfectly hot water rains down on me from the modern square fixture. I could stay in here forever.

I rinse my hair and survey all of the products Say has lined up along the edge of the tub. Of course, Say buys the most expensive shampoos and conditioners. I choose one purple bottle, examine the smudged sales sticker on the bottom: $134. I clear water from my eyes to make sure I am reading the price tag correctly.

Yup. I click open the cap, squeeze a healthy amount into my palm, and bring my hand to my nose. The shampoo smells like a high-end salon.

I wash my hair, condition, then daydream under the hot stream of water for a long time. Next, I scrub my whole body and shave my legs. When my skin starts to prune, I hop out, dry off, and go to Say's room to rifle through my carry-on until I find something to wear. I didn't pack much so my choices are limited. Maybe I will raid Say's closet like the good old days. Nah, I can't be bothered. My little black top and skinny jeans will work just fine.

We both return to the bathroom and face the bathroom mirror together. Say applies mascara while I try to tame my hair with my round brush.

Say tells me about her latest guy. "He just wanted to move in together too soon."

"You just didn't want to commit." I stare at Say in the mirror, holding her gaze.

She scowls, then sighs. "You're right. But...hey, let me change the subject again. I want to take you to a little Italian place not too far from here. People rave about the food."

"Sounds perfect."

We continue to get ready—*both* of our stomachs grumble now. After watching me try to dry my hair with the hair dryer and round brush, Say takes both from me. "Let me help you."

She pushes me down onto the toilet lid again while she first blow-dries, then straightens my hair with a flat iron. Next, she hands me the mascara, plus a little compact with an assortment of colors that you can apply universally to lips, cheeks, *and* eye-lids. The effect is subtle, clean and classy. I don't even want to know what that particular product cost her.

After we've gone through all of the necessary motions, Say surveys us both in the mirror.

"We look marvelous."

I run my hands through my pin-straight hair. "This 'do looks professional. You missed your calling."

Say clacks the wide ceramic plates of the hair straightener together with a maniacal look.

"This puppy is pure magic. I'll order you one for Christmas."

"Thanks, Santa," I singsong as she flips off the bathroom light.

We gather our coats and purses and head outdoors. We make the short walk to the restaurant in ten minutes flat. Of course, we do stroll arm-in-arm and cackle the whole way there.

At the restaurant, a young hostess stands stationed just inside the foyer. She wears jet black head to toe, and even her long hair shines like onyx. "Good evening," she says with a bright smile. "Do you have a reservation?" We shake our heads, and the hostess stops smiling.

Say gives her full name for the waiting list, but the hostess states, "A table for two will be at least thirty minutes, sans a reservation," without any hint of apology.

"Oh, dear god in heaven," I mutter. I am actually starting to feel faint again.

Say squeezes my shoulder. "I have some gum in my purse to hold you over. We'll have to wait no matter where we go."

"Ugh. Fine."

We plop ourselves down on a wooden bench by the door. I

pull out my phone and send Annie a text to let her know that I've made it to the city. I think about texting Matthew, but I don't. I'm here to spend time with Say.

When a chic couple comes in, Say glances up from her own phone, then fixes her eyes on the man for a hasty second. "Shit," she whispers and stares pointedly at the floor.

The man, with tousled brown hair and model-like features, sports a blue suit jacket and dark jeans. He greets the hostess warmly, his arm still curved around his tall blonde date.

"Just act natural," Say says out loud.

"What the hell are you talking about?"

Say shushes me. "He'll see me. Fuck."

The handsome man nods to the hostess and looks around for a place to sit with the blonde while they wait for their table. He stops when he sees Say.

"Sarah?" he asks.

"Christ," Say growls but pops her head up, widens her eyes.

"James, how have things been?" Say plasters a scary, fake smile onto her face.

James raises his eyebrows. "When did you get back?"

Say's face gets red. "Umm, a few weeks ago, I guess."

James squints. "How's your mom?"

"Much better. Thank you for—"

"Miles, party of two." Say turns immediately to the hostess, who shrugs her shoulders.

"We had a cancellation."

"Oh, thank god." Say jumps to her feet. "Well, James, I'll see you around, I suppose."

"Great to see you, Sarah...."

The blonde date looks back and forth between James and Say. Say grabs me by the hand, pulls me up from the bench, and we plow our way over to the hostess's stand. The hostess leads us through the restaurant and seats us at a table by the window. She hands us each a menu, smiles perfunctorily, and walks away.

I scoot my chair forward. "What was *that* all about?"

Say leans in. "Remember that clingy guy I told you about this past summer?"

"Which one? You've had so many."

Say flips me off, then continues. "The one who wanted to meet my parents right away. The guy who listened to Enya?"

"Ohhhhh, him. No grown man should listen to Enya. Dealbreaker right there."

"I may or may not have told him that my mom was sick and that I had to leave town for a while to help take care of her."

"Say! Why didn't you just tell him the truth?"

"The man is forty years old and listens to Enya. And he was clingy. And he was moody. He would have jumped off the balcony of my apartment, I just know it."

"You're horrible!" I hiss, but she gives me a shrug.

I strip off my coat, and Say, too, starts to settle in for the meal.

We chat and bicker while we wait, debating the menu items. Finally, a smartly-dressed waiter with slicked-back hair approaches. "May I start you ladies with something to drink?"

I study the exhaustive drink list again. So many "innovative" cocktail choices, half of which don't seem palatable. Say orders a glass of wine. I decide that I don't get to get away often enough. I order a tried-and-true Long Island Iced Tea.

"Wait, we're going to have *that* kind of night?" Say high-fives the air with both hands. Looks at the waiter: "I've changed my mind. Nix the wine, and please, bring me a Long Island Iced Tea as well. And we're hungry. May we order our food now too?"

"Of course. What will it be?"

Say orders the chicken parmesan. I order the eggplant, as usual. It's my favorite.

The waiter grins at Say. "I'll put that order right in for you."

"And will you bring some bread over...when you get a chance?" Say winks at me.

"Of course." The server takes our menus.

Very soon, a food runner drops off a miniature loaf of bread, complete with its own little cutting board and serrated knife. Say seizes the tiny loaf of bread and rips it in two. A *Seinfeld* "man hands" reference. We know each other so well that we no longer need to say the punch line out loud.

Say slathers a torn-off chunk of bread with soft butter, motions for me to sit forward, then shoves the piece into my mouth. She then readies a piece for herself. "Tell me more about the Liam and Matthew situations," Say mumbles around her first bite.

I take the time to chew and swallow. "Things feel pretty crazy right now. I really cared for Liam and all that, and I like Matthew, but who knows. I don't want him to just be a rebound guy. You know me. All I've ever wanted was to be truly, *madly,* and deeply in love."

Say butters more bread and passes it to me, but she's got that drama-girl glint in her eye.

"You stay alive," she begins to recite, "no matter what occurs. I will find you!"

"Don't even go there," I protest. "Don't trash the most romantic love scene in any movie ever made."

Say finishes the monologue in a stage whisper: "No matter how long it takes...no matter how far...I will find you."

I slow-clap, which cracks Say up.

The cute waiter arrives with our very potent drinks. He sets down our tall glasses, both adorned with multicolored paper umbrellas. "Careful now," he warns us with a crooked grin.

As he walks back to the kitchen, I raise my drink, and Say clinks her glass against mine. We both take long, slow sips of our Long Island Iced Teas. My first taste almost makes me cough, but Say seems as suave as ever as when she replaces her glass on the tabletop as her phone buzzes on the table. Without so much as a glance, she tosses her cell into her bag. "I'm going to ignore that tonight. I want you all to myself, so you better silence yours too, missy."

"Aye, aye, sir," I say with a salute. I bend down, tuck my phone into my purse stashed under my chair. I feel the pinch of my stomach roll as it hangs over my pants, and I adjust my waistband as I sit up. I need to tell Say about the baby and Annie, but I'm not sure now's the time either. Fuck it. I want to continue to enjoy tonight. Maybe later, but not yet.

We gossip until the meal arrives—old high school frenemies and scandalous movie stars. We could gab for hours. We never run out of topics.

I actually gasp when the server sets my plate on the table, and not from hunger. It's been a good long while since I've seen such a presentation. "This meal could be on a cooking show." Say agrees and even claps when she sees her own plated food. I can't get over how delicious our meals look.

My breaded eggplant sits on a bed of steam-wilted greens, which still retain their vibrant garden-fresh color: delicate spinach and arugula, tender baby kale leaves. They've garnished the fried slices of eggplant with swirls of chunky, and no doubt house-made tomato sauce. The whole plate is dusted with grated parmesan cheese, basil, and cracked black pepper.

"It almost looks too good to eat," I gush to the waiter. He catches my eye, and I blush, wondering if I've said too much. I blush deeper, and this time, I decide I can indeed blame it on the alcohol, and not my apparently raging hormones.

The waiter asks, "Anything else, ladies?"

Say looks up at him. "Nope. We're good, thank you," she says.

Say lops off a hunk of her chicken and drops it onto my plate. She snags some of my eggplant in return.

I bring the first bite to my mouth, blow on it, and shovel it in. The eggplant itself is not too soft but not too firm either. Perfectly crisp on the edges. "Say! Oh my god. Try a bite right this minute."

Say cuts and stuffs a bite into her mouth, closes her eyes, and puts her hand to her chest.

She moans, and of course, I think of Annie.

"So good, right?"

Say nods and keeps eating. She alternates bites between the chicken and the eggplant. I sample her chicken, rave over it, and sip my drink. I start to feel cozy, and gratefully full. Say always knows the best places to eat out.

The waiter returns to ask how we're doing. I joke, "Did you write down the correct drink order? I said I wanted a Long

Island Iced Tea, but this drink tastes so smooth, I think you gave me plain iced tea instead."

He grins again. "No, you've got the real deal there. Can't you tell?"

But then his attention is redirected by new arrivals in his seating section. "Keep enjoying yourselves, ladies. I'll check in again."

We slow our pace: nibble our food and nurse our drinks. I sit back and enjoy the ambient sounds of cutlery against dishware, the light undercurrent of ongoing conversation, and the bustle of the restaurant whenever the kitchen's doors swish open. Say grabs my hand every now and then and gives me a squeeze as we chat. I haven't felt this content since...I was on the swing in the barn with Matthew. I smile wide when I picture that day. I must look like a goofy moonstruck teenager, but Say only smiles back at me. The good food and good drinks have mellowed us both.

Eventually, the waiter clears our dinner plates and asks if we want to see the dessert menu. As much as I'd like to prolong this glorious meal, I'm much too full already. Say declines dessert as well but asks for the check. "My treat," she announces. I start to protest, but she kicks me under the table. I hold up both hands in surrender.

"You deserve a treat," Say declares.

The waiter drops off the check.

I sober up a little. "Thank you," I tell Say, in all sincerity. "And not just for dinner—"

"I know," she interrupts again. "I've got you." She tips her glass toward me, and we both take a final gulp. We slug our waters, too, for good measure, before we gather our stuff to leave.

20

Outside I feel too tipsy. Say's every word strikes me as just a little too hilarious, and I have to lean on her to steady myself. We laugh like idiots, and other people avoid us on the sidewalks. It's a beautiful night. At one point in our meanderings, I can feel my phone vibrate.

Suddenly, Say stops. "Wait, where did you get that snazzy purse? What happened to that old potato sack you've lugged around for years?"

"My friend Annie gave it to me."

"Well, let me be the first to welcome you to the twenty-first century!"

"Hardy-har." I check my phone, since we're stalled here anyway. There's a text from Annie. My heart thumps in my chest. What if something is wrong? I bring the phone closer to my face and read the text.

I think Chance is autistic.

Say reads over my shoulder. "Who's Chance?"

I sigh and chuckle. "Her dog. I can't even. I don't even have time to try to explain. Give me a sec."

I hit the call button. Annie picks up in less than half a ring.

"Chance only wants to be picked up when he stands on

your left side. The right side makes him freak out. What do you think? Autism? Or a stroke?"

"Annie, I'm out with Say right now, and I'm not sure dogs get autism. Don't worry."

"Oh, okay. Sorry, honey. Let's chat tomorrow. When you're on the train. Or when you get back. Wait. Just one more thing." Her voice takes on a subtle echo. "We've got a guy over here working on the living room." I picture Annie cupping her hand over the receiver, but she still speaks loudly enough for anyone within fifty feet to hear her. "You should see his biceps when he tears at that old carpet. My. God."

I have to laugh. "We'll talk about Chance and the hot guy tomorrow, Annie, I promise. Love ya."

"Love you too."

I hang up.

We pass by a bar with tacky, big-bulbed Christmas lights in the windows. "Say, I'm here for just one night. Can we go in? Please?" I pant like Chance.

"Hell yes, let's do this." Say yanks the door open.

A poster with neon writing advertises "80's Nite" just inside the doorway. Bon Jovi blares from speakers. A waitress in a hot-pink tee shirt and neon-green leg warmers struts by with an overloaded tray of drinks. We proceed directly to the bar. People are packed in like sardines, and it's noisy as fuck, but I love it. Say shouts a drink order at the bartender for us, opens our tab with her credit card. We scope the area while we wait. When the bartender slides the drinks across the sloppy-wet bar, Say hands them to me. She points to the sign for the bathroom and finagles her way across the bar again.

I clutch an ice-cold drink in each fist. A man with a lazy eye, stained white beard, and a sailor's cap swivels around on his barstool, gawks at me, and winks. *Great.* He leans toward me and clunks his beer mug down on the bar. Foam spills over and runs down the side of the glass.

"Hey, sweetheart. Can I have your number? I seem to have lost mine."

The man slurs every word, and I can smell the booze on his breath. I want to laugh out loud, but instead, I smile to be polite. "My girlfriend is in the bathroom," I say very clearly.

"Sweet. You've got a girlfriend, huh?" He laughs through jack-o'-lantern teeth. "Nice," he says. He rubs his beard and continues to snicker as he stares at me.

What in the actual fuck. I so don't want to engage with this man.

"Call me Cap'n," the man says as he extends his hand.

Christ. "Yeah, maybe I'll see you around." I turn my entire body away and focus on the bathroom door.

I take a sip of my drink through the tiny black straw. Gin and tonic. A double, probably.

I am going to feel this one tomorrow. I sip again and wait, alone.

Finally, I spot Say. She waves toward the other end of the bar—far away from Cap'n, thankfully. I meet her there, set our drinks down on soggy cardboard coasters. We talk while we watch people dance. The bartender sets down two more cocktails before we've finished the first round. "These are from that guy down there." He points to where Cap'n raises his beer glass and grins.

Say asks, "Friend of yours?"

"Yeah, we got real close while you were in the bathroom."

"He's cute." She nudges her elbow into my ribs. "Shall I call him over?"

"You wouldn't."

"Wouldn't I?"

I pinch her forearm, and she slaps my hand.

"Ouch!" I say, and she laughs.

We continue to try to talk over the growing noise as the crowd gets rowdier. At a certain point, I know I'll be as plastered as Cap'n if I drink any more. I can already see the kaleidoscope splotches in my vision, which is my cue to call it a night. "Time to go," I tell Say. "I'm about to turn into a pumpkin."

"Okay, Cinderella. Unless...you want one last dance with Prince Charming?" Say teases. I try to pinch her again, but she snatches her arm away and raises her hand high to close out the tab.

Back in her elevator, Say leans against the mirrored wall with her eyes closed.

When the elevator lurches up, I swallow hard to keep the contents of my stomach down.

Back in her kitchen, Say opens a cupboard and takes down two tall glasses. I already have my hand under the faucet, waiting for the steady stream to get cold. Say fills both glasses, and we chug the contents. My head has started to throb, and I can hear her every swallow. Say sets her glass down on the counter, wipes her mouth with the back of her hand. "Let's go to bed."

Say takes my hand and leads me through her dim apartment

to the bathroom.

I wash my face while Say brushes her teeth. Say looks at me again in the mirror, and this time, we don't look so "marvelous." Toothpaste foam slides down her chin. Say lets her toothbrush dangle from her own mouth while she rummages in the medicine cabinet. After too much racket, she eventually hands me two ibuprofens. I put them on my tongue, bend to the tap, and slurp more water.

When we climb into bed, the room spins. For me, at least. I put my hand on the headboard to steady myself. "Don't I promise to not drink like this every time I drink with you?"

Say kisses my cheek. "Yes, you do." She pulls the down comforter up to her ears and rolls over. "I love you."

I stare at the ceiling. Gather my nerve. Now or never. "Say. I want to tell you something."

I sit back up in bed. Say rolls back over to face me.

"Okay. Tell me."

"Well, it isn't a big deal, but I think you should know."

Say props herself up on her elbow. "What's going on?"

"I had a miscarriage."

"Wait. What?" Say sits up too, then clicks on the side-table reading lamp.

"Again, no big deal. Honestly, I didn't even know I was pregnant. You know how my periods can be."

Say blinks. "When was this?" Her eyes bulge. Then, "Are you okay? Jesus!" she shouts.

She then takes my hands in hers. "Tell me," she repeats.

"I lost the baby a couple of months ago. It did...shake me a little. So much blood. And I still sometimes lie in bed, stare at the ceiling like just a sec ago, and picture what life would be like if Liam and I had a baby. That baby. And now Liam's going to have a baby with...."

I can't even say her name. I pause and then tell Say about Annie. As I talk, Say puts one hand to her open mouth. She has tears in her eyes. She swipes at her cheeks. Her mouth hangs open while I talk.

When I'm finally done, Say leans forward and tucks my hair behind my ear. Holds both my hands in hers. "Grace, I just can't. I mean, I can't imagine."

I shrug, try to smile. "Hey, life happens, right?"

Say studies my face. "I mean, I just can't believe all that you've been through in such a short period of time. What can I do to help?"

"Nothing. This," I say with a half-smile.

Say squeezes my hands. "But you'd tell me if there's anything I can do?"

"I will. I promise." I lie back down: too exhausted, and already hungover.

Say turns out the light. "Jesus. You've been through so much. You'd tell me if you weren't okay, though?" she asks in the sudden darkness.

I see many yellow blobs behind my eyelids. "Yes. I promise. I just wanted you to know."

I focus on the faraway ceiling again.

Say hovers over me. "Why didn't you tell me any of this sooner? I would have dropped everything and come to you."

"That's *exactly* why I didn't tell you. It's no big deal!" I raise my arms and slap them down on the comforter.

Say shakes my arm. "It *is* a big deal, Grace! All of it is."

I clutch Say's hand. "I'm fine, really. Let's not talk about it and go to sleep."

Say wiggles close and kisses me goodnight again, this time on the top of the head. "I love you more than anything, you know? We can, and *should,* talk more. But whenever you want, okay?"

"Deal. I love you."

Say throws her arm over me. "Because I'm here for you—"

"Say. Let it go. Just for tonight."

"Whenever you're ready...." Say pulls me close to her, and miraculously, I fall asleep.

When Say's cell phone alarm goes off at 5:00 a.m., I groan and pull my pillow over my head. Say announces, "God. I feel like dog shit."

"Ditto."

Say closes the bedroom door behind her to block the light, but I can still discern bits of her morning routine. I hear the toilet flush. She turns the faucet off and on, off and on. When she starts the shower, I am lulled back to sleep.

I wake again when Say returns in her fuzzy bathrobe, a white towel swirled atop her head. My face rests in a puddle of drool on the pillow, so I guess I've been out for a bit. Felt like two seconds. The bathroom light silhouettes Say's body through the open door. She's quiet as she bends to dig through her drawers.

I struggle to sit up. "Hey," I mutter.

"Go back to sleep. Your train doesn't leave until 8:30, right? Reset your alarm for 7:00. You'll have plenty of time to get ready and make it back to the station if you take an Uber, okay?"

"Yes, no taxis." My head pounds so much I have to lie back down. "I just need to...close my eyes...."

Next thing I know, Say's by the bed again. She whispers, "Safe travels, okay?"

"Wait. How did you get dressed so fast?"

"Grace, you were snoring again before I even left the room. You can't hold your booze, old lady. Not like you used to."

"I think you may be right."

"Oh, I *know* I'm right. You smell like a distillery. Get some rest, okay? And call me later. We have a lot to discuss—"

"Yeah, yeah. I know."

"Hey. I love you. Call me anytime. I mean it."

Say leans over and kisses me on the forehead, and then she's gone.

I doze in fits for an hour more, plagued by chaotic dreams. In one of them, I get into a car accident, and my vehicle ends up submerged in water. I can't get Chance or Annie out fast enough, and I panic more when I can't unbuckle Annie's seatbelt. But then Annie somehow gets out and makes it to shore, and she looks at me like I am the crazy one for being in a panic.

The alarm buzzes at seven, and when I sit up, I need a minute to focus my blurry vision.

An hour later, after a hot shower and a quick Uber ride, I arrive back at the station. I'm actually a little early, so I buy a plain bagel at a kiosk on the street to soak up the booze. I find a bench in Grand Central to nibble on my breakfast.

On the train, I drift in and out. When the hiss of the brakes jolts me at various stops, I keep my eyes closed and picture

Matthew: At the farm. In the car. On my porch, holding apples. Holding me. When I nod off for real, my fuzzy daydreams fade to black. I don't fully wake again until home.

Ten minutes later, I'm on the sidewalk in front of the station. My head throbs. Annie arrives with the usual fanfare: tires screeching, horn honking, free hand waving me over.

"You stink," Annie says as soon as I get buckled into my seat.

"Thanks."

Annie checks over her shoulder for oncoming traffic. "What in god's name did you drink last night? You smell like you've got turpentine oozing out of your pores." She guns the gas, and my head jerks back against the headrest. I suck in a breath, but Annie doesn't seem to notice. Instead, she talks a mile a minute about how nice the laminate wood floors look in her living room. "The guy got the work done fast, but I can always give him your number, if you want."

"Annie, I don't need any more complications in my life but thank you anyway." I look out the window as we pass through the marsh.

We ride in quiet. Well, I'm quiet, and Annie is Annie. She tones it down the less I respond.

When we get home, Annie smacks the car into park, tells me to "Go sleep it off, will ya?"

I give her a half hug. "Are you okay," I say, tearing up.

"Yeah, I'm just fine. Just a little tired is all. Now go get some sleep, okay?"

I look Annie in the eyes. "I love you so much. You know that don't you?"

Annie winks at me. "Right back at you, kid."

Back in the kitchen of the rental, the house is eerily silent. I'm too exhausted to eat. I go plop onto the couch. I lie back and turn on the television. At some point, more sleep comes.

21

Annie and I spend the next two weeks engaged in our usual activities: morning coffee and walks on the beach with Chance. New to the mix are extra-long naps for Annie. I help her with little projects around the house to give her easy tasks to focus on. Bill brings us tea and insists we take breaks. Work piles up. Sometimes I bring my laptop over and work at their kitchen table while Annie rests. On one of her better days, I spend an afternoon with Annie at her church and help sort nonperishables into boxes for needy families in town. Matthew and I text often; he always asks about Annie and my stories-in-progress. Last night when we were on FaceTime, he insisted I read some of my writing to him. It felt good, sharing with him.

Today, Annie has asked me to take her shopping even though she looks exhausted. I want to tell her that she should stay home, but who knows how many more times we'll be able to have outings like this one. As I pull up to the curb, I can't help but offer to help her to the door.

Annie narrows her eyes. "Go park the friggin' car."

"I was just making sure—"

"I can still walk, you know!"

"You're right. I'm sorry."

I watch and wait as Annie moves slowly toward the entryway of the department store.

She pauses at the entrance, glances over her shoulder at me, then mouths, "Go!"

I expect her to flip me off, but she simply turns and shuffles through the automatic doors and disappears inside. I'm struck by how much thinner she looks, her walk much less confident than it once was.

Once inside, I find Annie in the women's section. She slides dresses to the left on a rack one by one. Annie sighs, nabs a black drop waist, surveys it, throws it in the cart, and continues to move dresses along the rack. She snags a few more.

"Aren't all of those a little dark and dreary? Don't you want some color?" I reach for a patterned pencil skirt. "Something brighter?"

Annie says nothing, just stares at me. Thins her mouth.

"Oh, okay," I barely manage to say. Christ. We're here to find a dress for her funeral.

I follow her to the dressing room area, trying to swallow the bile rising into my throat. Annie snatches a red ticket with the number six on the front from the woman behind the counter, nods in my direction, and says, "She's with me."

I gather the garments from the cart. The dresses feel too heavy in my arms. Annie stops in front of the last door on the left. I hang her choices on the hooks in the stall. "I think this is a good start," I say as I step out and she steps in.

In the waiting area, I sit cross-legged on the floor by the full-length mirror. Each time Annie comes out to model another dress, I say, "I like it," because I don't know what else to say.

The fifth dress is the color of slate; it's floor length, and the neckline shows some serious cleavage. Annie shakes her chest back and forth with her arms spread wide. "What do you think? Bill will die when he sees me in this one. Make sure the undertaker pushes 'em up real high."

Annie hoists both breasts as high as they will go, practically to her chin.

"Stop it!" I say louder than I should.

Annie props her hands on her hips. I've never spoken to her in such a terrible tone.

"I'm sorry. I don't know how to feel about shopping for...for your.... I hate all of this."

"You think this is fun for me?" Annie snaps back. "Do you know how it feels to know your life will end sooner rather than later? I hate it too, even more than you, I'd bet, but I'm trying to make the most of the time I have left. I just needed you with me today to do this, Grace," her voice cracks, "to make this thing that I have to do feel at least a little bit normal."

I hang my head. My cheeks flare. How selfish of me. I need to get my shit together.

I hoist myself to my feet. I look Annie right in the eyes. "I'm truly, truly sorry. I think this dress looks great. The style's perfect on you." I give her shoulders a gentle rub.

Annie pinches my cheek, says, "Thank you," then reenters the dressing room to change into her street clothes. I grab ahold of the wall to slide down onto the cold tile floor once again.

My mouth feels very dry. What I want to do is drop my head into my hands and sob, but I don't. I sit under the fluorescent lights and wait for Annie to reemerge.

Next, Annie suggests we find something for me to wear while we're here. Again, I don't like the idea, but I'll cooperate. Annie holds dresses up to me and either tosses them in the cart or shoves them back on the rack without asking my opinion.

I try on somber dresses for what feels like an hour while Annie commentates: "Too big. Too small. That one makes your boobs sag. Your ass looks weird in that one." When I step out in a navy-blue wrap dress that hits just below the knee, Annie looks me up and down and says, "That's the one."

"Okay, then. Let me change, and then we'll head home. I need to read at least twenty articles this afternoon, and you look...tired."

Annie doesn't protest.

After I'm done, Annie grabs the items I don't want, scrunches them all up in a giant ball. I carry our dresses on their hangers high over my shoulder so that Annie's won't drag. At the end of the hall, Annie hands the fitting room attendant the mess. Hangers poke out every which way.

The woman drops the bundle on the counter in front of her. "Thanks, have a nice day," she deadpans.

Annie scoffs at the woman's sullen reaction, so I take her arm and move us toward the checkout to avoid a scene.

"Annie Whitney," I warn.

"Does that woman have anything better to do with her day? Isn't it her job to put the clothing back on the hangers? Jeez."

On the way to the registers, Annie redirects us to the shoe section. She stops and surveys the shelves then looks over at me. "Wait. Do dead people wear shoes in their coffins?"

Sick acid races up my throat again. "Don't know," I choke

out. "I've never looked."

"You know what?" Annie shrugs. "Let's wait on the shoes. I'm pooped."

To distract myself in the checkout line, I study the items they put by the cash registers as impulse buys: children's books, iPod earbuds, socks, and specialty candy. I read the ingredients on the side of a bag of coffee. Annie studies the display of dog toys. Suddenly, I hear a horrible smacking sound followed by a shriek. "Oh my god!" a woman yells.

All heads turn toward the commotion. I stand on tippy-toes and spot a twentysomething woman with a ponytail over by the jewelry counter. She scans the store's floor in front of her shopping cart: "My baby! Help me!"

Annie only pauses for a second, then jogs off. I stay in line but watch the scene unfold. The salesclerk at the jewelry counter calls 911 on a store phone, one usually reserved for pages and announcements. People gawk. An older woman behind me holds her hand over her mouth. The mother continues to cry out. I can't see her anymore. I assume she's on her knees, her baby in her arms. The jewelry clerk paces with the phone between her ear and neck, her voice shrill.

I see Annie next. She's got a toddler balanced on her hip.

"What happened?" the older woman behind me demands.

A man behind her says, "The mom was helping her older child tie her shoe, and the baby in the seat of the cart toppled forward."

Others in line gasp. I shudder as the smacking sound replays involuntarily in my head.

The little girl Annie holds sobs. The baby on the ground

doesn't make a sound.

Approaching sirens overpower the music on the store's speakers. A fire truck races up, doors fly open, and firefighters rush in. An ambulance arrives next. While several of the EMTs tend to the baby, I see one of the firefighters near Annie. He takes down some information on a small pad of paper then gives Annie a final nod.

Moments later, Annie comes up beside me with the toddler in her arms. The girl rubs her eyes with chubby fists as tears roll down her cheeks. "Okay, now. I've got you. Everything will be fine," Annie singsongs.

The little girl stops crying but hiccups with both hands balled against her mouth. Annie snatches an oversized rainbow-swirl lollipop from the rack behind me, hands it to the little girl.

"You want that?" Annie asks.

The little girl nods. Annie looks at me. "Help her open it."

I unwrap the cellophane and hand the stick back to the little girl. "Here you go."

Annie positions herself in a way so that the little girl doesn't have a view of her mother or the paramedics. Voices bark out of walkie-talkies.

A few minutes later, the first responders wheel the baby out on a stretcher, and one of the EMTs helps the mom through the sliding doors and into the back of the ambulance.

Annie grins when the firefighter she spoke to earlier returns. "This is Firefighter Ben. He's going to take care of you for just a minute until your daddy gets here. Isn't that right, Firefighter Ben?"

Ben smiles at us. He's young, maybe late twenties. He's dressed in his faded black-andyellow fire suit, which seems odd because nothing is on fire, though I'm sure the uniform's protocol.

"What's your name?" Ben says as he reaches toward the little girl. She recoils, puts her head on Annie's shoulder.

"Did you know that Firefighter Ben is a good friend of mine? He's one of the nicest people I know."

Ben chimes in, "Hey, what kind of lollipop is that? That's my little girl's favorite too. She's just about the same age as you."

"What's her name?" the girl asks timidly.

"Her name is Hannah. Hey, I need some help turning on the lights of the fire truck. Would you come help me?"

The little girl nods, and Annie sets her down on the ground. She gives Annie one last look before she takes Ben's hand.

The checkout line comes to life once again, and I know I need to get my legs to move, but I can't. Annie takes her dress from me and pushes me forward. We pay like normal, but the store manager talks to a police officer out front, and the cashiers look shaken. I walk through the parking lot, still feeling numb.

When we settle into the front seat, Annie asks how I'm doing. I stare out the windshield. "That really shook me." A sob spills out before I can stop myself. Annie rummages a napkin out of the glove box, hands it to me. I blow my nose. She hands me another, and I wipe my eyes.

"Take a few deep breaths," Annie instructs.

I breathe in and out twice. I clear my throat, pull my seat-belt across my lap, and buckle, but then stop. "Did you hear that baby hit the floor? Did she move when you were over there?"

The tears come again.

"Try to let it go, Gracie. The doctors will take care of her now."

"But how'd you do that? I couldn't even move, and yet you ran right over. I feel like such a fool, a coward."

"I don't know," Annie says. "When I heard that mom yell, that could have been my baby on that floor. Did you see all the other women in line? When she cried out, we all felt her pain. I guess I just knew that I had to help."

"Unbelievable," I say.

"Sometimes, you just have to answer the call. Even if you don't want to."

I stare straight ahead. My phone vibrates in the console. I glance at the screen and see that I've got a text from Matthew. He's asking how I've been. I'll talk to him later. Right now, I can't find the words, and I've got to get us home.

22

Thanksgiving came and went. I'd gotten behind at work, so I stayed home and plowed through fifty articles. Annie stopped by in the afternoon with a plate of food for me after she and Bill spent the day feeding the homeless a turkey dinner at their church.

Matthew and I communicated throughout the day. Lately, he mostly texts between study sessions for the National Architect Registration Exam. Looks like I may not see him again until after the new year. I haven't heard a thing from Liam.

Now it's just a couple of weeks before Christmas, and Annie's symptoms have worsened. She moves at a slower pace and tires more quickly. We still have coffee together most mornings, but sometimes, Annie goes home to rest before she finishes her second cup. She can't walk much anymore either, so I've started jogging again on my own.

I'm about to go into the house after today's run when I see Bill by their backyard shed.

He's struggling to maneuver a giant cardboard box out through the narrow door.

"What's up?" I ask as I approach him.

"Annie wants to decorate for Christmas."

I don't want to bruise his ego, but I have to ask: "May I help?"

"If you like," he says and gives the box one final tug.

Bill and I haul in seemingly endless cardboard boxes and plastic totes. Annie applauds each time I step into the living room. She flips the tops off the storage containers and marvels at the treasures inside. Chance puts his paws up on the edge of each bin and sniffs at the contents.

"Christmas happens to be my favorite time of year," Annie says as she opens a long box with a fake tree smooshed inside.

I set down a cumbersome container and say, "Really? Hadn't noticed."

Annie grins and points a finger at me. "You'll stay and help decorate, right?"

"Of course I will." I do have more articles to get through, but those can wait. I bend to position more boxes within her reach, but Annie touches my shoulder, turns me to face her.

"Grace, I really need you here."

"I just told you I'd stay."

"No, I mean...in the end. Will you be here?"

I take her hand as I shift my feet to steady myself. I meet her eyes: "Of course I will." My voice rings clear, final.

"Look, I know I'm asking a lot—"

"Until the end, I promise. I wouldn't have it any other way."

"Thank you, Grace. I want to be at home in the living room with my hospital bed in front of the window so that I can see every sunrise and sunset over the ocean. I want Kelly to be here too, but she won't be able to handle it. Ever since she found out, she hasn't come to visit. Not once. And she's been calling less and less. Poor thing has never done well with stressful situations. She tries to outrun her feelings. Always has."

I pull a strand of gaudy silver garland from a box. "I was going to ask you about her."

"We'll see what she does the closer I get to…." Annie looks out the window, then rounds on me, hands raised. "But I want you to know this, if the situation gets unbearable, like you don't think you can do it anymore, just promise me you'll hold the pillow over my face."

"Annie!"

"I need to speak my truth. If the end becomes a real shit show, do me in. Take me to the pier and shove me off if you have to."

I shake the string of garland to untangle it. "Don't worry, Bill and I already drew straws. If it gets nasty, I get to be the one to yank the plug," I say.

"Like if I shit the bed—"

"Stop it," I say. "I'll take good care of you." I drape the garland over Annie's shoulders, and she cups my cheeks with her palms.

"I love you, kid. You know that?"

"I love you too."

In the two hours before lunch, we unpack Annie's antique nativity scene, angels, and too many snowmen. Bill works outside on the house lights and sets up Santa's sleigh and reindeer in the front yard. Annie sits most of the time but provides explicit directions on what goes where as she unwraps. She tosses paper and packing peanuts over her shoulder and hands me the special items.

When she passes Baby Jesus to me, I start to walk across the room to find his spot then stop. I stare at the figurine. His arms are held open as if he's reaching up to me. I nestle the tip of my pinky into the palm of one of his hands, run my thumb across the top of his head. Wavy brown hair. Brown eyes. He feels lighter than a beach pebble in my hand. Yup. That was just about the size of–

Behind me, Annie snaps her fingers. "Earth to Grace. The manger scene is over there."

She points to the parlor table by the front door.

"Okay, okay," I grumble. I shuffle toward the incomplete nativity scene, plunk the little guy into his cradle, and return to the living room.

Annie's standing now, fidgeting with the crooked branches of the fake tree. "I've been meaning to ask you something else too. What's your plan?"

I help Annie straighten the tree limbs closest to me while she fusses with her side. "Well, after this, I'll go home and work all afternoon."

Annie huffs. "Grace, I'm talking about the future."

Chance prances around my feet, paws at my leg. I start to fluff the boughs to fill in the plastic tree's gaps. "Well. The lease runs out in May, I think. I haven't given it a lot of thought beyond that."

"Any ideas of where you *might* want to go?"

I shrug. "I may go spend some time with Say."

Annie leans past the tree to look at me. "Will you make any stops on the way there?"

I glare at her.

"What?"

"I know what you're asking, and I don't know the answer to that question yet."

"Fine," Annie says, "to be continued," and I can hear the smirk in her voice.

When I've stacked most of the emptied boxes by the back door, I plop down next to Annie on the couch and admire our work.

Annie stares ahead. "When I'm gone, this will all just be stuff to sort through."

I just look at her, not sure what to say. Again.

She continues: "You spend your whole life collecting things that mean the world to you, and you can't take any of it with you. Everything you love ends up in a yard sale."

"Not...everything." I put my arm around Annie's neck and rest my head on her shoulder. My nose tingles, and I'm afraid if I *do* say anything, I'll start to cry. Annie doesn't need my sobs right now, so I just stay quiet until Annie pokes me in the ribs, and I yelp.

She holds her belly and laughs. "You know what? Let's talk about something less depressing. Are you going to go see your folks for Christmas?"

"They said they'll come to me instead."

"Well then, you and your parents should come over to our house for Christmas dinner."

I sit up, grab her knee. "Annie, is this an official invitation?"

Annie huffs again. "I just assumed you'd be *here*. If you were in town, that is."

I can't hide my cheek-to-cheek grin. Mom's gonna love

Annie. "Speaking of Christmas, what do you want this year?"

"Don't waste your money on gifts for me. Remember what I said," Annie swirls her finger in a circle around the room, "yard sale."

I start to change the subject, but Annie beats me to it: "Have you heard from Liam at all, by the way?"

"Nope."

Annie looks like she wants to say more, but Bill comes in and distracts her. He looks around and lets out a low whistle. "You ladies want some fresh hot coffee after all that hard work? My fingers are frozen to the bone."

"I should go home to work for a few hours. Maybe tidy up before Say's visit tomorrow."

"I can't wait to meet her."

I clap Annie on the knee. "Get some rest, okay?"

"Wait. I want to give you something." Annie pushes a smaller gray tote toward me with her foot.

Inside I find a miniature Christmas tree already strung with delicate white lights, plus some handcrafted ornaments.

"This year's been an awful mess, I know, but you should decorate your place too. Holiday cheer and all."

"Aww, thank you, Annie." I try to hide a sniffle.

Despite the work waiting for me, I decide to go for a walk to clear my head. As I bundle up and head out the front door, I contemplate a stroll on the beach, but the wind would feel like needles on my face so close to the shore. Instead, I veer down a quiet side road off Main Street.

Annie's church is about halfway down the block. Wide stone steps lead to the double wooden doors. I tip my head back and admire the tall steeple. I wonder if they leave churches open during the day these days, or do they only unlock the doors for service?

I give one of the shiny brass handles a hearty tug, then step into the smell of incense and lemon polish. The overhead lights aren't on, but the front altar glows. Two giant Christmas trees tower above everything, both lit—one a couple of feet taller than the other. Twenty-five or so red poinsettias line the steps to the altar. Candles burn all around and flicker against the walls.

I peel my jacket off as I make my way down the aisle. I pause by the front pew, drop to one knee, and make the sign of the cross—an almost-forgotten instinct from my childhood. Then I slide my rear across the cool bench. I'm not one to pray, but something compels me to speak aloud. I close my eyes, bow my head. "Please give Annie mercy in the end. Give her dignity. Give her peace."

When I raise my head, I stare at the immense stained-glass window high behind the altar. I take in the deep and various shades of blue. I squint to try to focus on Mary and the baby, but the candlelight blurs my vision. I blink a few times, shake my head, but no matter what I do, I can't get my eyes to fully clear. I can see Mary, but a jagged greenish splotch covers her torso where the baby should be. I glance back at the two trees instead, and just as I do, the lights on the taller, more majestic tree start to fade in and out in alternating patches. My heart flutters, then squeezes in my chest. I'm not ready for her to go.

I close my eyes, try some meditative breathing. Picture me and Annie at the beach again. We both float on our backs with arms outstretched. We hold hands to keep from drifting too far apart. Warm water rocks our bodies. I smell the fresh salty air, and coconut. I lift my head, look over at Annie, and smile. She smiles back but then lets go and swims toward shore. I watch her strong, steady strokes.

When I pop my lids open, the taller tree snaps completely dark, like a blown fuse. I suck in a sharp breath, choke on my spit.

When I recover and look around, of course, no one's here with me except me. No Annie. No priest. I think I need a nap, a real one. Some real rest. I lean left, prop my head on the ornate curve of the bench's end. I relax even more, slouch down sideways into the pew, but jump when my phone vibrates in my pocket. I sit up straight, glance at the screen. It's Matthew. I send the call to voicemail and slide the phone back into my pocket, for now. I need to sit still for a few more minutes, to clear my head.

Much later, on the sidewalk outside the church, I dial Matthew's number. It's time I tell him about losing the baby.

23

The next morning, I work some more but stop to bake a batch of chocolate chip cookies right before lunch. Then I do some last-minute cleaning upstairs. When I run the Swiffer under the bed, one of Liam's black dress socks appears with a dust bunny. *Lovely*. I pick it up with two fingers and throw it into the trash.

Just before dinnertime, when I hear a car pull up outside, I run to the front door. In the driveway, Say stands next to a sleek black SUV, a BMW.

"Where'd *that* come from?" I holler. Say's never owned a car.

Say adjusts her cat-eye sunglasses on her nose. "Some guy, I don't know. My neighbor. I'm pretty sure his name is Robert." She smiles. I laugh and hold out my arms to her.

Say's winter boots thunk on the front steps on her way onto the porch. "Please tell me you have something sweet in there for me to eat."

"I know better," I tell her as I fold her into my hug, "than to let you get hangry."

Say comes into the kitchen fifteen minutes later dressed in some of my sweatpants and an oversized sweater. She has on two of my socks—mismatched, of course. I slide the plate of cookies on the table in front of her and hand her a mug of herbal tea. Say shoves a whole cookie in her mouth and chases it with a gulp of tea. With a full mouth of gooey wet crumbs she says, "Spill it. Tell me everything."

I tell her all about how much Matthew and I have been talking. Say walks to the refrigerator and stands there with its door open. "I'm listening," she assures me.

"What do you need?" I ask.

"I don't know yet. Milk for the cookies, maybe. Or, ooh, this!" Say snatches a can of whipped cream from the fridge, tips her head back and the canister upside down, and fills her mouth with a loud, long squirt.

As I watch her do shot after shot of whipped cream, I have to remind myself that Say runs her own company in the city. She completes complex projects for very important clients. I don't have big days *or* famous clients. *I* should be the one doing whipped-cream shots.

"You look so happy when you talk about Matthew. I don't think I've ever seen you so giddy over a guy."

"He's pretty amazing."

"Ah, see, we've gone from *pretty nice* to *pretty amazing*." Say grabs two cookies and covers one in an obscene amount of whipped cream. She makes a sandwich, and the cream oozes out and drips onto her sweater. I point to the spot, and she shrugs and grins.

I laugh, then shrug myself. "I don't know. I guess I don't want people to think I just jump from guy to guy. You know me—serial monogamist. I've had long-term boyfriends in my life since the sixth grade. Maybe I should stay single for a while."

"Sure, but who cares what people think? Do what you want. I certainly do." Say hands me a whipped tower of cream atop a cookie. "You know, I'm sure people have something to say about me and the men I date. I'm with someone right now named Patrick, and I know he's more into me than I am him. But whatever, I'll stick around to see what happens."

"Wait, you're not dating Robert, the car guy?"

Say shakes her head. "Hell no. He's just a good neighbor. But get this...Patrick wants to keep a toothbrush at my place. Is that weird, or what?"

"Wouldn't you rather have this guy use his own toothbrush and not yours?"

"I'd rather he not spend the night at all. He snores. And twitches." Say thinks for a few seconds as she chews. "I have my career. I love the city. I have great friends. And you know I want to adopt a baby someday. Do I need someone else in my life to attain or possibly thwart anything on that list? Nope. I don't."

"Nope," I agree. "You're great at your job, and you're going to be a great mother."

"I'll teach her to be a woman of grace and dignity. This world needs more of us."

I nod, then lean over to wipe whipped cream off Say's nose.

She giggles as she play-smacks my hand away. "But back to you. About this Matthew: Have you made that list yet?"

"Say, are you turning into my mother? Already?"

"Hey, your mom's technique has saved my ass so many times over the years."

"Okay, I'll work on an inventory. Just not right now. Let's go be lazy on the couch."

"Wait." Say grabs my elbow. "Did my talk of adopting a baby...bother you? I hate when I just blurt insensitive shit."

"Stop it! You know you can say anything to me."

"Well, you haven't talked about what happened very much. How are you doing with all of that anyway?"

I squeeze her hand on my arm. "It's alright, I think I'm healing. Well, obviously I'm physically healed. It's the mental part I'm still working on."

Say grabs the cookies, takes me by the arm, and steers me toward the couch. I flop down.

As soon as we're snuggled under the throws, I tell Say all of the agonizing details of that morning when I lost the baby. I don't cry. I simply recite the facts. Say continues to say nothing.

For the first time, I don't leave anything out—the pain, the blood, the shock.

When I'm done, Say leans her shoulder into mine. "I'm so sorry you had to go through all that. You know, Gracie, maybe you should go talk to—"

"Yoo-hoo!" Annie yodels from the back door.

She charges into the living room dressed in a bright red jogging suit with crisp white stripes down the sides, her arms spread. "Who is *this* cutie?"

Say stands up, and her blanket falls to the floor. Annie hauls her in for a hug, and Say doesn't resist. She's heard all my Annie stories.

"Jesus. You're even taller than I thought you'd be," Annie says as she takes a step back. "What'd they feed the two of you as kids? You're Amazons, the both of you."

"You're *pretty amazing* yourself," Say counters and winks at me.

I wag a finger at Say then pat the couch next to me. "Have a seat, Annie."

Annie shakes her head. "Oh, no. I want to give you girls your time together, but I had to run over real quick to meet this one." Annie beams at Say, and Say, bless her heart, beams back.

Say says, "Won't you join us, Annie? Really, I don't mind."

Annie waves a hand but continues to stand in the middle of the living room. "I can't stay, honey, but while you're here, you have got to see the ocean and eat at The Creamery, maybe head out to the farm—"

"Say's only here for the night."

"Well, all the more reason for me to skedaddle," Annie points at Say, "but you have to promise me you'll at least check out The Creamery. My friend Babs makes the most *amazing* muffins."

Say cracks another wide grin. "Definitely," she says.

"Annie, at least have a cookie before you go." I hold the plate out to her.

Annie places a hand on her stomach and looks in Say's direction. "I don't know.... Annie's stomach has been on the fritz these past few days."

"Well, let me just wrap up a couple for you to take to Bill."

From the kitchen, I hear Say tell Annie, "Grace told me about what's going on with you. I'm so sorry."

"Well, thank you, but we don't need to go into all of *that* today. I want you girls to have a fun visit, so I'll excuse myself. You don't need this old lady hanging around."

"Annie, you really should stay," I call from the kitchen.

"You really should," Say echoes.

"I need to go home and make dinner for Bill," she calls back.

Annie lowers her voice to one of her infamous stage whispers—I can still hear every word when I stop wrestling the tinfoil. "...you know, Say, you really mean the world to Grace. And she needs good people like us in her life, especially after the baby and everything with that jackass Liam. I was hoping Matthew'd be back sooner—"

"Hey," I cry out, "I can hear you!"

"Pipe down in there," Annie squawks then continues. "The kid has been through hell. I'm glad she has you."

Say matches Annie's volume and tone as she announces, "And she'll always have me, Annie, don't you worry."

They stroll into the kitchen arm in arm, and I hand Annie the cookies.

Annie spins on her heel. "Say, it was so nice to finally meet you. Now get over here for one more hug." Annie gives Say a squeeze and a shake. She pats my cheek with her free hand on her way out. "Talk soon. Thanks for these."

As soon as the door closes, Say drawls, "Oh my god, Grace, she is exactly how you described her. What a character. I love her already."

"She's something, alright."

We spend the next couple of hours on the couch gabbing. Matthew sends a few texts, which Say reads aloud to scrutinize every word. "He's way into you," she decides.

"You think so?"

"Oh, I *know* so."

Say squints as she scrolls through the latest text. "Being

honored at the grand opening of the museum he helped design. Just outside the city. Big ribbon cutting two days after Christmas. My my," she says, then: "Oh, here we go. He says he thinks the exam went well today."

"What? Let me see!" I yank the phone from Say's fingers, but she just scooches closer to read over my shoulder.

Sure enough, Matthew's trying to downplay the importance of his accomplishments, but I tell him how proud I am of him anyway. I end the text with the smile emoji with hearts for eyes.

Say snorts, then pinches the back of my upper arm. "You're so in love with this guy, it's not even funny."

I swat her hand away and frown at her.

"Come on, girlfriend, you know you—"

"I mean, I do really, really *like* him."

"That's all you need for now. But keep this one around for a while, will ya? Could be good for you."

"Could be," I say, "could be."

We order pizza for dinner, and I tell Say more about Annie while we eat.

"You're such a good person," she says. "You have always taken in every three-legged blind dog in the neighborhood."

I slap Say's arm. "Annie's not a stray mutt!"

"That's not what I mean," she says as she takes another bite. She gets quiet again as she chews. "I just worry about you. You tend to take care of other people and neglect your own needs in the process. Just make sure you take care of yourself through all of this."

"Fine, Mom, I'll make another list," I snark.

Around ten, we go upstairs to sleep. Say jumps onto the bed, stretches diagonally across the length of it. I roll her over and get under the covers. We talk and giggle in the dark like we're sixteen again.

At one point, we even have an old-fashioned foot fight, pushing our feet together in an attempt to shove each other off the bed, but we don't shove nearly as hard as we used to when we were kids. We give up at the same time and pull the blankets to our chins.

"Goodnight, Gracie."

"Thank you so much for coming to see me. I didn't realize how much I needed to talk about...everything."

"Anytime, girl, you know that."

I roll onto my side, grab my phone from the nightstand to send Matthew a goodnight text, but he's already beaten me to it.

24

Two days before Christmas, in the early afternoon, my folks arrive. Dad drove the entire three and a half hours, of course. Mom's much more comfortable directing my father's every move from the passenger seat—even on short trips, let alone longer rides.

Mom stands in the doorway and gasps with her hand on her chest. "Look at this place!" she says as she marvels at the cute décor.

Dad nudges Mom from behind with the edge of a suitcase, his arms full of luggage and grocery bags. I rush over to help.

"I've got it, kiddo. Just show your mother around."

I grab a few bags from him, anyway.

Mom explores on her own while I go to the kitchen. "Look at this view!" my mother yells from the top of the stairs.

"Your cottage is lovely," she says, "just lovely," when she enters the kitchen a few minutes later.

I have to say, "Well, it's not *mine*, per se," but she waves off the comment with a smile. She pulls a container from one of the reusable shopping bags, sets it on the counter, and removes the lid from the oversized Tupperware. The smell of cinnamon wafts my way. I'd know that container and that scent anywhere.

"You made them!" I squeal and clap, then snatch a sweet roll and take an enormous bite.

"At least use a plate," Mom says as she opens my cupboards until she finds one.

"Oh my god," I moan.

"Don't talk with your mouth full." Mom puts the meager remains of my roll on a plate for me. I moan again as I lick the white glaze off my fingers. Mom squints at my atrocious manners.

Dad comes in and sets his hat on the table. He hugs me and kisses my cheek.

"How about I make us some coffee, perk you two up after your long drive?"

"That would be great, honey," Dad says. "I'll be right back. I'm going to carry the rest of your mother's things upstairs."

I fill the coffee pot with water, scoop in four giant heaps of dark coffee grounds, close the lid, and press the start button. The coffee pot starts to gurgle and drip. I rinse my hands then open the cupboard above my head to pull out the mug Annie likes best, but it shifts in my wet hands and tumbles to the floor and shatters. I jump back from the spray of exploding porcelain chips and put both hands to my mouth.

"Oh no," Mom says and rushes toward me.

I hold up a hand to keep her at a safe distance then bend down to scoop up the pieces. Instead, I sit there on my haunches, staring at the shards.

Mom says, "Honey...let me help."

I point toward the broom and dustpan tucked beside the refrigerator. I'd just finished sweeping before they arrived.

I stay crouched, unable to move. "Annie loves this mug," I

somehow manage to explain.

Mom squats too and gingerly gathers the bigger chunks by hand. She drops the pieces into the trash can, then returns to sweep up the rest into a pile. When she finishes, I grab her hand, and she slides down onto the floor next to me, wraps an arm around my shoulders, and rocks me side to side. "Gracie. Honey. I'm so sorry."

If only she knew how bad it's really been. I'm not telling her about the baby, though. Soon, but not today.

"It's all going to be okay, Gracie girl. Life might be hard for a while, but you'll get through it."

I chew the inside of my cheek then swallow, but louder than I mean to.

Mom pulls me closer. "Hey, is there anything else you want to talk about?"

My mouth goes dry. I shake my head.

"Because you can tell me anything, you know."

I lick my lips. "I know, Mom."

She kisses my cheek. "I'm always here for you. Always."

I rest my head on Mom's shoulder and close my eyes. After a few more minutes, Mom pats my knee. "I love you so much, honey."

"Love you too. Now, let's get going. I want you to meet Annie."

"I'd like that."

I hoist myself up and then help Mom to her feet.

A half hour later, we're in Annie's kitchen. Bill sets the paper down on the kitchen table and stands to shake my mother's hand. "Nice to finally meet you," he says in his usual shy way.

Chance scampers in and jumps at Mom's legs. She runs both hands down his back.

"Look at you, you little cutie. You're even cuter than I thought. Yes, you are!"

Chance's rear sways back and forth and my mother's voice gets even higher. "I want to take you home with me. Yes, I do!"

I have to speak louder over her cooing. "We thought we'd invite Annie to go shopping with us today."

Bill sighs and says, "She was pretty beat last night. Went to bed early and napped most of the morning."

"Well, if she's too tired—"

In comes Annie in a pink sweatsuit, her house slippers scuffing along the linoleum floor.

She attempts to put her glasses on with one hand. "Did somebody say *shopping*?"

In the car, Annie talks to my mother nonstop. She pauses only when the farm comes into view up ahead. I put on my blinker and look left. Santa sits in the front seat of the old truck at the entrance to the road and waves. Annie leans across my chest and waves back, then looks over her shoulder at Mom. "You're gonna love this place."

Mom smiles at the old barn and the building that houses the bakery. "I want to live here," she says. "Look at that swing in the barn!"

We both take an arm and help Annie across the dirt path to the entrance. I open the door with my free hand, and as we step in, the smell of spiced cider hits me. I can feel the warmth radiating from the woodstove, and carolers sing in the corner.

"Isn't this great?" Annie asks my mother.

"It is."

After we get Annie situated at a small table, Mom helps pull her coat off and drapes it on the back of the chair.

"Hey, Mom, why don't you take a look around? Annie and I will wait here for you."

Anne blurts, "Oh, for god's sake, Grace, go show your mother the shop. I'm perfectly fine right here." She crosses her arms and gives me a sharp look.

"Okay, okay," I tell her. I stroll away with Mom.

Mom browses but eventually selects a couple of Maine-themed ornaments: a silly moose wearing four mismatched mittens, and the other a mini burlap sack tied with a green ribbon and smelling of pine needles. I order some raspberry pie and assorted donuts, still warm from the display case.

We three sit knee to knee at the tiny table and graze. The carolers sound angelic in the background and are accompanied by the jingling bell above the door when new shoppers enter.

Annie greets almost every person with a big wave. She knows practically everyone in this town, and she also knows every detail about their lives.

"How's Dicky?" she asks an older woman who clutches a metal cane. "Did you ever sell that car?" she asks another woman in a sweater adorned with crocheted kittens in a basket.

I love to see Annie interact with folks. "A fixture," most would call her.

My phone vibrates in my jacket pocket—a text from Matthew. *I just wanted you to know I'm thinking about you today.*

Hope to see you soon. The text ends with a heart emoji.

I type in a reply: *Miss you too xoxo.* My finger hovers above the cell screen. Too much? But what have I got to lose? I hit send.

The carolers begin to sing an old Shaker song. Annie hums along loudly, terribly out of tune, which at first makes me giggle, but then my chest begins to ache. What am I going to do without her? Mom must've seen my expression fall because she squeezes my hand under the table. Annie continues to butcher the song—I grin at her and hold back my tears.

One of the owners ambles over. "I hope you ladies enjoyed your visit to the farm today."

We all nod. "Really wonderful," I say. "Thank you."

The lady nods too and asks, "You'll come back again next year?"

My mother's smile fades. She looks at me and then at Annie.

"Wouldn't miss it," Annie says.

Mom excuses herself to the bathroom and as she does, a young mother strides by with a baby bundled in a purple snowsuit. I smile as they pass. It hits me then that at least a week has passed since I've thought about the miscarriage. A sick guilty feeling creeps through my body. What kind of mother forgets to make the time to think about her dead baby?

Annie asks, "Hey, what's wrong?"

"I'm okay." I dab at my eyes with a scratchy, crumpled napkin.

"Bullshit," Annie says.

I laugh, then sigh. "You're right. Sometimes...I feel like I'll never be okay."

"You know, you'll never forget your loss. But, one day, it will be okay to remember the pain and still be happy. I promise."

Annie rests her hand on top of mine. "It just takes...more time, though I hate to say it. Time. That damn four-letter word."

I snort. "Where do you come up with all your nonsense?"

"I'm full of gems. You should write them down before I go. You could write a book—"

"Are you *trying* to depress me more?"

"Just doing my job," Annie says with a wink.

When Mom gets back from the restroom, Annie announces she would like to go home. As we stand to put on our coats, I turn and look at the mom and her baby one last time. The mom balances the baby on her knee, and the baby clutches a mashed donut in her fist. Shiny drool rolls down her cheeks. The baby looks up at me and shows me her gooey pink gums. I wave back. A wave of nausea rolls through my stomach when I think about Liam and Sophie and *their* baby. But I shove those thoughts away for another day, telling myself to enjoy my time with Mom and Annie.

25

I hear my dad in the kitchen early on Christmas morning. I feel around for my phone from the nightstand. Two new text messages.

Merry Christmas. I hope you have a great day xoxoxo.

Matthew. And he's upped the ante with extra hugs and kisses.

The next message makes me pause. I sit up straight in my bed.

I'm thinking of you. Maybe we could get together sometime and talk? I've got some things I'd like to say. Enjoy Christmas.

Liam.

I toss my phone down. Rub my eyes. Pick it back up and read the message again. I stare at the screen for a few moments. *Okay, weirdo, whatever.* I respond to Matthew's text only.

Mom, Dad, and I have a light breakfast of coffee and fruit as we open gifts. I got my folks gift certificates to their favorite restaurants back home, plus earrings for my mom and a sudoku book for my dad. Afterward, we get ready to go to Annie's house for Christmas lunch.

Mom offers to help Annie as soon as we walk through the door, but she shoos us to the table and tells us to sit back and relax. Just as we get settled with our glasses of sparkling wine, the back door flies open and in strolls Annie's clone. The two are built the same, only Kelly is slightly taller. Two rambunctious boys gallop past us all into the living room.

"Honey, I'm home!" Kelly bellows, arms out, shimmying her sizable chest. She beelines for her mother and gives her a resounding smacker of a kiss on the cheek. Not only does Annie's daughter look just like her, but she acts just like her too.

Kelly grabs Bill by the shoulders and squeezes his neck. Then she plants her hands on the table. "You must be Grace. I've heard all about you from Ma." Kelly motions for me to stand and as I do, she wraps her arms around me and lifts me off the ground, only to shake me side to side, like Chance with his favorite chew toy.

Finally, she turns to my parents. "And you must be Grace's folks?"

A man with dark brown hair walks in through the open doorway and flops into the chair at the end of the table. He plunks down a six-pack of beer. He pops the metal cap off one of the Corona bottles with the edge of a pocketknife and then takes a long swig.

"And you must be Tommy," I say with my hand out.

Tommy looks at my hand blankly. He's short, a little handsome, definitely Italian, and even if a bit crude, not at all the monster I'd expected after hearing Annie's rants. When Kelly cuts her eyes at him, Tommy straightens to shake hands with me and my parents.

One of Kelly's boys runs through the kitchen and bumps into Annie. "Go on, get out of here, you rascal," Annie says as she brandishes her whisk in the air. "Nana will be in to hug you in a minute, but I have to finish this gravy first."

Kelly corrals her children into the living room. Tommy sips his beer, seemingly both bored by and oblivious to the ruckus.

Maybe Annie's right about Tommy. He's so...what's the word—disengaged? Cocky? Maybe *lazy* is correct, after all.

About fifteen chaotic minutes later, we're all seated at the formal dining room table crowded with platters of food. Annie clinks her fork against the side of her glass. Even the grandsons settle into silence. "I just wanted to thank you all for being here. It means a lot to me, and I'm so glad we can all be together—even you, Tommy." Annie laughs, lifts her glass, and we all cheer her toast.

Annie moans with each tiny bite of her mashed potatoes and turkey gravy, as does Kelly in unison. Annie's putting on an elaborate show of enjoying her own cooking, but I can tell she's not really taking in that many calories.

"Delicious," my father gushes as he helps himself to seconds.

Mom wipes her mouth with her cloth napkin. "Annie, my goodness, I think that is the best stuffing I've ever had. I'll have to get your recipe before we leave."

"Thank you, Carol. My mother's recipe. Might be a little off this time, though. I didn't have the strength to give it a good stir like I usually do. I hope the seasoning got mixed in."

"Well, I think it's heavenly," Mom says before she takes another bite.

I watch Annie push food around on her plate while chatting with everyone. Eventually, Annie sets down her silverware with a clank. "Phew, I'm full," she announces.

"It's always good to save some room for dessert," Mom says with a wink.

Annie burps against the back of her hand. Her grandsons

giggle, and Kelly gives them a mock-stern look, which only makes them laugh louder. Then one of them starts telling made-up knock-knock jokes, and the dinner conversation devolves into the worst punch lines imaginable, with the adults egging the boys on. Annie laughs until she cries, then wipes her eyes with the neckline of her blouse.

And then she gets serious very suddenly. "Shoot. I almost forgot. Bill, would you grab that covered plate over there on the sideboard? The one with the striped cloth."

Bill pushes back his chair. "Sure thing, sweetie."

He returns to set a cake stand in front of Annie. She pinches the top center of the cloth and then whips it away like a magician.

Kelly gasps when she sees what's underneath. "Ma, you made it!"

Before us sits a beautifully braided loaf of fresh bread with a bright green hard-boiled egg in its center. The crust has been baked to a perfect gold and decorated with red sprinkles.

"Annie, that looks amazing. What is it?" I ask.

"My famous Easter wreath."

I scrunch up my face and tilt my head to the side.

"Well, I typically make it for Easter dinner, as you could probably guess, but I figured, what the hell. Might as well make it now while—" She stops, takes a long deep breath through her nose and then continues:

"Usually, I dye the egg pale blue, but I thought it would look festive this way. I meant to put it out on the table earlier as a centerpiece."

As Annie prattles on about the bread, talking about the egg-white wash, her voice starts to sound like it's coming from far away. My throat feels too tight, like I can't take another bite. Or another breath. I look up at my mother. Her face is flushed. I look at Kelly next. She shrugs her shoulders, smiles at me, but with tears in her eyes. She turns away from Annie.

I jump in to say, "That looks truly divine, Annie," but even my own voice sounds distant in my ears.

Kelly clears her throat. "You should take some home with you, then dip a piece of that bad boy into a nice hot cup of coffee tomorrow morning." She gives my foot a gentle tap under the table with her own. Shit. I should be trying harder to console Kelly, and here she is trying to comfort me.

I nod numbly. "I'll have to try that. Thanks."

After that, everyone goes quiet, and for so long that I'm afraid no one is going to say anything for the rest of the meal. Finally, Kelly tosses her napkin onto the table.

"Lordy, lordy," she sings out. "I'm stuffed!"

"Same here, honey," Bill says.

"Wait. Before we all get up, I have some gifts." Annie scoots her chair back, grabs a large paper bag from the corner of the room, then comes back to the table and claps her hands together. "Every family should have one of these in their kitchen." She tugs out a few elaborately wrapped gifts. She hands one each to Kelly, me, and Mom.

I tear into my package to find a spiral-bound presentation book. On the cover is a photo of Annie. She's wearing a tall white chef's hat and an apron. She has Chance tucked under one arm and a wooden spoon in her other hand. She has an enormous grin on her face. I laugh out loud at the picture. "Annie's Café" is printed in bold red lettering along the bottom border of the photo.

"A book of my best recipes."

"What a lovely gesture," Mom says.

I flip through a few pages and stop on "Annie's Magical Meatloaf." I read through the ingredients list and chuckle when I get to "a handful or two of those breadcrumbs with the green and white label."

Kelly leafs through her copy of the book. "Ma, this is so cool!"

"This is awesome, Annie. Really," I say.

Annie steadies herself on the edge of the table and beams. She looks around at all of us, then says, "You want to know something? I am the luckiest."

I reach over and give her hand a squeeze.

Annie nods as she leans over to collect the dirty plates, but I wave her away at the same time Mom does. Annie does not protest. Her skin has that gunmetal gray look to it again.

"Ma, why don't you go watch the boys play in the living room while we clean up?" Kelly says.

Annie nods again and moseys toward the living room. It sounds like the boys are starting to fight, and I hear Annie say, "Don't make me pull this car over."

The cleanup happens quickly; we all pitch in except for Tommy, who continues to sit at the table as we work around him, another cold beer in his hand.

Annie sleeps the rest of the afternoon in her bedroom. Mom and I play *Life* with the boys while Dad and Bill chat about cars and fishing. Tommy scrolls away on his phone, and Kelly talks my ear off to the point where I can hardly concentrate on the game.

I gravitate toward the kitchen now and then and pick at the desserts. I text Matthew here and there, checking in on his day. He sends photos asking for my opinion of dress shirt and necktie combos for the upcoming ribbon-cutting ceremony at the museum.

Just as it starts to get dark out, Annie enters the living room and flops onto the couch. Even though she's just slept deeply for hours, she still has dark circles under her eyes. Her face is puffy too, with lines from her pillow.

My mom leans over and gives Annie's shoulder a gentle squeeze. "Don, we should go and let these folks spend some family time alone."

"That's not necessary," Annie protests. "Please, stay as long as you like."

"Thanks, but it's been a long day for us too. We'll get out of your hair and get some rest ourselves."

Annie kisses Mom with a big *mwah* then asks, "How long will you and Don be in town?"

Mom sighs. "Oh, I don't know. What do you think, honey?"

"You tell me, dear. You're the boss, applesauce."

Mom turns back to Annie. "Well, then I think you're stuck with us for a few more days, if you don't mind."

"Perfect," Annie says. "Let me show you out."

Annie rocks her body back and forth twice, then manages to hoist herself to her feet with the help of the armrest. I take her by the arm and lead her toward the kitchen.

Everyone except Tommy stands.

"Nice to meet you, Tommy," I say over my shoulder.

"You too," Tommy says without even looking up from his phone.

After extra hugs and goodbyes, my folks and I step out into the cold night. I pull out my phone to check my texts again but stop in my tracks when headlights wash over the side of Annie's house. A silver truck pulls into the driveway at my cottage. My heart thumps in my chest. *What the fuck is* he *doing here?*

Liam climbs out of the truck in his knee-length dress coat. He's got a potted plant in his hand.

Mom slaps at my arm, squints in the near dark. "Is that—"

"Yes, it is," I practically hiss.

Liam waves and grins before he begins to walk toward us. The outdoor motion sensor light kicks on. "Well, Merry Christmas, everyone!" Liam shakes Dad's hand and nods at Mom.

"I took a chance that you both might be in town, so I wanted to stop by and drop this off."

Liam lifts the plant higher, then hands it to me—a red amaryllis already in full bloom.

I don't even know what to say. Or think. I smile back, trying to be polite, but he's intruding, and he knows it. I kind of want to kick him in the shins.

Dad glances at me, clears his throat, then turns to Liam. "Well, it was great to see you, but it's a little chilly out here, so I think Carol and I will head inside."

Liam nods. "I understand. I won't keep you. I just wanted to say Merry Christmas."

"Thank you for the flowers." Mom gives Liam an awkward half hug.

After my parents disappear into the house, Liam pulls a square envelope from an inside coat pocket and hands it to me. I tuck the envelope under my armpit and cross my arms. Liam says, "I know it's probably weird that I'm here."

I say nothing.

"I'm sorry, I'll let you enjoy your holiday in peace. It's just that—" Liam looks down at his feet. Kicks at the frozen ground. Looks back up to meet my eyes. "I just...needed you to have that." He points to my armpit. "Merry Christmas, Grace." Liam squeezes my upper arms. He stares at me for a brief moment, then turns away, gets into his truck, and drives off.

As soon as the truck is out of sight, I rip the envelope open. When I tug on the card inside, something cold and shiny slithers out. I'm able to catch it before it drops to the ground. It's a delicate silver chain with a pendant. At first glance, it appears to be a circle—almost, but not quite; actually, it's in the shape of a heart. I study the design then have to plant my feet more firmly when I realize it's an abstract, intertwined mother and child. The mother's head touches the baby's head, and the heart's curves are the mother's arms embracing the baby.

I clutch the necklace inside my fist and flip the card open. *Dear Grace, What we went through was not nothing. I'm so sorry I wasn't there for you. You're going to be a wonderful mother one day. Love, Liam.*

*We? Did he just write...*we*?* What did *we* go through? "Are you fucking kidding me?" Both my ears start to ring, and I can't quite breathe properly. I suck in a gulp of fresh air, but the bitter cold burns my lungs.

I stare at the spot where Liam's truck had been parked—for a long, long time. So long that the motion sensor light turns itself off and then one of my parents flicks on the porch light. Only then do I realize I'm shivering.

26

New Year's Eve is here, and my folks will drive back to New Hampshire late this afternoon. Before they leave, we're going to have finger foods with Annie and Bill.

We've all spent the last few days together. We played cards or dominoes with Annie when she was awake. Bill and Dad went to Cabela's two days ago and came back with matching fly-fishing vests. That night, Annie brought over an enormous tray of meaty lasagna. Yesterday, we ordered Chinese takeout. Annie continues to eat less and less.

I've somehow managed to find time to work and write in between all of those activities. Liam has sent me a few texts. I haven't responded to any of them. Matthew and I communicate daily.

My folks use the day to pack and perform perfunctory tasks while I work. Mom sweeps the entire house and dusts. After borrowing some tools from Bill, my dad fixes the dripping faucet in the downstairs bathroom.

I take a break to visit with Mom after lunch. I settle into a chair in the kitchen and pull another close to rest my feet on. Mom slides a pecan pie into the oven, then washes her hands.

She turns to me. "You know—"

I stop her with a held-up hand. "Mom," I say, "please, don't go there."

"I just want to make sure you're okay. I know you and Liam loved each other, and I was surprised when you called to say you'd taken a break, that's all."

"Mom, I'm fine." I'm more annoyed with her than I should be. She's got every right to be concerned about me. And she still doesn't know the worst of it. I just can't seem to tell her that I lost her first grandchild. "I think Liam and I shouldn't be together," I admit instead.

"Hey, if you're happy, we're happy. Your father worries about you here all by yourself, though. He almost brought you your old baseball bat."

I laugh. "Yeah, that's all I need."

Mom rolls her eyes. "You know your father."

"Besides, I'm *not* all alone here. I have Annie and Bill. Plus, it feels good to be living on my own. In that respect, I'm happy, Mom. I promise." I pause, drum my fingers on the table. "You know something? I can honestly say that, despite everything, I'm more content than I have been in a long time."

"That's all I needed to hear." Mom kisses the top of my head. I pull her close to me and wrap my arms around her waist, rest my head against her belly. "I love you so much."

"Love you too, Gracie girl."

Just before three, Annie and Bill arrive at the back door. Annie comes in and unwraps a gray knitted shawl from around her shoulders. She tosses it onto the back of a chair but then bear-hugs herself. "Brrr. Do you need me to pitch in for the heating bill over here or something? Jeez. Are you running a butchery? I can see it now. Cattle hanging from hooks in the ceiling."

"Okay, drama queen," I say as I drape her shawl over her shoulders again.

Bill sets down a wooden platter of cheese, crackers, and veggies.

"Hello, hello!" Mom sings as she walks into the kitchen. She goes directly over to Annie, runs her hands over the shawl. "This is gorgeous."

"Thank you," Annie says and pulls Mom in for a hug.

I snag some paper plates from the top of the fridge and toss them onto the table. "I'm starving. Let's eat."

Dad grabs a fistful of napkins. Mom opens a bag of tortilla chips and dumps them into a ceramic bowl. I pop the casserole dish of Mom's chili cheese dip out of the microwave.

We all sit and chat as we eat. Annie eats one or two chips with the dip but then stops to sip some ginger ale. We talk about mundane things like the weather and New Year's resolutions. After only about a half hour, Annie's got her head propped in her hands on the table. Bill notices and says, "How about we get going, sweetie?"

Annie opens her mouth, but I cut her off. "I think that's a good idea. And before you even ask, no, you may not help clean up. It will give me something to do after everyone leaves."

Annie sighs. "Fine, fine." Bill helps her to her feet.

"Well," Mom says. She gives Annie a tender smile and takes hold of her hands. "I'm so glad I finally got to meet you, Annie. You're just as wonderful as Gracie said you were."

"I pay her to say those nice things," Annie says with a wink.

Dad shakes Bill's hand, but Bill pulls Dad to him, and they pound each other on the back, as men do.

Mom steps back, looks at Annie. "Take care of yourself, okay?"

"How can I not, with these two constantly hovering? I hardly have to lift a finger these days."

Mom laughs. "Well, take advantage of them."

I give Annie a half hug. "I'll see you tomorrow for coffee, right?"

"I hope the hell so. You never know."

"Annie! I *will* see you tomorrow." I kiss her on the forehead.

Dad places his arm around Mom, and she rests her head on his shoulder. Annie waves goodbye as she and Bill walk out the back door.

Mom pulls a tissue from her sleeve and starts to dab at the corners of her eyes. "You're brave in ways I'll never know, Gracie. Don't know if I could do it."

My throat closes. I tug at the neckline of my shirt and choke out, "Sure you could, Mom." I smile through my tears. "You taught me everything I know."

I help Dad load the last of their luggage into the car. After hugs, Mom presses her forehead right to mine. "If you need anything, you give me a call, okay?"

"Will do."

I stand on the porch and wave as my parents leave.

Back inside, I notice Liam's plant on the floor by the door. I give it a small nudge with my foot to move it out of my way. I had meant to make Mom take it back to New Hampshire.

My goal is to stay awake just long enough to see the ball drop. I clean up then read articles about the latest car recall for a couple of hours. At around eight, I plop onto the couch, turn on the television, and watch the people in Times Square all bundled in their hats and mittens. Though it looks too cold to be outside tonight, I'm still jealous that all of those people get to hang out in such a cool spot, and I'm here, on my couch, about to ring in the new year alone. I alternate my attention between the live coverage and finishing my report for work.

At 10:30, I close my laptop for the night and get into my pajamas. I wash my face with a washcloth and stare at myself in the mirror. My landlord left all sorts of cosmetic products in the drawers under the sink. I dig around and find a fancy facial mask. The instructions say to rub the stuff on, let it harden, then wash it off "for a silky-smooth feel." I secure my hair in a high bun, open the tube, squirt what appears to be textured green toothpaste into my hand, and smear the goo in circles. I leave a little circumference clear around my eyes. Next I survey my landlord's selection of glossy polishes and decide to go all out and paint my toenails a racy fire-engine red.

Soon enough, I'm back on the couch, toilet paper stuffed between each toe, polish still gleaming wet. I lean back with my bare feet propped on the coffee table to rest the leftover dish of dip on my chest. I've already eaten half of another bag of tortilla chips, and I know I won't stop until I finish the dip then put the bag up to my face and drink the crumbs at the bottom. On TV, the revelers hop with anticipation as they try to stay warm and wait for midnight. Just as I settle in with my snacks, someone knocks on the front door, and I almost drop the entire dish of dip.

I safely set the dish on the coffee table and mute the TV. My toenails haven't dried yet, so I have to hobble on my heels to the door.

When I flip on the porch light, I can see the top of his head through the glass.

Matthew.

I suck in my breath and swing the door open. Then I grin coyly and say, "Perfect timing."

"Cute," he says as he touches the shellacked goop on my cheek.

I prop a hand on one hip, lean against the door with the other. "Pretty sexy, huh?" I rest the tip of my forefinger against my lower lip.

Matthew chuckles. "Very." He puts his arms around my shoulders, pulls me gently against him. We stand so close that our lips nearly touch. "Hey," he whispers.

"Hey."

"I missed you."

He strokes my rough cheek with his thumb, then runs his hand up and rests it just behind my ear. I peck him on the lips. "I missed you too. Now come in. It's cold out there."

Matthew bends to untie his boots by the front door.

"You're early," I say. "You said maybe next week."

"I know," he says. "Couldn't wait." He walks over to me in sock feet, takes my hands. "Plus, everything's done...except–" Now he leans in for a long kiss.

I feel my face mask start to crumble, and I pull away. "Let me fix my face first."

"Mind if I rummage in the kitchen for some food? Been a long drive."

"Help yourself." As I walk toward the bathroom, toilet-paper toe-separators pop loose with each step I take.

In the vanity mirror, I see the green goop has hardened and aged my skin with its cracks.

"You didn't tell me I look like the witch from *The Wizard of Oz*," I call out, and Matthew laughs.

After a vigorous scrub, I pat my face with a towel, then run my hand down my cheek. Damn. My skin does feel softer. I try to fluff my hair, but it lays limp. All my tools and toiletries are in the upstairs bathroom. I shrug at my reflection. Eh. This is as good as it gets.

I find Matthew in the kitchen with Annie's lasagna in one hand and a fork in the other. He eats the pasta cold, right out of the tray. He flushes when he sees me and sets the tray down on the counter. He speaks to me with the back of his hand against his mouth. "I'm sorry," he mumbles, "I meant to use a plate, but it just looked so good."

"Delicious, isn't it? That Annie can cook." I open my mouth, and he feeds me a bite.

I find a fork for myself and start to dig in too, but then I stop to look around. "Wait, wait. What time is it? We don't want to miss the ball drop."

Matthew checks his watch. "We still have time."

"Well, in that case," I say as I take another forkful. We both lean against the counter as we eat. I rip a couple of paper towels from the roll and hand one of them to Matthew, wipe my mouth with the other.

"What's your resolution?" Matthew asks between bites.

I think for a moment. "I want to make some big changes this year. I want to get going with my life. If that makes any sense. You?"

Matthew takes a deep breath. "Now that the end of my schooling is in sight, I'm ready to get going with my life too." He tries to stifle a yawn.

"You seem really excited about your new plan," I joke.

"Long drive," he says. He blinks at me, then smiles.

"Hey, how was that ribbon-cutting thing?"

"It was pretty cool, actually. I mean, the ceremony itself was kind of boring, lots of speeches and stuff. But I have to say, it was pretty neat to see something that began as sketches on paper in real life."

I make air quotes. "*In real life,* Matthew?"

He nudges me. "You know what I mean."

"I do. I'll shut up. Tell me more."

Matthew sets his fork down. He begins forming shapes with his hands again. "The way the light was coming through the entryway. When I sketched it out, I wasn't sure if I was overdoing it with the windows, but Grace, it was really something. All the angles looked so sharp. You've got to see it sometime."

"I'd love that. Maybe after Annie—" I stop and look up at the ceiling, having to take a steady breath before I can speak again. "Well, maybe this spring, I could take a drive down."

Matthew loops an arm around my shoulders. "Sounds like a plan," he says, then kisses my head. "I'm full. Are you all set?"

"Yes. Put that away before I eat all of it."

Matthew covers the tray and slides it into the refrigerator. He claps his hands together.

"Okay, then," he says. "Let's go relax until midnight."

I nod, and Matthew takes me by the hand.

In my bedroom, Matthew peels back the comforter, casts the flowered sheet to one side.

He strips down to his boxers and climbs into bed. I kick my sweatpants to my feet and join him.

He finds the remote on the nightstand, turns on the small television on the bureau, clicks until he finds the countdown. He then lies down on his back and pulls me close. I put my head on his chest, and he caresses my neck. He starts to massage my upper arm and my eyelids feel heavy.

Maybe I will have someone to kiss at midnight after all, if I can stay awake.

I rest my hand on his stomach. "How many people do you think are out there tonight?"

"I think I heard about a hundred thousand. But that sounds high."

"Jesus. Imagine the trash. And how do they even manage to stay out that late? I think this is the first time I'll have seen the ball drop in years."

"Same," he says, "but it's nice to have someone to stay up with this year."

We critique the musical acts to keep ourselves awake, and just before twelve, the crowd gets even more boisterous. Some of them shake noisemakers in the air, some jump in place, and the rest point their cell phones in the direction of the ball. When the group begins to chant, "Ten, nine, eight, seven..." I raise onto my elbows. After the ball finally drops and the fireworks start, Matthew tugs me back to him. "Happy New Year," he says into my ear.

"Happy New Year, Matthew."

The confetti rains down in Times Square like new-fallen snow. "Auld Lang Syne" plays.

Some couples kiss, others dance, and strangers sway and sing with linked arms.

We watch for a few more minutes, passing yawns back and forth. Matthew caves first.

"Are you ready to sleep?"

"Mmhmm," I murmur.

Matthew turns off the television. I turn onto my other side, and he rolls over with me, drapes his arm over my hip, and tucks me into him. He's still holding me tight when I drift off.

I awaken with a jolt when I hear someone knocking downstairs. I sit up. My pulse races. Matthew stirs. But then I remember that Annie and I had plans to have coffee this morning. Shit. I have to get Annie out of here.

I tell Matthew to go back to sleep, that it's just Annie. He mumbles and rolls over. I slink out of bed and snatch my robe from the hook on the back of the bedroom door. I run downstairs barefoot. At the back door, Liam stands there, not Annie. He doesn't even wait for me to invite him inside, as if he still lives here.

I step away from him. "What the hell are you doing here?" I bark out, but in a whisper.

"I just have a couple of things I want to say."

Liam speaks in a normal voice, and I shush him, while pulling my robe closed tighter across my chest. I feel strangely... naked, though I've worn this ratty robe in front of him a million times. "Liam, you can't keep stopping by unannounced," I say just above a whisper.

Liam looks past me at the stairs. "Wait, is someone here?"

"Liam, now is not a good time."

"Okay. I get it, but before I go—"

"Liam—"

"I want you to know that I take full responsibility for everything that happened. I lied to you, and I was wrong."

He takes a step closer. I take another step back.

Liam steps forward again and gently squeezes my chin, his signature move with me—the very definition of us, the old us. "I really do love you, Gracie. Not that it matters. I know I've ruined things between us forever, but I need you to know that. And I'm not with Sophie anymore. I mean, I'll still be there for the..." he pauses and looks at me, "... the baby. My mom said she'll help. But Sophie and I, we're through. We're going to try to make it work as friends. I just don't love her. And I'm so sorry for everything. Truly. I've been talking to this shrink."

Liam stumbles over his words. He stops. Clears his throat and I notice that he has actual tears in his eyes. "I just love you so much, and I'm so very sorry for ever hurting you. And I guess that's all I wanted to tell you."

My mouth hangs open. I can't seem to close it. Liam puts a hand over his eyes, and his chin begins to tremble. Then he swipes away tears as they fall.

On instinct, I reach out and grab his upper arm. "Liam," I

say, not knowing what to follow that up with. He pauses only for another second, then places a hand on my cheek. "Gracie girl, you're the best thing that ever happened to me."

He leans forward and kisses me, then turns and leaves. My jaw is still unhinged from my face.

As I close the door behind Liam, I hear a creak on the stairs. Matthew is on the landing, my comforter wrapped around his waist. He gives me a weak smile, then trudges back up the stairs.

I don't know what to do. I need to think. I put on coffee, because Annie is bound to be here any minute. Then I realize how unusually awkward our usual morning coffee klatch is about to get.

When Matthew comes back downstairs a few minutes later, he's fully dressed. "I should get over to see my folks."

"Matthew—" I stammer.

"I loved last night, but I feel like I should go now. It sounds like you've got some things to think over. Call you later?"

Matthew gives me a half-hearted hug. He kisses my cheek, then slips his feet into his untied boots by the front door. I want to tell him not to go, and that there's no way I'd ever get back together with Liam, and that I think I'm falling in love with him, but I'm honestly too stunned by all that Liam said to speak. "Matthew," I say, "I..." but nothing comes out.

Matthew gives me a sad smile, then turns and walks out.

I spin around when I hear someone at the back door. If that's Liam again—I rush to the door and haul it open, ready to tell my ex what I think of him, once and for all, but instead of Liam, I see Bill. He's out of breath, and his face is flushed. "I just called 911. She can't breathe."

27

I kneel in front of Annie. She's on the couch, hunched over. Sirens shrill in the distance.

"Just breathe. Just breathe." I make circles with my hand on her back. A knot forms in my throat.

Bill's voice cracks. "Did I make the right decision?"

"You did," I reassure him, but all of a sudden, I can't seem to swallow.

Soon several EMTs rush in. Their feet pound across the floor, and I jump out of the way. They put an oxygen mask on Annie's face. I rush to Bill's side and clutch his hand. He could probably use some oxygen too. Two men load Annie onto a stretcher, and then someone else takes her blood pressure. Bill follows as they wheel her out into the icy cold.

I grab Annie's keychain off the hook by the door. "I'll follow you to the hospital with your car," I call out as Bill climbs into the back of the ambulance. He waves over his shoulder.

I can see the top of the oxygen mask and Annie's hair through the square windows on the back of the rig. Bill bends his head to hers. The ambulance roars off, lights flashing.

I turn to Chance at my feet. "You'll be okay, boy." He, too, has the shakes. I stoop down and take the time to pat him. "Honey, she'll be right back. Don't worry."

I can hear Chance's tiny whimpers through the door as I leave.

At the hospital, I rush through the sliding doors of the emergency room. I bark out Annie's full name, and an attendant points down a hallway.

I scan doorways for Annie and try to push my way in when I find her.

"Family only," says a stern nurse. She extends her arm as a barrier.

Bill says, "It's okay. She's ours."

A doctor in green scrubs asks us both to go to the waiting room. Bill looks as if his knees might buckle. I take his arm and usher him out. We sit next to each other. I feel cold and jittery.

I hand Bill the car keys but then don't know what to do with my hands. He pockets them and rubs at his temples while my leg involuntarily jogs up and down and rattles our row of chairs.

Suddenly, Bill looks at me and whispers, "I need to call Kelly."

I pat his arm. "Call her on your cell. I'll go get us some coffee." Bill looks me over, hands me a few singles from his wallet. I realize only then I'm still in my robe, with no purse. Mercifully, I'd slipped on shoes at some point, but I don't remember when.

When I return from my short walk to the vending machine, Bill's eyes look glossy and red. He blows his nose on one of the white handkerchiefs he always carries in his pants pocket.

"Kelly's on her way."

I nod, hand him his coffee, and we wait quietly. I pick up a magazine off a side table and leaf through it. Bill stands and paces the room now and then. Nearly an hour later, another doctor arrives. She adjusts the surgical cap on her head, lifting her ponytail off her neck. "I'm Dr. Jenson."

Bill and I stand. "I'm Bill, Annie's husband."

"I want to explain some things to you. Do you mind if we sit down?"

Bill waves toward the hard plastic chairs, and we all sit again. "This is Grace, by the way."

Dr. Jensen faces me. "The daughter?"

I start to stammer, but Bill saves me. "Close enough," he says.

"Okay. I want to be straight with you both," Dr. Jensen says. "Annie's body is weak and will begin the process of shutting down soon."

Bill puts a hand to his forehead and looks down at his lap. I rub his back the same way I rubbed Annie's earlier.

"Now, it won't happen tomorrow. This morning, the tumors in Annie's lungs caused pressure in her chest, which made it harder and harder for her to breathe. Her lungs will, eventually, fill with liquid."

Dr. Jensen studies Bill. "Do you understand, Mr. Whitney? I know this is a lot of information to take in all at once."

Bill looks up at us. "You mean she'll suffer even more?" Bill swipes a sliding tear. "She'll suffer...then drown?"

Blood rushes to my head, and I can't hear anything but my pulse in my ears. My body starts to tremble, and I press against the back of the chair. I cross my arms to hold myself still.

Dr. Jensen's lips continue to move. Bill nods and nods. I

struggle to rein in my reactions.

She turns to me and, eventually, asks if I have any questions. I can hear her faintly now, but I still can't speak or think. I just stare at her.

"If you need anything, just let me know."

She pats Bill's shoulder. "Why don't you go see her."

Bill stands, and Dr. Jenson leads him down the hallway.

I stand to watch them leave. I don't know what to do. I need to call my mom. I slap at my empty pockets, then look around for my purse, forgetting again I left everything at home. I didn't even lock the cottage. I shuffle down the hall to the nurses station, and explain that I don't have my cell with me because I ran out of the house in a hurry. The nurse receptionist points me to a courtesy phone down the hall.

I put the clunky receiver to my ear and dial. When I hear Mom's voice, I choke out a sob. "Breathe," she says. "Just... breathe."

I do what she tells me to do.

"Okay, again."

I take several long breaths while she waits. My hand shakes; I lean on the wall to steady myself. The cinder block wall is cold against my forehead.

"Now, what's going on? Do you need us to come back? Is Annie...."

I take in one more gulp of air before I speak. "She's going downhill fast."

"Gracie, I'm so sorry."

I cry harder then but when I'm finally able, I share the details with Mom. The more I talk, the angrier I become. "Life is so dumb, you know? I mean, I feel like she's way too young to die. I used to think sixty was old, but the older I get, the more I realize just how young...."

Per usual, Mom comforts me by simply listening while I rant: "Like, friggin' robots can perform surgery these days, we can clone stupid sheep, and yet we can't seem to come up with a cure for cancer. How idiotic is that? I don't get it. I really don't." My voice continues to rise. "And to top it all off, the doctor basically said Annie's going to *suffer*, then die. So, there's that."

Mom repeats, "I know, hon."

"We're more humane to dogs at the end, for Christ sakes." I lean forward and let myself weep again. I squeeze my eyes shut, and when I open them, I watch the tears hit the vinyl tiles.

My shoulders shake, and my throat hurts from trying to hold the sobs down.

Mom tells me it's going to be okay. I try her breathing technique again. *Breathe in. Breathe out.* I blink a few times, then look to my left. An older woman sits in a chair down the hall, her hands folded across the purse on her lap. She smiles sympathetically at me. I pull the receiver away from my face. "Sorry," I say to her, louder than necessary. I wave, then turn back to face the wall. "Sorry, Mom. Didn't mean to trip offline like that."

"You've got a lot going on. It's understandable that you would feel angry. I don't blame you a bit. Life *isn't* fair sometimes."

"It really isn't," I say back and my voice breaks. The tears won't stop now.

"Your father and I will come anytime to help. You know that."

"I know."

Finally, when I get myself under control, I swipe my sleeve under my nose. "I should get back," I tell her. "I just needed to hear your voice. You can always calm me down. I'll call when I know more."

"Sounds good, sweetie. Call anytime."

I tell her I love her then hang up. I blink again, and when the spots clear, I see Dr. Jensen far down the hall.

I call out, "Excuse me. Could I ask you a couple of questions now?"

Dr. Jensen stops and turns to me.

"I know you're busy. My questions will take just a minute."

She nods, and we walk toward each other. When she gets close enough, she gives my forearm a squeeze. "Go ahead," she says, "ask away."

A few minutes later, as I stand outside the door to Annie's room, Dr. Jensen's words echo in my head: "Three weeks at least, maybe a month." I lean against the doorjamb, take a sip of coffee. It's gone cold. I realize I don't want to face Annie now that I have this new information. I gulp down more coffee and grimace. Tell myself to get my ass in there.

I open the door slowly to see Annie propped on pillows. She's got oxygen tubes in her nose. Machines beep to her left and right. Her mouth is wide open, and she's snoring. Bill sits in a chair by her bed, his head in his hands. I clear my throat.

Bill looks up, gives me a half-hearted wave, then hangs his head again. I tiptoe over to the chair on the other side of the bed, but on the way, my foot catches on the leg of the tray table.

The wheels are locked in place and scrape against the floor; the foam-and-plastic water pitcher shifts, almost topples. I wince. Annie jolts awake and looks around. She sits up straighter when she sees me, wipes the corners of her mouth with her thumb. "What, no coffee for me?"

I look down at the cardboard cup in my fist and shrug. "I can ask if they'll mainline you some through your IV if you want."

Annie smirks.

Bill stands and takes hold of Annie's hand. "Honey, I'll go ask the nurse if I'm allowed to get you something light to eat." Bill looks over his shoulder at me. "She didn't even get to finish her toast this morning." His voice breaks.

I reach across the hospital bed to pat his shoulder. "I'll stay with her. Why don't you go take a little walk too?"

Bill looks at Annie. "I'll be fine," she says and puckers up her lips. "I'll be even better if you can get me something good. A big pastry would really hit the spot."

Bill kisses Annie then faces me. "Thank you, Grace."

When Bill closes the door behind him, Annie looks me up and down. "Come here."

She pulls me closer to her by the belt of my robe. "I'm in bad enough shape. I can't walk around here with my ass out for everyone to see. Now give me your robe."

"Oh, you *have* lost it, haven't you?"

I sit on the edge of Annie's bed. "I don't have much on underneath, else I would share."

"Fine. I have a better ass than you, anyway. Who cares if people see it." She hesitates, studies my face. I can imagine how bloodshot my eyes must look. She reaches out and taps the back of my hand. "What a shitstorm, huh?" Her face looks bone white, and the wrinkles on her forehead and around her mouth seem more pronounced.

"Indeed." I feel the tears rising again and walk toward the window.

Kelly arrives just after one in the afternoon. From the room, we can hear her yelling, "Ma, Ma!" She gets louder as she makes her way down the hallway. She kicks the door open, and a nurse hurries in behind her.

"I got here as soon as I could," she says, out of breath.

"Stop it. I'm fine," Annie says. Kelly rushes to her mother's bedside and sheds her coat onto the floor on the way. I pick it up and drape it over a chair.

"I'll go," I say, "so the three of you can spend some time together."

Kelly spins around and takes hold of my shoulders. "Please don't feel like you have to leave just because I'm here. That's silly."

"Grace has had a long day already, and after, I suspect, a long night too." Annie gives me a cheeky smile. I realize she probably saw Matthew arrive last night. "Go rest, Grace," she insists.

"I at least need to change out of this robe."

"Okay, but come back anytime," Kelly says. "I mean it." She wraps her arms around me and won't let go. "Thanks for all you've done for Ma." Kelly gives me a smooch on the cheek.

Bill hands me the keys I'd given him earlier. "Take Annie's car. I'll ride with Kelly."

Annie says, "Will you check on my baby boy?"

I nod, kiss her on the forehead. "Sure will, and don't you

dare leave me yet. We have a lot to discuss."

"Oh, I'm sure we do," Annie says with a wink. Her eyes are shiny and bright.

28

As I tap away at my laptop, Chance lies on the floor with his head on my right foot. Every now and then, he gets up, spins in a circle, then flops back down with a sigh. "I know, buddy, I know," I tell him again and again.

When the lights came on at Annie's early this morning, I went straight over to see if they needed anything. Bill and Kelly were on their way back to the hospital. Bill mentioned that the hospice folks were coming to install the necessary equipment, so I offered to wait for them and then said I'd take Chance to my place until they came home. When the delivery truck backed into the driveway, I brought Chance outside and talked to him while they lugged in a bed, wheelchair, and commode. I doted on Chance until they were done and I could lock up Annie's house again.

I'm really trying to work today, but I keep having to stop to rub my eyes. Last night, when I couldn't sleep, I tried reading articles to occupy my mind but couldn't concentrate. Then I started having imaginary conversations out loud with the doctor, and all of my anger about losing Annie came back. So I got up and began cleaning the kitchen. I put away the clean dishes and swept the floor first. Next, I washed all of the refrigerator shelves, polished the doors of the cupboards, and took everything out of all of the drawers for sanitizing and reorganizing. I used my homemade concoction of dish soap and vinegar, a recipe of Mom's that's effective but hard on the hands. My skin puckered, but I turned on some music and set to cleaning the rest of the house, upstairs and downstairs. Around 10:00 p.m., I dropped to my knees and hand-washed all the hardwood floors with some Murphy Oil Soap I found under the kitchen sink. A couple of hours later, when I was truly and utterly exhausted, hands cracking and head pounding, I collapsed into bed but still had an awful, restless sleep.

Now I can't stop yawning no matter how much coffee I drink, but I have a deadline looming; I can't just *not* work. As I read and review, I massage Chance's back with my bare left foot, the one he's not using as a pillow. His fur is silky and warm.

Around noon, I bring Chance back to Annie's to start lunch for everyone. Their fridge is jam-packed. I drag out cold cuts and macaroni salad. When I hear the car in the driveway, I wipe my hands on a dish towel as I look out the window. Bill helps Annie out of the front seat while Kelly collects items from the back seat. I gaze down at Chance. He shakes his little butt back and forth. "She's here, buddy."

Kelly balances a kidney-shaped pink puke-bin full of stuff—bottles, soaps?—on one arm and carries a stack of assorted medical supply boxes under the other. A half-used roll of toilet paper tucked beneath her chin falls to the kitchen floor as they step inside. I rush to her. "Here, let me help."

I take the bin from her and begin to pick through the items. I shake out a washcloth with my free hand and look at Kelly then Annie.

Kelly shrugs. "Don't look at me. All that crazy lady's idea." Kelly jerks her head in Annie's direction.

I roll my eyes. "Annie. Seriously?"

"Hey, when we get the hospital bill," she says as she shuffles by, "you'll see why I took what I did. That right there adds up to at least a hundred dollars' worth. They *want* you to take all that for what you pay to stay at the hospital."

I laugh. "Well, I'm happy to see you acting yourself again."

When we get Annie settled into the new bed, she lets her shoulders slouch with a sigh. Even her cheeks and lips seem to be drooping with exhaustion. "I think I'll rest for a while."

"Okay, darling." Bill kisses Annie's forehead.

Chance comes bounding in, jumps on the bed, and settles at Annie's feet.

"You goof," she whispers.

We leave the living room to give Annie some peace.

In the kitchen, Kelly rummages around in the cupboards, and I flash back to my cleaning spree last night. I duck into the half bath to wash my hands.

I've left the door open, and Kelly comes in just as I get the water warm. "Can I talk to you for a second?"

"Of course." I wait for her to tell me what's on her mind while I lather my hands with vanilla-bean-scented soap—one of Annie's signature scents.

Kelly closes the door behind us, lowers her voice. "Look, I can stay for a few more days, but after that, I have to get home to the boys. You know my husband's no good with them."

I dry my hands. "Living so far away right now must be so hard for you."

Kelly squeezes my forearm. "I'm comforted knowing you're here. You know, Ma used to drag me to church when I was little. I hated it, and I didn't believe in any of it. But now, wow, I get it. I get it! Like, I'm not here, but you're here, and you're just what Ma needs right now, and you just happened to pick the house right next to hers to rent for the year. Her *last* year—" Kelly's face creases. "I don't want to be here...at the end. I don't think I can handle it. I want to remember her sassy and full of life. Ma says she asked you. Do you really think you can?" Her lip begins to tremble, and the tears come. She starts fanning her eyes. "Shit, shit," she says as she cries harder.

I put my still-wet hand on her shoulder. "Yes. I'll be here."

"You're the best," Kelly sobs. "This whole thing is so stupid, you know?"

Kelly braces both hands on the vanity and cries quietly. When she raises her head and gets a look at herself in the mirror, she stops. "Jesus. Why has no one told me in all of my years of life on this planet that I ugly cry? Look at me!"

I pat her on the back, meet her gaze in the mirror. "Go ahead and ugly cry. All the cool kids are doing it these days. I walk around with a grimace on my face, runny nose, and my eyes nearly closed with puffiness lately. The look is all the rage in this neighborhood."

Kelly gives a half-hearted snort. "I can see why Ma loves you so much." She rummages in a drawer, pulls out an eyeshadow pencil and an ancient-looking powder compact. "Give me a minute to fix this trainwreck." She takes the hand towel and drags it down both cheeks. "I'll put on a face, and then I'll be out. I don't want them to see me like this."

"Take your time. I'll get lunch started."

We talk, but only in whispers, while we eat. Chance has joined us at the table, to beg and sniff our food. We make tea and wait. And wait.

Eventually, Annie wakes. Kelly steps out to call the boys, to tell them Nana is happy to be home. Bill and I both go to the living room. Annie's in a pale, flowered nightgown, which makes the gray shade of her face seem even more pronounced. She's got a few discolorations on her arms that weren't there before. Bill sits on the couch, gives me the chair next to Annie.

Annie picks at her flattened hair. "I look like dog shit, don't I?" At the sound of her voice, Chance barks and begs to be lifted back onto the bed. "Well, excuuuuse me," Annie says to Chance. I scoop him up and set him down next to Annie. He snuffles her neck immediately.

I want to tell her she looks like a million bucks, but we both know I'm a bad liar. "I mean, you've looked better."

"Yeah, so has he. Look at this mop." Annie pushes an unruly poof of Chance's hair out of his eyes. "We could both use a trip to the salon, couldn't we, boy?"

Chance pants into Annie's face. "Don't suppose you've ever groomed a miniature poodle, have you?"

I laugh. "As you can see, I can barely groom myself these days." I run my fingers through my ratty hair until they snag at the ends.

Annie snorts and turns to look out the window. The line of her mouth thins into nothing, and then she croaks, "Those disgusting crows! Goddammit, Bill! Get those assholes out of here.

They've pecked the hell out of the trash again."

Without a word, Bill rushes outside. I hand Annie the plastic cup of water from her bedside table. I steer the straw toward her cracked lips. She takes a slurp, then waves it away.

"Okay, tell me everything. Now."

"Everything? Now? Even while Bill's out there murdering crows for you?"

Annie closes her eyes. "Don't be cute. You know what I want."

"I don't even know where to start. So much has happened."

She cocks open one eye. "Spill it," she demands, then snuggles back into her pillow like a child preparing for a bedtime story.

I tell her about Liam, and Matthew. How everything didn't suck, until it did. "I feel like life will never be normal for me, ever again. Everything is in limbo. The rental, my job. Matthew. Fuck. Just...fuck."

Annie lifts one arm and lets it fall back onto the bed. "And here we go with the pity party."

"I know, I know. These aren't real problems." Annie's close to literal death, and here I am, mid-complaint about my silly soap-opera life.

Lids still closed, Annie gropes for my hand. Due to the IV from the day before, the top of her hand sports new shades of sunset-purple and mottled-yellow. I bet she's been poked and prodded everywhere, poor thing.

Annie tells me, "Since the day I met you, you've lived in this la-la land where you expect life and your relationships to be all pansies and unicorns, and I'm here to tell you, sister, life isn't like that. Look, I love Bill, but love takes work, and relationships aren't easy. Grace, all in all, when you think about it, you've been dealt a pretty good hand. You're so smart and still young. Your tits are still perky, for god's sake."

I laugh but squirm in my seat. My voice catches and stalls when I try to speak again.

"When I go," Annie continues, "I want you to take some time to figure out what you want. Not what you think Liam wants or even what Matthew wants. Look at me, I'm sixty-seven years old, and I have, maybe, a couple of weeks left."

Annie squeezes my hands in hers. "You moved here, and I realized I had my perfect partner for the end. I've lived such a good life, and these last months have been—" She pauses to catch her breath. "These last few months have been beautiful. Because you are beautiful. We've shopped, ate like queens, and had a hell of a lot of laughs. You've been my...my best friend."

My throat burns, and I can't speak at all now, but I don't look away.

"When I'm gone, I want you to go too. Just go. Get outside and take lots of your crazy runs. Eat something sugary and fatty from the farm and order more and eat it for me. Watch your sad, sappy movies and have a good cry or twenty. Sleep with as many men as you want to until you figure out what *you* want. You deserve to live. So. Live. For both of us."

I lean down to kiss Annie's hand and let the tears roll down my cheeks. Within a few quiet minutes, she's snoring. Loudly.

I smother a laugh, swipe at my eyes with the flat backs of my fists, gather myself, then walk back to my cottage. My heart thumps when I see Matthew on my front porch. Again.

Waiting. For me.

29

Matthew and I spend the next few days together. He cooks for me while I work and leaves to visit his parents when I go to be with Annie. I've not given him any definitive answers, and he hasn't pressured me to do so. We simply enjoy our time together. When he does leave for Pennsylvania, I tell him I can't wait to see him again, and I mean it. We agree to keep in touch, but there's an unspoken understanding between us that the rest of my time here in Maine needs to be focused on Annie. For now, that's enough.

Annie spends most of the next two weeks asleep. She wakes long enough for the hospice nurse to administer meds and take her vitals. Nicole comes more often as the days wear on. Annie has a port for medication. Nicole teaches Bill, Annie, and me how to use it. We push the morphine, or Annie does, when she needs to ease the pain. "You really can't overdose, though. The pump won't administer medicine if you give it too often."

Nicole's a little thing with a great sense of humor, and she speaks matter-of-factly. We all laugh and joke, and I love that she treats Annie with kind patience and never talks down to her. She always makes eye contact with Annie and speaks to her even though I'm not sure she hears a lot of what any of us says through the meds.

Bill and I take shifts. I like the night shift. I sleep in the recliner by Annie's bed. Bill takes the day shift, which allows me time to go for walks with Chance, writing, and working at their kitchen table. Neither of us has to cook. Annie's frozen a lifetime supply of meals in the freezer in the basement. I put dishes in the oven to warm them; Bill and I eat at the table together every night.

For relief, I talk to Mom often. She calls me, or I check in with her every single day, sometimes twice a day. I also talk to Say. I feel like they all know Annie as well as I do now. I call Kelly daily, as well. I hold the phone to Annie's ear and let Kelly talk to her.

Annie still sits up and eats when awake, but she hardly ingests anything. Just a bite or two here and there. Nicole says this process is normal. I feel helpless. On one of the bad days, I ask Nicole a horrible question—out of Annie's earshot—that I've had on my mind: "Is she eventually going to starve to death?"

Nicole rubs Annie's cheek. "I don't think she's hungry anymore."

One night after Nicole leaves for the evening, I start to pull out my laptop and get to work. But Annie moans from her bed, so I rush to her side. Her eyes pop open. "You're here," she says. The small lamp on the table beside the couch illuminates her face. "Remember when we went to lunch that day?"

I'm not sure which day Annie means—there were so many lunches and other outings— but Nicole says to just go with whatever Annie says, even if she may be hallucinating. "How could I forget?"

"What a great day, huh?" Her eyes close for a moment and open again. "While you're here, would you help me with something?"

"Sure, what do you need?"

"You see that water all over the walls?"

I look around the room. "Why yes, I do."

"I need you to mop it up. Kelly always takes too long in the shower when she gets ready for school. Now look, water is running down the walls."

"I'll get some towels in just a minute." Annie's eyes close again before I can even finish my sentence. I sit at her side and watch her as she sleeps. I rub her hand and talk about other fun memories we've made. I work and nap, off and on, when she's quietly settled.

The next time I wake, I'm still by Annie's bedside. I roll my sore, stiff neck in circles.

Bill stands in the doorway with a tray of teacups. "Good morning, sunshine," he says to Annie. No response.

"How was she last night?"

"Good. We had a good night, didn't we?" I clasp Annie's hand.

Nicole arrives before lunch and takes Annie's vitals. As she tucks the stethoscope into her bag, she asks Bill to come to the kitchen with us so that we can chat out of earshot of Annie.

"Her body is shutting down now. We need to focus on comfort from this point on. Annie's already got a little fluid in her lungs." I think back to that quiet rattle I heard this morning while I did her mouth care with the sponge swab. "That rattling noise will get louder and louder as the days wear on. When the death rattle increases in volume, you'll know the end is near."

The muscles in my neck seize again.

"They like music," Nicole continues. "Play any music Annie would like. It soothes them."

"How...." Bill stops. I know what he wants to ask. So does Nicole.

"A day or two, maybe. She won't suffer, though. Annie's already somewhere else, transitioning into her next place. She's here, but she isn't."

Bill nods but clutches my forearm.

"I don't think I need to come back, but if you need me, don't call the agency. Call my personal cell." Nicole pulls her phone from her purse. "Let me give you my direct number."

When Nicole prepares to leave, Bill looks left and right and wrings his hands. Nicole leans over and whispers something in his ear that I can't quite hear, but when she finishes, Bill winks in my direction and says, "I know she is."

Nicole comes to me next and gives me a hug, but I hold on too long. She holds me back. *What do we do when she dies? Who do we call? How will it feel?* Too many questions swirl in my head. Nicole releases me, locks her eyes with mine. "It will be okay. *You* will be okay."

Nicole wraps her scarf around her neck, adjusts her hair, buttons her coat, and leaves.

Bill and I sit in the kitchen. We don't talk for a long time. We just listen to the drone of the refrigerator, the winter clinks in the water pipes. I can't begin to imagine what he's thinking, poor man.

"Do you want something to eat?" I blurt.

Bill shakes his head.

"Me neither."

"But I'd take a cup of coffee in one of Annie's big mugs, if you don't mind?"

I brew a fresh pot and bring Bill his coffee, grateful for the mundane but useful task. Bill sits beside Annie's bed, rubs her forehead, and hums a nondescript tune. I settle in on the couch with my own hot cup of coffee.

Not long after, Annie stirs. Her eyes blink and blink. Bill stands.

"Honey?"

Annie forces her eyes to stay open to stare at Bill. She clutches the rails of the bed and tries to hoist herself.

I'm on my feet in a second. "Easy now." I try to help Annie sit up, but she stretches her arms out for Bill. He leans in, and Annie drapes her arms around his shoulders. Annie begins to sway back and forth ever so slightly. Bill closes his eyes, holds Annie close. I feel like an intruder right now, in one of their most intimate moments. I step into the kitchen.

To pass some time, I send Matthew a text. He responds right away, says he's thinking of me, missing me. After a few minutes, I go back into the living room, and Bill lays Annie back on her pillow.

I feel exhausted, maybe in a way I've never known. "Bill, do you mind if I get some air?"

"Of course not. Take your time."

The cold air slaps me in the face when I open the door, but I don't care. I walk around the front of the house and sit on the steps of the porch. I pull out my phone again. Say answers after the first ring. "Say, I don't think I can do this much longer."

"You can," Say reassures me. Her voice is soft but strong. "Do you want me to come up to be with you?"

"You're sweet. No. You stay there. I know you're busy. It just makes me feel better to talk to you. Tell me about anything that doesn't have to do with cancer or hospice. Anything."

"Well, I've got a new guy."

I slip into Say's story.

"His name is Ted. He's a lot like me. He's even my age. I did a project for his boating company a few weeks ago."

"Does this mean he wears white pants and L.L.Bean boat shoes and ties sweaters around his neck all the time?"

"You know, that's what I pictured when I talked to him on the phone for the first time too, but he's not like that. The first time I went to his office, he was in black Chuck Taylors, jeans, and a blue tee shirt."

"Shut up!" I squawk into the phone.

"I shit you not. He's so down-to-earth and loves to work like I do, but he also loves to have fun. We both left work early last week to go to dinner and an art opening."

"Haha, very funny," I say. Say *does not* leave work early.

"I'm serious!" Say protests. "Ted doesn't annoy me. And...."

"What?"

"I let him keep a toothbrush at my place."

"Holy shit!"

"I know, right? I think this might be serious."

I'm happy for her. Say's never taken any man seriously, ever. "You're growing up so fast." I sniffle into the phone and pretend to cry.

"Screw you," she says.

"I'm kidding. I'm truly happy for you. You probably need to go, huh?"

Say pauses. "No. I have all the time in the world for you."

"I know you do, Say, but I also know that you're a very busy woman. I love you."

"Love you too, pretty girl. Talk soon?"

"You've got it," I promise.

I hang up the phone and sit in silence. A car pulls into the driveway. I stretch, trying to get the kinks out of my back as I stand.

Matthew's mother gets out of the driver's side door. A few other ladies step out onto the driveway too. Nancy holds a paper shopping bag. "We wanted to come by with some food, should anyone need it."

"Thank you so much. What a thoughtful gesture."

Nancy comes close, loops her arm through mine. "I know things have been hard for you."

I fight back tears. "I'm just so...tired."

Nancy tucks me tighter to her side, a sweet, gentle movement that reminds me of Matthew. The tears gush then—I can't help myself. Nancy just holds me and lets me cry.

"I'm sorry," I say as I stand back. "I don't know you all that well, and here I am blubbering all over you."

Nancy grabs my hands. "You have such a big heart. Do you know that? No wonder my son likes you so much."

Nancy reaches into her coat pocket. "Matthew wanted me to give this to you in person." She hands me a book. I touch the cover, which feels like coarse recycled material. The book is printed with a watercolor image of a hill, and a calm blue lake in mellow, muted colors at its base. Two sketched figures paddle a canoe. Inside, the book's blank, lined faintly. A journal, with a note tucked inside.

"I know he would be here with you if he could, but as you know, he's on that required program tour. If you need anything, I'll leave you my number. Just call, and I'll drop whatever to help in any way that I can. We all will, won't we, ladies?"

The other women nod their heads in unison. One wipes her eyes with a tissue.

Nancy takes a piece of paper out of her purse and writes her name and number down. "Anything, you hear me?"

"Yes, ma'am," I say as I tuck the scrap of paper inside the journal too. I wave as Nancy backs the car down the driveway and out onto the street. When they are out of sight, I set down the bag of food and unfold the note from Matthew.

Dear Grace, I don't know why I'm here when I should be heading north to be with you. I'll come there if you want me to. Just say the word. Until I see you next, I'll take you with me wherever I go. Love, Matthew.

I tuck the note back into the envelope and sit to feel the cold sunshine on my face for a time. Then I go in the back door to the kitchen, curious to see what the ladies brought. I peel back the lid of the Tupperware container on the top. Chicken parmesan. Still warm. I pluck a piece with my fingers and take a big bite. When was the last time I ate? I didn't even realize I was hungry. I take a few more bites right from the tray then replace the cover. Bill comes into the kitchen.

"Bill, why don't you take a break too?"

"You've been busy, huh?" He points to the grocery bag.

"Not me, some ladies from town."

"How nice of them." Bill peeks into the living room. "I don't want to leave her."

"Some fresh air will do you good. Take your cell phone with you. If anything changes, I'll call you."

Bill does not like this idea at all, I can tell, but I also know that he'll go crazy if he stays cooped up a minute longer. "Okay. I'll take Chance for a short walk on the beach." He hasn't been out much either. The little guy just sits at the end of Annie's bed and whimpers.

"You could both use a walk." I help them toward the door.

Bill puts on his jacket. "You're sure?"

"She'll be fine. I'll call you if anything changes. I promise."

Bill takes one more look around the room, nods, then leaves.

When I turn to go into the living room, I trip on one of the throw rugs. I curse then smile when I think of that night, we sang karaoke, and I fell right in front of Matthew. I straighten out the rug with my foot.

I go to see Annie and rest my head on the edge of the bed.

"Annie, I don't know if you can hear me wherever you are right now, but I have something to say, and you've never been this quiet. I'll say it now because you can't interrupt me." I pause too long, then choke out, "I love you so much, you cranky old woman." I press my hands to my eyes.

I'm sure Annie's laughing wherever she is, but it feels weird not to hear her cackles. I rub her hand. "I know you want to hang on, to stay for us, but if you need to go, go." I stare at Annie.

I want her to sit up and make a joke. I want to see her sit up and call me a rude name. Anything. Annie remains silent, her mouth half-open.

Bill returns a few minutes later with Chance. As soon as he unhooks the jeweled leash, Chance jumps onto Annie's bed and snuggles her feet.

"You held out longer than I thought you would. I'm proud of you."

Bill shrugs. "I knew if I came back right away, you'd send me right back out. I've been on the porch for at least five minutes. How is she?"

"Same," I say.

"Maybe I should share the night shift with you."

"I think you should."

30

I don't dare leave Annie's side. I can't even seem to make myself go next door for a change of clothes, and I must stink by now. Nobody cares, especially not me.

I comb Annie's hair in an attempt to get the bangs just right. I know she'd wake up and slap me if she could because I'm doing a terrible job. I have no real reason to style Annie's hair, but it's something to do. Anything. Maybe my touch soothes her too.

Around midnight, the mood in the room shifts. Annie becomes restless and irritated. Her body moves involuntarily. She groans. I don't like it at all. I call Nicole. She tells me to push the meds to make Annie as comfortable as possible. As we speak, I feel more and more agitated myself, and by the end of the conversation, I can't sit still. I need to do something, everything, but there's nothing I can do.

By 2:00 a.m. Annie's breathing becomes labored, and the rattle in her throat gets louder. I want to cover my ears, but I know I can't block out this wretched fucking noise—a crackling of papers, on fire. I jump to my feet. "Bill, I can't. I need a break. I have to go home. Ten minutes."

The lines on Bill's forehead crease into ridges. "I understand," he whispers as he continues to rub Annie's hand.

I bolt for the front door and place my hand on the knob, but before I can turn it—

"Wait!" Bill shouts.

Something in his tone stops the crazy in my head for a moment.

Bill's voice trembles. "Grace?" he says again above the rattle.

I look over my shoulder to see that Bill has Annie propped with one arm.

I walk back to the bed and slip my arm around Annie's back opposite Bill and raise her a bit more. Annie's eyes flutter and then roll open. Only whites at first, but Annie struggles to focus. She looks toward the window, it seems.

Bill leans into her field of vision. "Hi, hon," he says.

Annie continues to gaze ahead. Her eyes show no emotion, but I know she sees us. I know she knows we're here for her.

Bill starts to cry but stops suddenly and stares down at Annie's hand. I follow his eyes. Annie's finger twitches. We both glance down, and moments later, her finger moves again, and this time, she inches it toward Bill's hand.

Her mouth's been open for hours, but now her lower jaw has some tightness to it. She tries to move her mouth, which works like a rusty hinge stuck open. Annie's got something to say.

I know Annie's trying, in her own stubborn way, wherever she is right now, to get back here. To us. Her jaw moves again, but no sound emerges.

"Did you want to say something, sweetie?" Bill says into Annie's ear.

I strain to hear, swallowing my own sounds.

When Annie puts her lips together again, a noise comes from between her clenched teeth. Bill and I both lean in even closer. Just a whisper at first, but then one word. I don't understand what she says, but she squeezes both our hands to the best of her ability.

Bill says, "Say it just one more time, Annie, please? If you can, just one more time."

Through her far-away stare, I see Annie concentrate, and she speaks again.

Bill and I repeat her last word: "Home."

Annie's eyes struggle to turn themselves to meet ours. Her eyes lock onto Bill's the longest.

Moments later, Annie's eyes close. She sighs, a rough sound she can't control from deep within her chest. Bill nods at me, and together, we lay Annie back down on the pillow.

I look and wait to see Annie's chest rise again, sure it won't. I remember what Nicole taught us, and I begin to count aloud: "One-Mississippi, two-Mississippi, three-Mississippi." I make it to nine-Mississippi before she breathes. "Oh, thank god," I say, but I am not sure why. Kinder to let her go, I know.

There beside Annie's deathbed, I realize that death is a lot like birth. I imagine what it would have been like had my baby lived. There would be a lot of standing around and waiting for someone to transition from one place to another. Pacing. In the end, all our lives would have changed forever.

At around 4:00 a.m., I hear the door open. It's Kelly. She rushes into Bill's arms.

"Daddy," she cries, "I couldn't stay away."

Bill wipes her tears away for her. "I'm glad you're here, sweetie." Kelly hugs me next. I rock her back and forth, then we all settle in. More waiting.

The minutes drag on. Bill and Kelly chat over Annie. I try to give them their space, but Kelly and Bill both insist I stay in the room with them. We laugh and cry, and they share their favorite memories. Annie's jaw hangs back in its slack position, her eyes closed. We determine that we can step away for just a few minutes in shifts to get a bite to eat and maybe one more cup of coffee. Bill and I excuse ourselves to the kitchen first.

The coffee pot's green light has been on for days. I pour a cup and head back to stand in the doorway of the living room. Bill debates whether to eat the last of Annie's famous coffee cake with his coffee. He removes the tinfoil-wrapped package from the freezer as delicately as you would lift a newborn baby, then sets the bundle on the counter. Kelly walks into the kitchen, and they both stare at the package as if it might come alive. The last of Annie's food, the last touched by her live hands.

Kelly waves me back into the kitchen to share the still-frozen coffee cake. She manages to cut a couple of slices. She puts them on plates and pops them into the microwave for ten seconds each. Kelly sets them on the table, but we can't eat. No one takes a single bite.

"How about I wash the dishes," I suggest, "and you two go sit with Annie."

I plunge my hands into the warm water, press them to the bottom of the sink. I lean forward and force an exhale. I close my eyes, inhale, then begin to wash plates and glasses.

Minutes later, Bill comes to the doorway of the kitchen. "Eyes open," he says.

I sling soapy water across the kitchen as I swing around. "What?"

"Eyes open," Bill repeats, and I dry my hands on my clothes as I run for the living room.

I look down at Annie. She is positioned the same as before, but I know she's gone now.

Her eyes are open, blank.

This moment isn't what I thought it would be. I pictured something different, something more panicked—not this terrible, too-quiet release.

The room is overwarm but Annie's body somehow already feels cold when I touch her. Bill cries in Kelly's embrace, and someone, somewhere, is saying over and over, "It's okay, it's okay, it's okay." It takes me a moment to realize that the voice I hear is my own.

Annie came into my life less than a year ago with a powerful, obnoxious jolt, and just like that—in this stupid fucking silence—she's gone.

31

When the hearse arrives, the attendants act very professionally. The whole process is much more dignified than I thought it would be. Honestly, I don't know why I expected otherwise.

Two men, both in black coats, stand in the kitchen. One's got white hair, the other man's steely gray with flecks of black. The white-haired gentleman presses a folded homemade quilt under his arm. A personal touch. "Would you like to see us bring her out? You don't have to."

Bill and Kelly sit in the living room with Annie. I decide I do need to watch Annie leave her house for the last time. I wait in the kitchen, though; I don't want to see them move her out of her spot in the sun.

The attendants return to the hearse to retrieve a stretcher, which surprises me. Of course, the coffin comes later. I guess I've never thought about what this exact moment would look like. I start with a silent prayer to the universe. I ask that these men be gentle with Annie during the hearse ride, and later, at the funeral home. I'm truly thankful she won't suffer anymore. I wonder where her soul is right now. She already feels so far away from me.

The two men wheel the stretcher out to the car through the

back door. Annie is under the handmade quilt. At least now she won't be so cold, I think. Isn't it funny? I know she's gone, but I'm still worried about her. Kelly and Bill follow the men outside, with no coats or hats.

I stay back, scoop Chance into my arms, give him a million kisses on the head. He struggles to follow Annie to the hearse but then gives in to my comfort. He knows she's gone.

The church ladies arrive first that afternoon. They show up at the front door with casserole dishes and plates of cookies. By early evening, trays and tins litter all the countertops. I'm impressed to see how much Annie has impacted this small community. Poor Chance spends the afternoon wandering from room to room, whimpering but accepting pats from visitors.

The next three days go by in a blur. I accompany Bill and Kelly to the funeral home, although Annie's already taken care of everything. We don't have much to do. Many people come in and out of the house. Annie's already planned the funeral, but there will be no wake or visiting hours. Annie had insisted on that much. She didn't want Bill to have to stand all night and shake people's hands. She always put him first.

On the morning of the funeral, I stare at the dress I have laid out on the bed. I'm in my robe with my hair in a towel. I wonder what color to polish my nails. If I went with the fiery red, Annie would say it's too sleazy. I laugh to myself. I can hear Annie teasing me, and all at once, my chest feels heavy. I'd give anything for Annie to play-scold me just one more time.

Annie would've liked the crisp blue sky today. When I drive up to the front of the funeral home, men in suits stand guard at the doors. They could be the same men that carried Annie out. I'm not sure. They nod and smile politely when I get to the entrance. I hand them my car keys for the complimentary valet service. I glance over and wave to Tommy and the boys, who are in their SUV with the engine running. I guess they're going to meet us at the church.

I've always hated the smell of funeral parlors—so stale and musty. I see Kelly and Bill through the large archway in front of me. Kelly puts her hand on Bill's shoulder, and they laugh. They look rosy together, in pink lights.

I actually hate the pink lights as well. Why can't they put traditional lamps in these places? Why the gross, creepy lighting? At least Kelly and Bill are keeping close to support each other.

In the end, Annie chose to be cremated. I guess she couldn't decide on the shoes after all. All that's left of her sits on a table in a wooden box. We three stand and face her. I look down at the container, not even as big as a shoebox. How does an entire human fit inside such a box? I stretch out one hand to touch her one last time. My friend Annie, so large in life, sits quiet and still in a small, simple box.

The funeral director approaches us. "Time to go, when everyone's ready."

In the limo, Bill holds the box close to him. Kelly and I ride in silence.

The church parking lot overflows with cars. Two men in neon vests direct the parking. Cars line the street.

The driver opens the door for us—icy, bitter air swirls into the limo. I step out first and then Kelly, and then Bill with what remains of Annie.

We climb the slick brick steps to the doors of the church. The air bites at my legs despite my thick tights.

The doors open—standing room only in the church. This turnout would please Annie. The music starts. Hundreds of solemn eyes fall on us as we pause in the threshold, and I feel strange, like an actual...stranger. Like I don't belong. Kelly takes my hand.

People sing; others cry. I'm taken aback when I see Liam at the end of a pew in the back, close to the inner aisle. He has on his navy-blue suit.

The pastor nods to us from the front of the church, and we begin our walk down the long carpeted aisle. As I pass, I brush Liam's hand out of habit, but my focus quickly shifts when I see Mom and Dad near the front. I try not to weep at the mere sight of them. They must have gotten up very early this morning to get here on time. My mom catches my eye and mouths, "You're okay," while my dad swipes at his eyes.

When we reach the front of the church, the pastor bows to us, and we take our seats in the front pews. Bill cradles Annie's ashes in his lap.

I hate church as much as funeral homes, but I enjoy the readings Annie's chosen for today—the songs too. The pastor talks, and I like that she took the time to get details about Annie's life from members of the community. I admire all of the enormous flower arrangements. Bouquets of white roses and stargazer lilies adorn the platform. My eyes stop on an arrangement of pink carnations. If Annie were here, she would have something to say about the carnations. I can see her now. She'd lean over and say, "So tacky." I'd slap Annie's arm. She'd say it just loud enough for everyone around us to hear.

When it's time for the eulogy, Kelly walks up onto the altar. She bows and makes the sign of the cross as she makes her way over to the podium. She adjusts the microphone to her level while she clears her throat. Annie would have been proud of her daughter, her only child, today: People laugh at all the right parts. People laugh so hard at some of the stories that they cry. I'm touched and brought to tears once more when Kelly mentions my friendship with Annie. The pastor ends the ceremony on a light note. The ladies in the choir stand in their majestic purple robes and begin to sing. I try to sing along. Annie would have wanted me to sing and be joyful, but I can't. Bill sings every word and carries Annie out of the church with his head held high.

When we get outside, Liam comes up to me and kisses my cheek and squeezes my hand. My parents hug me again and offer their condolences to Bill and Kelly. Bill tells them to stop by for coffee and pie later. Mom offers to bring more supplies, but Bill shakes his head. "Annie thought of everything," he says.

All of the people file out of the church, and all of them want to talk to Bill. He's cordial, but the air's frigid. He and Kelly get back into the limo. I hang back to ride with my parents this time. I glance around the parking lot and spot Liam. He's looking at me. I raise my hand and give him a wave. He smiles and waves back. And for the first time in a long time, I genuinely have no more hate left in my heart for him. All of that's done with.

Annie and Bill's house bursts with people within the hour. Bill does very well. Kelly talks to every single person and laughs a lot. Everyone's got something warm to say about Annie. My mom washes dishes and refills coffee all afternoon. My dad buses for her.

When the afternoon light fades, the crowd disperses, and we all start to clean up in earnest. Bill comes into the kitchen as we work. "Stop," he pleads. "I'll need something to do to keep me busy for a while, and it may as well be more dishes."

I hug Bill. "I'll be here tomorrow to help."

Kelly hugs me for a long time too. "Thank you," she whispers.

"Please stay in touch," I tell her. She's so much like Annie, she's my best, last connection to her.

My parents get their coats. I insist they stay the night or at least stay for dinner.

Mom says, "Your father and I have booked a nice hotel in Ogunquit for a few days. You should come with us."

I pull both of them close to me. "Do you know how much you both mean to me?"

Mom smiles and says, "Does that mean you'll come with us?"

"I want to stay here. I could use a few days to gather myself, and then I need to get caught up with work."

My mom squeezes me tighter. "Have you decided where you'll go yet?"

"Would you believe me if I said I have no clue?"

"Your mother and I don't care where you go," my dad says, "just as long as you end up happy and safe."

"You sure you don't want to come with us? Even for one night?"

"I'm sure. I need some time."

"Okay. Don, go warm up the car. I'll hit the bathroom one last time and meet you out there."

Dad and I chat for a few minutes then he exits the living room onto the porch but almost trips over a potted orchid on the welcome mat.

I lean down to pluck the card. I open the envelope but don't have time to read the message before my mom comes out onto the porch and gives me another big hug.

"Love you, little girl."

"Love you too." We hold each other for another minute before she gets into the car.

I wave goodbye to my folks, eager to step inside to read the card. *I'm thinking of you all day today and every other day, for that matter. Love, Matthew.*

I look up to the sky and listen to the quiet here. For the first time in weeks, I have nothing to do with myself.

32

I'm on the beach and can't believe this will be my last run in this town.

A few months have passed since Annie left us. Bill is going to live with Kelly for a while and get to know the grandkids even better. Annie and Bill's house sold after only a week on the market. I've packed the few things I've collected since our arrival here. The rocking chair is wedged into my backseat. The rest, I'm leaving behind.

Today's also Bill's last day in town. I've made sandwiches for the road for him and some cookies for the grandkids. I know none of my treats will be as good as Annie's, but I want him to have something. I quicken my jogging pace so I can get back to the cottage. I don't want to miss our goodbye, and I still have a couple of tasks to complete while on the beach.

I scan the beach for an intact sand dollar. I guess I'm still hoping for a clear sign from Annie. After she died, I made a whole pot of coffee almost every morning for a week straight. I can finally now remember to make just a couple of cups for myself, but I still can't get used to coffee without her.

The horizon glows pink and orange. In the soft light, seagulls swoop, looking for scraps of forgotten food on the sand.

I check my watch; I still have a few minutes.

At the edge of the water, I shed my sneakers and socks. I know the ocean water will be freezing still, but I want to feel it one last time.

It's low tide. The cold-water rolls over my feet in waves no taller than a few inches high. I close my eyes and try to open all my other senses. I smell the sharp brine of the sea and hear the gulls call out to one another. I say another silent goodbye to Annie.

When I'm ready, I push my sandy feet halfway into my sneakers and hobble across the street.

I scramble like a scarecrow up the front steps and into the house. I wipe as much sand as I can off my feet on the mat inside the front door. When that doesn't work, I wash my feet one at a time in the downstairs bathroom sink.

I hear a quick, light knock at the back door, and when I lean out to look, one wet foot still in the sink, I can see Bill. "Come in, come in," I call to him.

Bill tsk-tsks as I dry my hands and feet. "I see your half bath is still in working order despite such abuse," he jokes.

I laugh and pull Bill to me. He lets me hug him for a long time. When I finally let go, he produces a small box from his jacket pocket. "Annie wanted me to give this to you."

I open the black velvet box, and I see two precious items: a perfect sand dollar, and a gorgeous ring—the silver ring from the craft fair, in fact, the one with the striking green stone.

"Son of a bitch," I say and smile. "She bought it out from under me."

I stare at the ring for a long while. "Stunning, isn't it?" I put the ring on my right hand.

"Very pretty." Bill pauses. Then he says, "I can't thank you enough for everything."

"Bill, I wouldn't have missed a minute."

"Keep in touch?"

"You bet."

We hug one more time. "You're all set?" he asks. "And you're sure you still want to take—"

"All set," I say.

"Love you, kid."

"Love you too."

When Bill opens the screen door to go, we hear the tiniest little creak. Bill smiles at me, then closes the door behind him.

I climb the stairs to clean up and get ready to leave. Halfway there, I stop to look at the framed picture of the couple on the landing. I realize that I came to Maine for more than one reason. Sure, I thought I would get my fairy tale with Liam, but I also wanted to devote a lot of time to my writing. Like all aspiring writers, I wanted to write the next Great American Novel. The best love story in history—with a handsome man, a romantic beachside cottage, plenty of fun in the sun, and above all else, unending love. As it turns out, I ended up with all of those elements as vital components of my storyline, just not in that particular sense or order. Now I think of Annie, and I think of Matthew, and I think of Liam. We're all here, still in my story.

In the shower, I think more about the writing I've done this past year. Who knows when I'll finish this book, the most effortless work I have ever written. Yes, at first, the words felt labored and forced, but the more I wrote about Annie and our adventures together, the more the story seemed to write itself onto the page.

I get dressed and jog down the stairs. In the kitchen, I grab the mug I bought at the craft fair—the one item I haven't packed yet. I smile as I trace my fingers over the fine lines of the Vitruvian Man. I tuck the mug under my arm, put my purse on my shoulder, and wheel my wonky suitcase behind me. At the front door, I stop to take one final look around. No one's here. Just me. And I'm okay. Say was right. Mom was right. Annie was right. I'm okay.

Outside, I stop at the end of the walkway and look over at Annie's house. A crow squawks and lands on the SOLD sign. I half expect Annie to walk out onto her porch to yell and shoo that crow away. So much good has happened here, I remind myself again—a whole novel's worth, actually.

I hop into my car, wedge my mug safely into the middle console's cupholder, and toss my purse onto the back seat. I look to my right. I think he's ready to go too. It wasn't a hard decision whether to include this guy in my life forever or not. He leans his head to one side and stares at me, deep into my soul. I realize I've found yet another love I never expected. I pat Chance on the head, turn the key, and put the car into gear.

As the two of us embark on our journey, I haven't decided where we'll go first. We might swing down through Kennebunk to see if that older man who sold me the antique rocking chair put his beautiful old house on the market yet. We'll definitely stop in Pennsylvania, and I'm guessing we'll spend some time in New York too. And who knows, we may end up right back here for another long stay in Maine. All I know is that we're just going to drive until we find one simple thing: home.

Acknowledgements:

My deepest thanks to Kevin Atticks and the folks at Apprentice House Press. You've made my lifelong dream of seeing my name on the cover of a book come true, and for that, I will forever be grateful.

Endless thanks to Court Harler. Without her, this novel would have never been published. She believed in this manuscript, even in its earliest, most terrible stage. She guided me in making this story what it is today. I'll never be able to thank her for the countless hours she spent working on this project. I wouldn't be half the writer I am today without her guidance and support.

Thank you to Kate Reagan, Jill Harrigan, Heidi McCurdy, Karen Landry, Melissa Johnson, and countless others who read earlier drafts of this novel.

Thank you to my writing community. Thank you, Jen Dupree, for all of your guidance and wisdom. Thank you to Olivia and Cass for helping me refine my work. Our writers group and your friendship are such bright spots in my life. Brandon Dudley, thank you for reading my very first terrible short story and still agreeing to be my friend anyway. Thank you Justin Tussing, and Penny Guisinger for allowing me to take part in the Stonecoast summer program. You both made me feel like I had something important to say for the first time in a long time.

Erin Towns, thank you for always reading my crappy first drafts, and for constantly reminding me that it's a long way to the top if you want to rock and roll. I forgive you for forgetting about that time my house almost burned down.

Dad, thank you for everything. You've always been my biggest cheerleader.

Alex, Maxim, and MacKenzee, thank you for your love and patience over the years while I wrote, even on the nights I didn't stop to make supper.

Dicky Bird, thank you for always answering my "How would you describe this?" when I'm writing, with exactly the words I need.

About the Author

Jennifer lives in Maine, where she teaches high school English. Her chapbook, Reclamation Days, was a runner-up in The Masters Review 2024 Chapbook Open and was a finalist in the 2025 MWPA Chapbook Competition. Her work has appeared in McSweeney's Internet Tendency, The Stonecoast Review, Free Flash Fiction, and various other places. She's a volunteer reader for The Masters Review and a member of the Maine Writers and Publishers Alliance. This is her first novel.

Apprentice House is the country's only campus-based, student-staffed book publishing company. Directed by professors and industry professionals, it is a nonprofit activity of the Communication & Media Department at Loyola University Maryland.

Using state-of-the-art technology and an experiential learning model of education, Apprentice House publishes books in untraditional ways. This dual responsibility as publishers and educators creates an unprecedented collaborative environment among faculty and students, while teaching tomorrow's editors, designers, and marketers.

Eclectic and provocative, Apprentice House titles intend to entertain as well as spark dialogue on a variety of topics. Financial contributions to sustain the press's work are welcomed. Contributions are tax deductible to the fullest extent allowed by the IRS.

To learn more about Apprentice House books or to obtain submission guidelines, please visit www.apprenticehouse.com.

Apprentice House Press
Communication & Media Department
Loyola University Maryland
4501 N. Charles Street
Baltimore, MD 21210
Ph: 410-617-5265
info@apprenticehouse.com • www.apprenticehouse.com

www.ingramcontent.com/pod-product-compliance
Lightning Source LLC
LaVergne TN
LVHW012338100826
845148LV00018B/2834

* 9 7 8 1 6 2 7 2 0 6 2 2 8 *